NO RIGHT TURN

A MIAMI JONES FLORIDA MYSTERY

AJ STEWART

D0920928

JACARANDA DRIVE

For Yvonne Jennings. As beautiful a person as I ever had the privilege to know.

And Heather and Evan. Home is wherever you are.

Jacaranda Drive Publishing

Los Angeles, California

www.jacarandadrive.com

Cover artwork by Streetlight Graphics

ISBN-10: 1-945741-10-4

ISBN-13: 978-1-945741-10-4

CHAPTER ONE

THEY DON'T MAKE THEM LIKE THEY USED TO. WHEN IT comes to houses in South Florida, they generally build them better now. Especially when you're talking about taking a battering from a hurricane. All the McMansions on my street had fared pretty well. I could hear the sounds of generators and industrial pumps and wet-dry vacuums clearing the floodwater from marble tile patios and polished concrete garage floors. There was a convoy of trucks from various cleanup companies outside the homes along the Intracoastal, crews hard at work making it as though Mother Nature had never dared spew her angry tirade across their travertine patios and Brazilian cherry outdoor settings, and doing it all before the homeowners had to cast their eyes upon it.

The odds were that my old seventies rancher would not have fared well at all, but once again it had proven the bookmakers wrong. The king tide that had surged down the Intracoastal had taken over my back lawn and patio, and the sandbags we had placed around the rear sliding door had fought the mighty fight but eventually succumbed. As had the old sliding door. After the water had retreated I was left with a sunken living room that resembled a tide pool in a children's museum, and unlike many of my waterfront neighbors, I didn't have the number of a disaster recovery team on speed dial.

What I did have was a rag-tag team of my own. We undertook our efforts on a triage basis. My fiancée, Danielle, had been given leave from her stint at the Florida Department of Law Enforcement Special Agent Training Academy in Tallahassee to help with the post-hurricane relief effort. My business partner, Ron, arrived in his beat-up Camry. The apartment he shared with the Lady Cassandra was opposite the ocean in Palm Beach so it had taken a pounding but other than a flooded underground parking area and a disheveled balcony, it had survived more or less unscathed. They had a homeowners association to take care of their cleanup so Ron had clearly decided that the quicker we got my place tidy, the sooner we would get onto fixing up Longboard Kelly's, and the quicker we got that done, the sooner we would again be enjoying a beer under Longboard's palapa bar.

The three of us removed the strewn sandbags away from the patio and piled them along the side of the yard. We worked around the speedboat that had parked itself in my backyard. My buddy Lucas dropped off a bilge pump from the marina he managed in Miami, and Ron attached it to a garden hose to drain out my living room. Danielle and I collected clothes and other bits and pieces and loaded them into the pickup she had bought while in Tallahassee. I wasn't sure if the truck was a cop thing or if she just liked the high ride, but either way, it proved useful. Although most of my furniture had gotten water damaged, none of it appeared beyond repair, which meant once it dried out, I would go on using it as if nothing had happened, so we tossed the truly deceased items in the back of the truck and mopped up the rest. The electricity was out and I didn't have a generator, so the fridge was pretty ripe, but I figured I could eat out until regular service resumed. Other than that, a fresh set of sheets on the bed gave us a place to sleep, even if we did have to dry our feet after lifting them from the sodden carpet.

I dropped a box of old baseball gear into the back of my Cadillac SUV and looked up at the Greek wedding cake of a home next to mine. I had never seen the owners. I often saw the maintenance staff. Cleaners, gardeners. After the disaster recovery team had sucked all the water off the property, I was sure the staff would descend en masse to sweep the floors and polish the andirons. A guy wandered out through the large wrought-iron gates and dumped an armful of palm fronds in the gutter. He looked up at me and nodded.

I nodded back and then turned to watch a car drive down my street. It wasn't a street that went anywhere. You came in off Blue Heron and then hit the houses on the Intracoastal and then followed the road right on back out again. But we often got lost tourists just trying to get a glimpse of the water. Sometimes folks stopped and asked where they could see the water. Some of my neighbors got rather put out by them, but I just recommended they drive north up to McDonald State Park, where they could see mangroves and lagoons and an almost empty beach, with not a Margaritaville in sight.

Ron wandered out, mopping his tanned brow, and we watched the car slowly cruise by and come to a stop at a house three doors down. It was such a vanilla vehicle I couldn't tell what the make was. If asked by the police to describe the getaway car, I would have provided the following details: Sedan. Whitish. That's all I could say. We watched a guy in suit pants and a polo shirt get out with a briefcase and walk to the door. He waited for the door to open and went inside.

"Insurance guy," said Ron.

I didn't argue. Ron had worked years in the insurance game,

so he knew the species. We wandered back inside. I collected more of my belongings that had spent time below the water line and put stuff to keep in plastic tubs and stuff to discard in plastic bags. Danielle took the job of donning gloves and emptying the refrigerator. She was a trouper. I carried my saxophone out to my SUV and found the bland sedan had migrated. The guy in the polo was looking up at my house. He consulted a clipboard and then looked up again.

"Mr. Jones?" he asked.

I said nothing.

"Great Southeast Permanent," he said.

"Morning," I said.

The man walked up the path to my house. It was still damp, but so were his feet.

"You put in a call to our claim center?" he asked, as if this was a mysterious thing to do after a hurricane had passed through.

"I did. You want to come inside?"

"Surely."

He followed me in, stopping in the living room just before it became a primordial swamp. He made some notes on his clipboard.

"She's held up rather well," he said. "Do you mind if I take some pictures?"

"Knock yourself out."

He wandered around the place taking photographs with his phone before stepping out the back. I stayed inside and watched Danielle handle sodden produce that seemed to be breaking off onto a new branch on the evolutionary tree. The insurance guy came back in and asked me to sign a document on his clipboard that confirmed that he had visited and he had assessed.

"What now?" I asked.

"Your roof looks remarkably good, considering. I think your neighbor might have sheltered you from the wind."

"I'll be sure to thank them if I ever see them."

"Most of your damage looks flood-related. We're trying to expedite processing, but obviously there are a lot of clients to get around to. Expect a confirmation letter from us in a day or two." He slipped his clipboard under his sweaty armpit and offered his hand to shake.

"I'd try and get a quote for the work ASAP, if I were you. Contractors are going to be up to their noses in work so it might take a while. Best of luck."

I walked the guy out, and he got in his car and drove back up toward Blue Heron, about halfway, where he stopped and did it all again. He was stepping inside the next client's house when another car drove by him.

This car was one of those glossy electric sedans that imply that the driver never goes far from home. It slowed as it reached the end of the road and came to a stop outside my house. It seemed like my place was Mardi Gras central today. There was a moment of pause, as if the driver was summing me up, standing there as I was in a sweat-soaked University of Miami t-shirt and board shorts. I waited by my front door for the tinted window to roll down, but it didn't. The door opened instead. That was the first hint that I wasn't dealing with a lost tourist. The second hint was the guy who got out. He was middle-aged and tanned like a hide, and he wore an expensive-looking black suit that sat perfectly across his shoulders. He closed the door with a dense thunk and then tugged at his cufflink.

Then he looked up at me. He didn't smile or make any kind of facial expression. His hair was slicked back and he had the nose of a hawk, and everything on him stayed perfectly in place. I wondered if Madam Tussauds in Orlando was missing anyone.

"Mr. Jones," he said, with an accent so heavy he sounded like he was pretending to be Latino.

I said nothing.

He took a couple steps up the damp concrete path toward the house.

"Mr. Jones," he said again, as if I hadn't heard the first time.

I said nothing. It wasn't how I usually handled myself, at least I liked to think not. I was generally a more friendly guy to strangers. But my Spidey senses were tingling with this guy. As my father used to say, I didn't like the cut of his jib. The neighborhood looked like a hurricane had recently ripped through because that was exactly what had happened. At best, it looked untidy; at worst, homes had been lifted up and deposited in a new city, and in a million pieces. There were palm fronds everywhere, and sea debris and trash, and all the lawns were bogs. This guy in his sharp suit didn't fit at all. He sure as hell wasn't an insurance agent.

The guy got halfway up the path to my door and stopped where it was starting to dry out. That's what alligators do. On dry land, they are clumsy and too long for their own good, but in the shallows, there is nothing more deadly. The metaphor just popped into my head and I knew it wasn't fair to the guy, but my mind worked like that.

"Help you?" I finally asked him.

He gave me a smile with no teeth. "Such a mess," he said.

"Aha."

"Lots of damages," he said.

"Plenty."

"Expensive," he said.

I had no more words. I was sweating where I stood. My living room was a swamp and some poor soul's speedboat had decided to stop off in my backyard. Standing in my front yard listening to Captain Obvious was not part of my plan.

"Let me cut to the chase," he said.

"Whenever you're ready."

"I'd like to turn this disaster into an opportunity for you."

What a swell guy. I wondered if he was going to offer me a set of steak knives just for listening to his pitch.

"This whole mess will be expensive," he said.

"That's why we have insurance."

"If the insurance covers you. This might have been a hurricane, might have been a flood. Whatever makes it harder to get a claim."

"Your point?"

"Even if you are covered, it will take years to claim and then rebuild, and I have no doubt you'll need to rebuild." He looked over my house like it was a car wreck. But not just any car wreck. A cheap Chinese import of a car wreck. The kind of car that wasn't worth that much less after the accident than it was before.

"I can make that all go away," he said, looking back to me. "I'd like to buy your house."

I nodded like I might be considering the offer, but in fact I was thinking about what the nearest weapon was and how I might use it to chase this lowlife off my island.

"I'm prepared to make a more than reasonable offer, given the condition. Cash. You can start again fresh. Somewhere new. Maybe on a golf course."

Vultures aren't bad birds. They have a PR problem. In many ways they are necessary. Dead animals spread disease, and the scavengers clean them up. It's the circle of life. Which was why calling this guy a vulture was unfair to the bird. This guy didn't care about the cleanup, or my imaginary new condo overlooking a nine-hole executive course out in Wellington. He and his ilk were in town to make a killing, not clean one up. When people had their lives torn apart before their very eyes, they became susceptible to the charms of snake oil salesmen. Make the pain go away, sell your house for pennies on the dollar.

"I don't play golf," I said. It wasn't strictly speaking true. I had played golf. I didn't know many professional baseball players who hadn't. I had even caddied in a tour tournament once. I wasn't that good at it, though, and I didn't care much for the artificial nature of golf courses. They reminded me of French gardens. Free to grow in whatever way we humans deemed acceptable. I liked my nature a touch more organic. Like mangroves. I liked the randomness of mangroves. A mangrove had saved my life, but I had liked them even before that. I wasn't a fan of the idea of cutting back mangroves to put in a manicured sand trap on the back nine.

"Your choice," said the guy.

I nodded. "Well, my choice is to stay here. Have a nice day." I didn't move, but I felt like the *have a nice day* was fairly definitive. I was wrong.

"Don't be hasty, Mr. Jones. I understand the emotional attachment to a home." He gave it the Chinese car wreck look again. I don't think he could help himself. "But you don't want to end up in financial ruin because of it."

"I'll be okay," I said. "You know your way back off the island?"

He gave me the toothless smile once more. "I'll be in touch." He turned and stepped back to his car, his fine leather shoes slapping in the water on the path, and then he slipped in behind the wheel. He didn't drop the window or say goodbye. He didn't seem to start the engine. The vehicle just pulled away and headed back from where it had come. I watched it until it turned onto Blue Heron. Mine was not the only house on the island in a state of disrepair, but it seemed to be the only one catching the guy's eye.

CHAPTER TWO

My house hadn't fared as well as the neighboring McMansions, but Longboard Kelly's had fared worse still. The courtyard was like an Everglades exhibit at the natural history museum. There was kelp and seagrass and dead purple sailor jellyfish everywhere. The palapa over the outdoor bar had been blown away, leaving a framework that reminded me of a dinosaur carcass. Mick had gotten most of the water out of the courtyard and was using a shovel to scoop up the kelp and the jellies into a wheelbarrow. The sun was out and the sky was blue and Florida was pretending that nothing bad had ever happened. The smell of rapidly rotting marine life harshed the effect.

Danielle swept out the indoor bar and Ron climbed a ladder that was the mortal enemy of men his age and stretched a plastic tarp over the naked roof. Muriel, Mick's longtime bartender, arrived to take an inventory of damaged bottles and glasses. I helped Mick with the jellies.

"Insurance guy come yet?" I asked.

Mick shook his head. "It's the city I need."

"How so?"

He held up a shovel full of sea debris up. We were wheeling it out into the parking lot and dumping it in the garbage hopper, but that was really only shuffling the deck chairs on the *Titanic*. If the city didn't get by soon to pick it up, the stench was going to become a force of nature itself.

"I can't open until the health guy inspects."

"You can't open?"

"Technically." He plopped some more jellies into the wheelbarrow.

"What about the palapa? How do we fix that?" I asked.

Mick grunted. "Thinking about ditching it, going with shiplap."

"You're gonna get rid of the palapa? Say it ain't so, Mick. That thatching *is* Longboard's."

"It's expensive is what it is. Every time we get a flippin' hurricane, it's the first thing to blow away. It didn't even make it through the afternoon. Besides, there's not many guys who do it. Every guy with a hammer can put up shiplap."

"You're making me want to weep, Mick."

He grunted again. "How's your place coming?"

"Getting there. The insides are a mess. I'll need new carpet, that's for damned sure. The rest I can't say until I get a contractor in there, and they all seem to be busy right now."

We scooped up all the marine debris and then swept out the courtyard. Then we collected the outdoor furniture from inside the bar and put it back where it belonged. Once the umbrellas with beer brand logos on them were back in place, the joint started to look right again. Ron found an electric drill, and we took the surfboard with the bite out of it that had been ripped from the back wall and we fixed it back in place. Longboard's was close to being Longboard's once more. Except for the palm thatching over the outdoor bar. I had never realized how much I loved that until it was gone. Ron's tarp flapped in the breeze to remind me.

One thing that had never stopped working was the beer taps. Mick had stayed bunkered down in the bar during the storm and had flushed the lines and replaced the CO_2 before anything else. Once we had done all we could do without more materials and some professional help, Muriel poured some beers and a tonic and lime for Danielle. We took our usual stools which were solid wood items and would survive the apocalypse.

"Here's to Longboard's," I said.

Ron smiled. "Here's to another sunny day in Florida."

His love of the so-called Sunshine State was unrivaled. Even the governor didn't pimp Florida like Ron. He loved everything about it, up to and including the hurricanes. They kept the riffraff out, he said. Or in, he wasn't sure. His wrinkled face and the marks from the removed skin cancers spoke of a Floridian life.

We clinked glasses and drank. Without the shade from the palapa, the outdoor bar was hot and I was already sweating. I could feel the moisture rising from beneath the pavers. Danielle guzzled her tonic and slammed the glass down on the bar.

"I'm off," she said.

"Where?" asked Ron.

"They've opened up a shelter at the Ballpark of the Palm Beaches. The National Guard is setting up a tent city for people who can't get back into their homes. Lots to do."

Danielle slipped off her stool and kissed me. "I'll see you later."

She wasn't halfway across the courtyard before Ron turned to me.

"She's one of the good ones," he said.

"I know, and I know where you're going with it."

"Not going anywhere," he said. "I just think you want to hold on to one like that."

"I already asked her, she already said yes. The rest is just details."

"The ceremony is a pretty big detail."

I waved my hand around at the half-restored bar. "We've got a few other things to get through first."

Ron shrugged and offered a mischievous grin. "Just saying." He glanced back at Danielle as she walked out into the parking lot.

The fence between the lot and the courtyard had been blown away, so we saw the woman coming the other way as soon as she stepped from her car. She nodded to Danielle as they passed and then continued into the courtyard. She didn't look like a tourist. I wasn't sure there were any tourists left in Florida. I knew any that were here would be most unlikely to find themselves at Longboard Kelly's. It was no kind of place for tourists, which made it distinctly un-Floridian. It wasn't on the water and there was no view. You were more likely to hear I-95 than the waves lapping against the seawall on the Intracoastal. But here she was anyway.

She wore a pink polo shirt with a logo on the breast, the letters DBR over a checkered flag. Her capri pants were blue and she wore white running shoes on her feet. She was wide in the hips but nowhere else, and her auburn hair was tied back in a ponytail. She wasn't young but she wasn't old. If she had attended college, it had been a couple decades ago.

The woman looked over each of us as she approached the bar. He eyes landed on Muriel, as often happened at Longboard's. Muriel favored tank tops that highlighted both her toned arms and her considerable bosom. As the woman reached us, however, her eyes dropped to me.

"Miami Jones," she said as if we knew each other from a party long ago.

"Have we met?" I asked.

"No, sir."

"But you know me?"

"I was told I might find you here. And your t-shirt is kind of a giveaway."

I glanced down at myself. My gray t-shirt had Miami emblazoned in orange and green across it.

"You wear that in case you get lost at the mall?" she asked.

Ron smiled.

"No. I went to school there. University of Miami."

"Did you have that name before or after you went there?"

"After. How can I help you, Miss . . ."

"Beadman. Angie Beadman."

She waited for that to sink in, as if I should know it somehow. I didn't.

"I want to hire you, Mr. Jones."

"My dad was Mr. Jones. Call me Miami."

"I'll try."

I put my beer down and offered her a stool and a drink. She took the stool but not the drink.

"What is it you want me to do, Miss Beadman?"

"Angie. Our property was broken into. We had some items stolen that my father would like returned."

"You call the police?"

"Of course."

"The police are usually in the best position to find stolen things. And they'll do it for free."

"Money is not the issue."

Even though I wasn't looking at him I felt Ron's ears prick up.

"What was stolen?" I asked.

"A car."

"You had a car stolen? Well, then I'd suggest the police are definitely the ones to help you. They have a whole department that can look out for your car. We're just two guys. Besides, we have a lot to clean up."

"To be completely accurate, it wasn't a car. It was a number of cars."

"What number?"

"Ten."

"Ten? You had ten cars stolen?"

"Yes, sir."

"Your family own a used car dealership or something?"

"No. My father collects cars."

"Who is your father?"

Angie frowned at me. "Dale Beadman."

I gave her my pouty mystified face.

Ron took up the baton. "Dale Beadman?"

"Yes, sir," said Angie.

"You live on the island," said Ron.

"Yes, sir."

Ron looked at me. "We should check it out," he said.

I wasn't exactly champing at the bit to take on a case. It was true, I did have a lot to clean up. And I was enjoying my beer. To cap off my antipathy, I found Palm Beach types difficult to work for. I recognized the conundrum in that, given that I worked on the Palm Beaches, and the island was where most of the money was. Perhaps that was the problem. Perhaps I was the problem. It could go either way. Regardless, I didn't have the faintest idea who this Dale Beadman guy was, but I trusted Ron's opinion on these things, so I picked up my glass and swallowed down my beer.

"Let's go."

CHAPTER THREE

CALLING THE HOMES AT THE NORTH END OF PALM BEACH island *houses* was like calling the *QE2* a *boat*. The roads were tight and surrounded on all sides by trees and hedges. Behind the foliage were homes that ranged from palatial to entire compounds. The lots weren't large like in Fairfield County, Connecticut, or neighboring Westchester, New York, where even with binoculars you couldn't see the houses from the road, but then the island wasn't that wide at the top end. One could only guess at the size of the houses behind the trees and the wrought-iron gates, or one could look at a satellite map.

Or one could visit. We followed Angie in my Cadillac SUV that had survived the hurricane with barely a scratch, which was new for me. Angie was driving a Camaro, low-slung and throaty, which made my vehicle look like it belonged to my grandmother. We passed through a high wooden gate that opened on approach and closed behind us, and I stopped on the sandy driveway behind the Camaro.

The house was large by most standards but moderate for the locale. It was a blue faux Colonial, about five thousand square feet, with a wraparound porch. Across the lawn from the house was another structure, long and low, more like a warehouse than an outbuilding. There were a couple of other outbuildings, small garage-sized units, for the ride-on lawn mower and such equipment.

Angie didn't take us into the house. We marched across the lush Bermuda grass toward the warehouse. Between the two buildings, the lawn stretched out toward the beach and the Atlantic Ocean. The view was sensational and the water sparkled and beckoned like a siren. I took a good look at the layout. Ron and I had spent the hurricane in a plush Palm Beach hotel—by good luck rather than good design—and I noted that the thing that had saved the hotel was that it was elevated in a way that the eye didn't really pick up. The lawns acted somewhat like a moat, so the storm surge that the hurricane had pushed across the island had broken around the hotel rather than pulsing through it. The Beadman estate was built in a similar fashion. The lawn undulated in a way that you barely saw, and certainly wouldn't notice if you hadn't just been through a hurricane, so that water flow from the ocean would funnel between the two buildings and down the driveway and go on to become your neighbor's problem. There was a small army of men positioned across the lawn, clearing debris and making it so the storm had never happened.

The driveway split into two—one arm reaching around in front of the house and the other making for the shorter side of the warehouse. Angie directed us to the other end of the warehouse, on the beach side. We walked around the bland white building and were surprised to find what looked like a beach-front bar. There was a large deck with tables and umbrellas and an outdoor kitchen that could have prepared a banquet. There was a framework similar to the one at Longboard's, where a pair of men were rethatching the palm fronds into a palapa awning.

The notion of shiplap jumped into my head, and it gave me a sense of melancholy.

Angie led us in through French doors that acted like portals in the space-time continuum. We stepped from a deck that was all Florida into a pub that was all England. The room was dark wood and dim lighting. On the right side was a bar along the outside wall with stools upholstered in green leather. There were booths along the opposite wall. The wall to my left had a big screen television mounted on it. Every other wall space was adorned with photographs and posters. Many featured one man either shaking hands with someone noteworthy or inside a car. There were just as many pictures of the car by itself. Like the leather, the car was green—my mother would have called it British racing green—and it wore the number 29 on the door.

There were large-screen televisions above the bar and below them a collection of scotches and bourbons and American whiskeys that would rival the fanciest Manhattan hotel. As my eyes adjusted to the dim lighting, I noticed that the wall opposite the bar, where the booths sat, featured large picture windows that looked out into darkness. I saw my reflection in the windows and felt a tad underdressed.

A man was standing behind the bar, polishing a glass in the time-honored tradition of barkeeps the world over. He was thin and wiry in a way that suggested he smoked a lot. He had a full head of hair and a thick mustache, both of which had turned salt and pepper. His face said he was beyond seventy years old, but his eyes belonged to a younger man.

The man looked us over without a smile, but he dropped the dish towel and came out from behind the bar. Despite the growing heat, he was wearing jeans and a blue work shirt with logos for a soda company, an insurance company and some kind of internet company over his heart.

"Dad, this is Miami Jones and Ron Bennett," said Angie.

The man extended his hand to me and Ron and we each shook it.

"Dale Beadman," he said twice in a gravelly voice.

I recognized him, but only just. Ron had filled me in on the basics as we drove over to the island. I'm not a huge NASCAR fan. I grew up in New England, where stock car racing was not really on the radar. Although it had developed a nationwide schedule, it was, to me, like mint juleps, the most Southern of sports. I only lived a couple hours from one of the most famous racetracks in the country at Daytona, and I enjoyed a fast car as much as the next guy, but I suspected the issue was that I didn't own a television, so I just never saw a race.

Dale Beadman was a legend in the sport. I knew that much. He was a winning driver and had gone on to be a winning team owner. He'd won at Daytona and Talladega and that was about where my knowledge ended.

"Mr. Beadman," I said.

"Dale, please. Thank you for coming."

I noted a slight Southern twang, as if he hadn't grown up in the South but visited a lot. I was about to ask why I was there when the phone behind the bar rang. Angie stepped around and answered it, and then she listened and then told whoever was on the line to send them over. Then she hung up and looked at her father.

"The police are here."

Angie walked out the French doors, and Dale Beadman turned to me.

"Mr. Jones, if I could ask you to do something for me?"

"It's Miami, and you can certainly ask."

"I wonder if you would remain behind after the police leave?"

"I wonder if you could do me a favor?" I asked in return.

"Name it."

"I'd love those guys fixing your palapa outside to drop by my buddy's bar and fix his."

I think Beadman was about to speak, but the words didn't get to come out. Instead, Angie Beadman walked back in through the French doors. The suit that followed her was a wrinkled wrinkle-free JC Penney special. Detective Ronzoni stepped from the heat without a bead of sweat on him. He just plain didn't sweat. It was a gland thing, or some such. But I got the sense that he came as close to sweating as he ever did when he caught sight of me. I smiled and watched the uniformed officer follow him in and then wait near the door.

Angie Beadman introduced her father to the detective and then made to do the same to me and Ron. I put my hand up.

"We're old friends," I said with a smile. Ronzoni did not return the smile. The last time I had seen him, he was motoring away in a Coast Guard tender from the hotel where he, too, had spent the recent hurricane. It seemed he had reached his limit for enjoying my company, so I let him take control.

"Mr. Beadman, I understand your car collection has been stolen."

"Yes, Detective," said Beadman. "Let me show you."

Beadman hit a button on a console behind the bar, and the space beyond the bank of windows exploded into light. Not just lighting, but light. Canned lights beamed bright in the cavernous space, bouncing off the white walls. The floor was black concrete polished to a shine. I could have shaved in the reflection. It looked like a hospital operating room. It was so stark the Palm Beach PD officer who had stopped by the door was drawn to the window, mouth agape, like a moth to a flame. The notable thing about the room, however, wasn't the spotlessness of it but the fact that there was nothing in it. The room pulsed its emptiness through the glass at us in the faux pub. The spaces didn't go together. The outside deck was a Florida watering hole, the pub was clubby English and the warehouse was clinical.

"So what's this?" asked Ronzoni, as ever right on top of things.

Beadman didn't take his eyes off the window. "This, Detective, is my garage. This is where my car collection was."

Ronzoni nodded deeply, as if discussing a deceased relative. Perhaps he knew more about NASCAR than I did.

"I see," he said. "How many cars did you have, Mr. Beadman?"

"There were—how many, Angie?"

"Ten," she said.

Beadman nodded to Ronzoni.

"And when did the burglary occur?"

"The night of the hurricane," said Beadman.

"And you know this how?" asked Ronzoni.

"Angie, my daughter, was here until that morning. She locked the garage. Right, darlin'?"

"That's right," said Angie.

"Were you the last to leave?" asked Ronzoni.

"Yes. I left with my mother. Everything was battened down and the staff had left."

"And Mr. Beadman, where were you?"

"I was in Charlotte, North Carolina. I had planned to be back but got delayed, doing some filming."

"Okay. And when did you return?" Ronzoni asked Angie.

"The day after the hurricane. In the evening."

"So the robbery could have happened after the hurricane had passed." Ronzoni looked at Beadman. "Not necessarily the night of the hurricane." He tried to cock his eyebrow, I assumed to show how his Holmesian detective brain was so far ahead of the rest of us, but he had to tilt his head to make the expression work and he ended up looking like he was having a seizure.

Beadman frowned and looked back to his daughter.

"The day after the hurricane the entire island was flooded," she said.

"I know," said Ronzoni. "I was here." He didn't look at me. "So there would be no way to get the cars out, would there?" Ronzoni nodded sagely, as if he had already thought of that but was glad to reconsider it. "We should make no assumptions, Miss Beadman. Until we know more, we have a time period of almost three days. The day of the hurricane—when you left—the day after the hurricane, and the day after that—yesterday, when you arrived back. Do you have any security video?"

"Sort of," said Angie. "The power went out during the hurricane. Before it went out, the cars were in the garage. It didn't reboot until I reset it when I got back."

"I'll need to see that video," said Ronzoni. "So tell me about these cars."

"They were my pride and joy, Detective," said Beadman. He looked wistfully through the glass at the empty garage. I glanced at his daughter, wondering where she fit in on the pride and joy scale.

"There was a range of vehicles. From an original Model T to a Ferrari 250 Testa Rossa. But mostly they were rare domestic vehicles."

"I'll need a full list of those," said Ronzoni.

"I can get that for you from my office," said Angie.

"Fine. Let's see the scene, then."

Ronzoni asked Angie to lead us to the garage. He whispered something to the uniformed officer, who then stopped Ron and me at the door from the pub.

"It's a crime scene," he said by way of explanation. His face was apologetic, as if he knew Ronzoni was playing games with me, so I let it slide. Ron and I took a booth in the pub and watched Ronzoni and the Beadmans wander around the massive garage. Ronzoni spent some time examining the rollup door at the end of the building that I figured led out to the sandy driveway. Then he wandered over to a long set of steel shelves. The shelves held what looked like parts for cars, but from a distance they all appeared to be far too clean to be car parts. I always imagined car parts to be covered in grime, but I supposed they weren't like that before they were used. I thought I could see a large piston attached to a connecting rod next to a small engine block that looked like a toy. Ronzoni examined all the parts without touching them and then spoke to Dale Beadman again.

"What do you think?" asked Ron.

"Ten cars? How do you steal ten cars?"

"Easy way is on a vehicle transporter. You know, a big semi-trailer."

"Right. Or you have ten drivers and you drive them off the island. Like *The Italian Job*."

Ron smiled. He had a touch of Michael Caine about him. "That takes a lot of planning, don't you think?"

"I do. And banking on the weather."

The uniformed officer opened the door from the garage, and Ronzoni led the Beadmans in. He shook hands with Dale.

"It's a tough one," he said. "Stolen vehicles are usually picked up where they're dumped or they're never found. Chop shops usually have them in pieces within hours. But your cars are more like art. That's how we'll find them. You display them like art and people will buy them like art. We'll get the feelers out to every auction house in the state."

"What happens if they take them to auction in South Carolina?" I interjected.

Ronzoni frowned. "Then it becomes a federal crime and we'll call in the FBI."

"That sounds a bit dramatic," said Beadman.

"We'll cross that bridge when we come to it," said Ronzoni.

He wouldn't want to cross that bridge. In my experience, law enforcement agencies worked better together than they made it seem in the movies and television. The rivalries were there, but they rarely got in the way. Most law enforcement types were too professional for that. The fact was, if a local crime became a federal crime by crossing state lines, the added resources of the feds were often welcomed by underfunded police departments. In the end, if the crime was solved, the local department got to claim that as a win in their statistics even if the Bureau did the bulk of the heavy lifting. Detective Ronzoni wasn't one for statistics, though. He liked the credit. He was a good cop, even if he was a terrible dresser, but he sure liked getting the credit, whether it was due or not.

"We'll need a police report for our insurance," said Beadman.

Ronzoni gave a look like he'd just eaten a bad pickle. "Of course."

Angie stepped toward the exit. "I'll take you over to the house and get you the list of cars."

"And that video."

"Of course."

Angie led Ronzoni away and he gave Ron and me a nod as he passed. They stepped out the French doors into the bright sun, which bounced off the television on the wall. I saw the reflection of one of the men fixing the palapa, up a ladder, yelling something at Ronzoni below. Probably telling him to watch the hell out.

I looked up at Dale Beadman, who stood at the end of our booth. I liked his fake little English pub. I could see myself enjoying a beer in a booth. I hoped against hope that he would offer me one.

"If you'll come with me," he said.

CHAPTER FOUR

Dale Beadman strode across the polished concrete. Ron and I followed. I, for one, wondered if I should take my shoes off, the floor was that clean. Beadman didn't remove his footwear, so I followed his lead. He made his way over to the long side wall where the shelves of car parts stood. He waited in front of the shelves as if they were important.

"You collect car parts?" I asked.

"I do," said Beadman. "Some of my collection is so rare you can't find parts, so when they come up I grab them. Other parts I have fabricated in my factory."

"So you're wondering why someone who goes to all the trouble of stealing ten cars would leave behind just-as-rare parts for those very cars."

Beadman glanced at me. "I wasn't, but I am now."

Then he grabbed the steel framework of the shelving unit and pulled hard. I thought for a second the whole thing was going to come down on top of us. It didn't. The unit was fixed to the wall and Beadman pulled the wall open. It slid like a barn door, revealing another section of the garage. He repeated the

effort with the second half of the shelving unit and then flicked
on the light.

It was an antechamber big enough for two cars to park side-by-
side, or one car if you really wanted to show it off. The walls and
floor were the same as the main area of the garage, white and black.

"A secret room," said Ron.

"Not secret," said Beadman. "Private. If you walked around
the building you'd figure out this section was here. It's not
hidden, exactly."

"But it's not on show," I said. "Why?"

"It's a special space for a special car. It might sound strange
to you, but it's for a car I wanted to enjoy all to myself. I
earned it."

"Okay, Mr. Beadman, I tell you what. You obviously
brought us here for a reason and I'm guessing this is it. So let's
get some stuff cleared up. We're pretty good at what we do.
We're not the Mounties, we don't get our man every time. But
our batting average is better than most. I don't need to tell you
tales like the police, reassure you that we'll find your stuff. If you
hire us, we'll search and we'll see what we see. That's what I
offer. All I ask in return is prompt payment and cutting the BS."

"I always pay my bills, Mr. Jones."

"It's Miami, and right now I'm more concerned about
the BS."

He frowned. He was a successful guy. At the top of his
totem. In my experience, the closer a guy got to the top of his
totem, the less honesty he heard. People generally liked to hear
what they wanted to hear, so other people generally gave them
what they wanted. I also knew from experience that those kinds
of guys often didn't appreciate the honesty. I didn't care what he
thought. I had a house to clean and a bar to fix.

"I heard you were a straight shooter."

"Where did you hear that, Dale? I never did get to ask Angie how she came to find me."

"BJ Baker."

I cocked an eyebrow. I did it a lot better than Ronzoni. BJ Baker had been a client. He had lost something and hired Ron and me to find it. Suffice to say he was a demanding client and we hadn't taken a shine to each other. I had certainly never expected to get a case on the recommendation of BJ Baker.

"You know BJ?" I asked.

"I do. We sometimes find ourselves in the same circles. I know you did the Heisman case. It was in the news. I asked him about you. He said you were a pain in the backside but he had to admit that you got the job done."

"You want to work with a pain in the backside?"

"I think BJ Baker is a pain in the backside and I consider him a friend. You, I don't know yet. But I don't care." He focused in on me and I noticed his eyes again. He had one hell of a steely glare.

"Let me tell you something about my business, Miami. It's cutthroat. There are lots of guys who want to do it and only a few who can. I have been a winning driver and a winning crew chief and a winning owner. And there's only one way that happens. Everyone on the team is the best at what they do, but they also work as a team. There are lots of egos in racing, and not just the drivers. I learned early on that everyone has different buttons to press, for good and bad. I learned to manage quiet guys and loud guys, guys who always think they're right and guys who never speak up but always add value when they do. I've managed guys I'd lend a million bucks to and guys I wouldn't give a dime, and I've managed guys that are lifelong friends and guys I didn't care to know socially. Call them pains in the backside if you want to. I don't care. In racing, only one thing matters. Results."

"I can't guarantee results, Dale. Your cars might have disappeared."

"They ain't been vaporized. They're still on God's green earth. You just got to find them. And I'm gonna make the job easier. I don't care so much about the cars in there," he said, pointing out to the main garage. "I got the police and I got insurance for that. Your job, if you're man enough for it, is to find one car. Just one. The one that belongs in this room here."

He didn't take his eyes from me, so I didn't take mine from him. It was a pissing contest, that was for sure. We're men, we do that. It's primal and feral and unnecessary and it's who we are. I believed what he said about managing guys. If he wasn't good at it, he wouldn't have been so successful. That was the case in all pro sports. It was certainly the case when I played baseball. You needed great players for sure, but a lot of pennants had been won by teams with less than all-star lineups. Good managers brought the best out of guys. As Beadman said, they knew how to manage the egos and press the buttons. I'd had managers I would have walked through fire for, and I'd had managers I wouldn't have rolled over if they were on fire, and I recalled well which ones were the winners. I knew in which category I put Dale Beadman. Despite the *if you're man enough for it* jibe. Danielle would have torn him a new one for that.

"All right, Dale. I guess the question is, do you want to tell me about this hot car, or do you not? Because without the warts-and-all truth, I'm confident you'll be paying me to find absolutely nothing."

"What do you mean, *hot* car?"

"I mean acquired by other than open and lawful means, Dale. I have a good friend who knows a lot of people who trade in things like illicit art and Heisman trophies. I've picked up a thing or two. So I asked myself, why would someone who has built an entire pub designed to allow him and his buddies to look at his car collection have a private chamber designed to hide one of his cars. And if said car was stolen from him, why would that someone not include it in the list of stolen vehicles for the police? Answer? He doesn't want the police to know about that car. Why? Because it's hot. Stolen. Acquired by unlawful means."

I had said my piece and I would say no more until Dale Beadman decided which way he would go. I did keep my eyes on him, though. He, on the other hand, looked at his feet and shuffled some. It was the first sign of uncertainty I had seen in him. Then he must have come to some kind of decision, because he took my eyes again with his steely gaze.

"The car wasn't stolen," he said. "By me, I mean. But there are issues with the—what do they call it? Provenance?"

"You can't verify the car's ownership history."

"Right. No one can. Because this car isn't supposed to exist."

"Okay. Tell me the story."

Beadman glanced at Ron and then back at me. "Can I offer you gentlemen a beer?"

Ron looked like a Labrador with a pork chop dangling in front of him.

We sat at the bar and Beadman poured ales from a tap. Once we had all taken a sip, he spoke.

"Have you heard of the F-88?"

I shook my head. "Sounds like a fighter jet."

"Same idea, I suppose. Those kinds of designations get given to concept projects, prototypes."

"Okay."

"This was the Oldsmobile F-88. It was one of the first concept cars. See, back in the fifties, General Motors ran these motor shows across the country they called motoramas. These concept cars were developed to show off GM's futuristic thinking. The F-88 was one of those. It premiered at a motorama in 1954. Have you fellas heard of Harley Earl?"

I shook my head and sipped my beer. It was good, not too hoppy.

"Didn't he invent the Corvette?" asked Ron.

"Sort of," said Beadman. "He was the head of the styling section at GM, basically the chief designer. You know all those sweeping lines and tail fin lights on those wonderful convertibles of the fifties and sixties? Harley Earl headed the team behind most of those. As you say, Ron, he was behind Project Opel, which was a secret development project that went on to become the Chevrolet Corvette."

Beadman took a sip of his beer. I was glad for it. I don't trust a man who lets his beer go warm in favor of flapping his lips. Beadman continued.

"The F-88s did the run of the motorama shows in 1954. Now, it was the policy at GM at the time that concept cars that had run their course at the shows or been replaced by a new concept should be destroyed."

Ron nearly dropped his beer. "Destroyed?"

"Yeah, I think it was a liability thing. See, a lot of the cars were never built out to run on the street. They were chassis and body and then just enough of a system underneath to move them from one show to another. The brakes weren't always production quality, that sort of thing. Lots of concept cars were destroyed. But not all of them. Harley Earl held a good deal of power in GM at the time, and the word was that a few of the concept cars found their way into the hands of his friends, top GM dealers, those sort of folks."

"And that's what happened to the F-88?" I asked.

"Sort of. Hold on a moment." Beadman found a device under the bar that looked like a tablet computer. He wandered back out to us, tapping on the screen. As he took a stool, one of the screens above the bar flickered to life. Beadman tapped a few more times. He seemed pretty comfortable with the technology. An image of a car appeared on the big screen.

"The F-88," said Beadman.

I could see his point. It was one hell of a sexy car. A golden convertible with a sweeping curvaceous hood and tail fin lights on the rear, and a wide, handsome grille like a smiling mouth on the front. It looked like something James Bond might have driven back when Connery held the mantle.

"That is a beauty," said Ron.

"She is. But she's more than a car. See, the F-88's history gets pretty murky. Despite its popularity, it was never put into production. The rumor was that executives from the Chevrolet division lobbied against the F-88 because the Oldsmobile would steal the limelight from the newly released Corvette."

"Dirty pool," I said.

"Yes, sir," said Beadman. "But the F-88 had one big fan. Harley Earl. The story goes that he liked the design so much that he had a second car built from the mold for his own personal use, which he had painted red. The red F-88 was known to have made appearances at a few shows and races, like the Sports Car Club of America races at Andrews Air Force Base in Maryland and Atterbury Air Force Base in Columbus, Indiana."

I nodded toward the screen over the bar. "So this clearly isn't the red one."

"Probably not," said Beadman.

"Probably not?" asked Ron.

"Well, here's the thing. The golden F-88 was reported to have returned to Detroit, but no one has been able to say what happened to it. What is known is that a shipment of crates was sent from GM to the California home of EL Cord, the owner of Cord Industries, which was the holding company behind the

Auburn and Cord car brands, American Airways and plenty of other transportation companies. Those crates contained enough parts to build an entire F-88. Some say it was the golden F-88 disassembled for shipping so as to prevent it from being sent to the crusher, others say it was the backup parts machined in case anything went wrong with the show version."

"Why send them to this guy, Cord?"

"No one knows for sure. But both EL Cord and Harley Earl had homes here in Palm Beach. They probably knew each other. Either way, Cord never did anything with the parts, and they were sold and on-sold a number of times. The car was partially assembled, sold again, and then finally assembled by a guy called Don Williams. It was last sold at the Barrett-Jackson auction for a touch over three million dollars and now lives in a museum in Colorado."

Ron let out a whistle.

"And the red one?"

"Disappeared. Harley Earl died in 1969 and left no clue. There was a rumor that the two F-88s were being loaded onto a transport when one of the engines caught fire. The story goes that the guy transporting them didn't know how to open the hood, so the car burned. No one at GM or Oldsmobile could recall such a fire. After that, the red F-88 disappeared."

I said, "Why do I think you've left off the words *until now . . .?*"

Beadman nodded. "It's well known that I collect cars, especially domestic cars. I have another Chevy concept car in my museum."

"You have a museum?" I asked.

"You don't follow racing, do you?"

"I don't catch it as much as I'd like."

"He doesn't own a television," said Ron.

"You don't own a television?"

"Nope."

"How do you watch sports?"

"I go to a bar, or I go to the game."

"What about news?"

"What news?"

"Any news."

"We just had a hurricane, and I know who the president is. You've had a car stolen. What did I miss?"

Beadman shrugged. He hadn't yet gotten a handle on my buttons.

"So the red car?" I asked.

"I was approached. By an intermediary. He said he could access a concept car, one of only two. We went back and forth a bit. Eventually I was taken to see it."

"Where?"

"Lansing, Michigan."

"Long way from home."

"We were at a race at Michigan International Speedway. It's a short drive to Lansing."

"And you saw the car?" asked Ron.

"I did. In a barn just outside of town."

I frowned. "A barn?"

Beadman nodded.

"So who had the car?"

"I don't know."

"You don't know?" I asked.

"No, sir, I don't. It was handled by the intermediary."

"Who was the intermediary?"

"I can't say."

"Dale, if you want this car found, you need to level with me."

"And I can't tell you who it was. I never met them."

"You never met them? Who was at the barn?"

"No one."

"You could have just taken off with the damned thing."

"It's not an easy car to hide. And we assumed they were watching."

"So whoever was handling the sale knew it was here. They might have stolen it back."

"We arranged the shipping, not them. So they didn't know where it was going."

"But this would be a decent guess."

"As might be my museum. Or any number of other places. And they wouldn't have known when it was going to arrive."

"When did it arrive?"

"Three days ago. The morning before the hurricane."

"The morning before the hurricane?" I shook my head. "You might have led with that. I need to see the security video."

CHAPTER FIVE

I DIDN'T GET TO SEE THE VIDEO. ANGIE BEADMAN HAD gone into West Palm Beach on some business, so I asked Dale Beadman to tell her to call me when she got back. We stopped off at Ron and Cassandra's apartment so he could change into fresh clothes. The Lady Cassandra was sweeping off the large balcony that overlooked the water across Ocean Drive. The beach was black with sea debris that the ocean was slowly but surely reclaiming with each new tide.

Getting back to the office was a chore. Flagler Memorial Bridge, the northernmost crossing, was still closed due to rebuilding, and Royal Park Bridge was closed as a result of the storm surge that had almost swept me away into the Intracoastal only days before, and was pending a structural engineer's okay to reopen. We trudged slowly down to Southern Boulevard and even more slowly back up into West Palm. Flagler Drive and the walking paths along the Intracoastal seawall were closed thanks to debris cleanup—things didn't happen quite as fast in West Palm as they did on the island—so we labored along South Dixie Highway.

Clematis Street was a shambles. The street had been

cleared of debris, and then the store owners and the restaura-
teurs and the bar proprietors had come in to mop up the mess
and had deposited their fresh debris back onto the street. The
second cleanup was yet to occur, and the sun was baking the
soiled food and waste into something to behold.

The bank branch on the ground floor of our building was
still closed. The floodwater had swept right through it and I
think they were reconsidering the choice of carpet in their foyer.
The elevator lobby to our office was tiled and had required
nothing more than a mop out, and someone had already done
that. Ron and I took the stairs up to the office. I figured I'd give
the elevator a few days of use to work out the kinks and make
sure it wasn't going to fail from all the rain before I tried it.
Besides, the stairs were a vital part of my fitness regimen. It was
incidental movement like taking the stairs that kept the beer
belly at bay. At least, that was the consensus of Danielle and my
office manager, Lizzy.

Lizzy was already in the front office when we arrived. She
had hair the color of coal and lipstick the color of a stop sign.
Her shirt was a white button-up and her skirt was tight but a
conservative length, and she gave the business a more professional first impression than we probably deserved. Lizzy gave
me a look up and down that ended with a deep scowl that
suggested my sweaty U of M t-shirt and workout shorts didn't
meet her standards. It was a fair assumption, but in my defense,
I had been cleaning up storm damage when Angie Beadman
had found me at Longboard Kelly's, and I was yet to get home.

"There are laundered shirts and shorts in the closet,"
she said.

"We have a closet?" I asked, glancing at Ron. He shrugged.

"In the second office," said Lizzy.

I found a crisp shirt with little maps of Florida all over it and
slipped on a pair of cargo shorts. It was a testament to how far

our relationship had come that Lizzy had stocked a wardrobe with shorts.

Ron was sitting on the sofa in my office sipping a water when I got there. Technically the second office was his, but he never used it, preferring the sofa in mine. Lizzy was in the visitor's chair in front of my desk but was turned around to face Ron. She looked at my clothes and nodded.

"Dale Beadman," she said.

"You know him?"

"Of course I know him. He's a legend."

"I didn't take you for a NASCAR fan," I said, edging around behind my desk and sitting down.

"What does a NASCAR fan look like to you?" she asked. Lizzy had a gift for turning my words around on me and tying me up in them.

"Male, large, bearded and Southern."

Lizzy shook her head. "I would expect someone about to marry a female law enforcement officer to engage a little less in gender stereotyping."

"That's not gender stereotyping," I defended. "I've only known one person who was a mad NASCAR fan and I just described him. You'd be the second."

"I'm not mad about it, I just follow it some. I like Daytona."

"Fair enough."

"Lizzy's going to do a little digging into Dale's personal life," said Ron. "I'll check out his businesses. See if we can't find any motivation for the burglary there."

I was about to say that was a good idea when we heard the front door of the offices open and close. Lizzy jumped up and stepped out of my office. The front area was her domain. She didn't close the door and I didn't hear any conversation. Lizzy reappeared in my door.

"Detective Ronzoni," she said, before she stepped aside to let Ronzoni through.

He looked the same as he had earlier, which was the same as he always looked. Disheveled was the word that came to mind. He really didn't have the crisp, clean look that one expected with the Palm Beach Police Department. I liked that about him. He did act like the personal stormtrooper for the rich and powerful folks on the island at times, but he was also aware that those same shiny folks were as capable of crime as any other human being.

Lizzy stepped out and closed the door behind her. Ronzoni took the visitor's chair and Ron tossed him a bottle of water, which he cracked open and guzzled half down. Then he wiped his lips with his suit jacket sleeve. The humidity was down since the hurricane, but it was still plenty muggy. I wouldn't have worn a jacket outside for a carload of cash. Even trousers were out for me.

"What's he hiding?" asked Ronzoni.

"What's who hiding?"

"Don't play dumb with me, Jones. Beadman."

"What makes you think he's hiding something?"

"He called me to investigate his stolen vehicles. He doesn't need you. So I have to ask myself, why are you there? And why does he want you to stay behind after I'm gone?"

"He didn't call you, Ronzoni. He called the police because he has to, in order to file an insurance claim. You have done his paperwork for him, haven't you?"

"Don't mess with me, Jones. This is a police matter." He took a breath and sipped some more water. "We worked together at the hotel. No reason not to do it again."

I smiled. Ronzoni was getting soft in his old age, and he wasn't that old. He was right, we had worked together to solve a murder during the hurricane. He had actually surprised me. He was pretty good at his job. And I think I had surprised him, as well. Mainly in my readiness to concede all credit to him for solving the crime. He was a puzzle, that was for sure. He loved getting the credit for solving cases, but he never seemed to use this credit to advance his career. From his current position, he might hope to become chief of detectives someday, but beyond that he was terminal. He'd never be chief of police, not in Palm Beach and probably not anywhere else, either. He just didn't have the political animal in him. The chief of police wasn't elected like the sheriff, but he was appointed by the mayor—who was voted in and out depending on the whim of the people—so the chief was as subject to the political process as anyone. Ronzoni wasn't the sharpest tack in the toolbox, but I think he knew where his skill set ran aground. Perhaps he just liked solving crimes. It was a cheesy thought but one that fit Ronzoni better than his suit.

"Okay, Detective. I'll play. No reason not to, right? Did you see the security video?"

If he noticed that I had started asking the questions, he didn't let on. "I did," he said. "What did you see in it?"

"Nothing," I said. It was the truth, given I hadn't yet seen the video.

"Me neither. The garage is locked up tight, the storm comes in, the cars are there, then boom, the power gets wiped out and there's no more video. When it comes back online there are no cars."

"Do we know if the video goes off due to a power outage or if it was cut?"

"Good question. Haven't had a chance to ask Florida Power and Light about that. And I got to get out to another call. Seems a lot of people get up to no good during a big storm."

"We'll be back out to the Beadman place later, so I'll see if there are any FPL guys around."

"Let me know," said Ronzoni, standing. He finished his water, crushed the plastic bottle and dropped it in the wastebasket. He walked to the door and stopped.

"How did they get ten cars off the island?"

I shrugged. "They drove them off, or they put them on a truck and drove the truck off."

"Two bridges were closed, that we know."

"Is there video on Southern Boulevard?" I asked him.

"There's video, but they don't record it."

"They don't record it? What's the point?"

"It's used for traffic management or some baloney. DOT says they can't afford to record it all over the state. Plus they'd have to hire people to handle all the requests they'd get from damn lawyers and such. What do you think about the idea of using a boat?"

"Would you have taken a boat out in that weather?"

"I wouldn't have stolen the cars. There's no telling what people will do."

He was right about that.

"I'll check out any possible spots that could have allowed a boat to load."

"Keep me informed," said Ronzoni, and he stepped out the door and was gone.

"Yes, boss," I said to no more than the thought of him.

CHAPTER SIX

I GOT LET BACK IN THROUGH THE SUBSTANTIAL GATES AND pulled my Cadillac SUV around in the driveway of the Beadman estate. In my absence, a pile of decomposed granite had been dumped in the open space between the house and the showcase garage, ready to replace the previous driveway surface, which had been washed across the island during the hurricane.

I was met at the front steps by a woman in tight jeans and a white cotton shirt. She had long blond hair and wore a full layer of makeup, I assumed, designed to mask her age. She gave me a warm smile that was all mouth and no eyes.

"Mr. Jones," she said in a syrupy Southern accent. "I am sorry we were not acquainted before. I am Missy Beadman, Dale's wife."

"Mrs. Beadman," I said, shaking her hand. Her hands were petite, but her grip was strong, and she had a magician's fingers. "It's a pleasure."

"The pleasure is mine, sir. And please, call me Missy."

"Of course."

"Now come inside for some tea."

She led me into the house, through a two-story entranceway

with a sweeping staircase and into a large great room with floor-to-ceiling windows and a killer view of the ocean. To the side of the great room was a kitchen. It featured two islands and the largest refrigerator I had seen outside of a morgue. Missy pulled at one of the refrigerator doors with both hands in order to get it open and then fished out a pitcher of tea.

"Iced tea, Mr. Jones?"

"Thank you." I had a mind to ask her to call me Miami, but I liked the way *Mr. Jones* rolled off her tongue.

"Is Dale in the garage?" I asked, taking a barstool at one of the islands.

"I'm afraid Dale had to return to Charlotte."

"What's in Charlotte?"

She dropped a coaster in front of me, placed a glass of iced tea on it and then took a stool beside me.

"Why, Mr. Jones, you are amusing."

"I try, Missy. So what's in Charlotte?"

She sipped her tea and looked out the window toward the white walls of the garage building. I could see the guys finishing up the palapa over the deck.

"You don't follow NASCAR, do you, Mr. Jones?"

"Not as much as I should, apparently."

She smiled again. It still didn't make it to her eyes. It wasn't until you met someone who only smiled with their mouth that you realized how much of a smile happens in the eyes. Danielle's smile did. Her mouth would crinkle up on one side and her eyes would light up. Missy's eyes didn't do that. I wondered if they ever had. She didn't have any wrinkles around her eyes, but that seemed too high a price to pay.

"Dale's team workshop is just outside of Charlotte. Most of the NASCAR teams are based in the Charlotte area."

"That's quite a commute."

She nodded, and I thought I saw something in her look.

Distance, like she went somewhere for a moment. Then she was back.

"It is," she said.

"Why is he based there?"

"Like I say, most of the teams are there."

"Why are any of them there? What's so special about Charlotte?"

"I can't honestly say, Mr. Jones. It's just always been that way. I'm sure part of it is geographical. A lot of the races are in the South, of course. But Charlotte is convenient for the races in the north as well."

"Is Dale there a lot?"

"Yes, I guess he is. Especially in season."

"That must be hard."

"Winning doesn't come easy, Mr. Jones."

I sipped my tea. It was sweet. I preferred my iced tea unsweetened, but sweet tea was the Southern way.

"How did you meet Dale, Missy?"

"At a racetrack, of course." For a moment I thought I saw the smile in her eyes, but then she caught herself. It must have taken a lot of practice. She stepped to a bureau. On top of it were two photographs in matching silver frames. She picked one up, looked at and then turned it to me. It was black and white but clearly taken at night under floodlights. There was a group of people standing in front of an old stock car. They all had beers. Some of them were facing away from the camera. A very young Dale Beadman was looking straight at the lens.

"He was racing stock cars in Alabama. I was at school in Tuscaloosa and a boy I knew took me to an evening race meet." She paused for a moment and I felt no need to fill the void. "We were in a sponsor's tent after the race—it sounds more glamorous than it was—and Dale was the number two driver for the sponsor's team. He was very charming. He asked me all kinds of questions about what I was doing at college and what I wanted to do with my life. . ."

"What about your boyfriend?"

"Oh, honey, he wasn't my boyfriend. Can't say that he even wanted the job, but after I met Dale it was irrelevant. He was the only man for me."

I glanced again at the photograph. Everyone was young and carefree and happy. Dale Beadman looked like he would live forever. And then I recognized the face two away from him. It was Missy. She wasn't looking at the camera. She was looking at Dale Beadman. She wore the look of love.

Missy placed the frame back on the bureau. "Did you know Dale arrived at my sorority house for our first date in a stock car? I had to climb in through the window."

"Is that legal?"

"Not street legal, no. It was a different time."

I said nothing.

"We moved to Daytona after we got married. Dale grew up on the Space Coast."

"You quit college?"

"No, sir. I graduated summa cum laude."

"Good for you."

"Did you go to college, Mr. Jones?"

"University of Miami."

She nodded. "That's where you gained the name."

"Yes, ma'am."

"Good football school. Not 'Bama, but good."

"Yes, ma'am." I glanced at the second of the two silver frames. It was a picture of Dale and Missy, a decade or two after the other one. It was in color. They were standing on a balcony overlooking a wide bay that was filled with large luxury yachts. The color of the water was the color of Missy's eyes.

"Monaco," she said. "Have you ever been?"

"No, ma'am."

"We went for the race, of course."

"Did you travel with Dale a lot?"

"Not by then. Angela Jean was born by the time that photo was taken. She was there, somewhere."

"Did you like France?"

"I didn't get to see France," she said. "Didn't even get to go to Paris. There was no race in Paris."

Her eyes drifted away again and then came back.

I said, "So how did you end up in Palm Beach?"

Missy collected our empty glasses and placed them in the sink. "That came later. I did travel with Dale for a couple years. I looked after the financials for the team. Then he got his shot at NASCAR. They have their own people, so they didn't need me. We moved to Charlotte but he was away a lot. Charlotte's nice, but it never really felt like home. When I was pregnant we decided to step outside of the bubble, so to speak. That was Palm Beach."

She tapped her thin fingers on the marble countertop and her rings made a sound like a meat mallet.

I asked, "Were you here when the F-88 was delivered?"

"The F-88? Oh, you mean Dale's newest darling. Yes, I was here, in the house. Angela Jean handled the delivery."

"Angela Jean?"

"Yes, she prefers Angie. Mothers can be so unnaturally attached to old names, can't they?"

I shrugged.

"Surely your mother doesn't call you Miami."

"No," I said. "Never." I kept to myself the fact that my mother had never lived to see me recruited to a college.

"And after the delivery, how did you get out of town?" I asked.

"We drove."

"To where?"

"Charlotte. We still have a home there."

"You drove to Charlotte?"

"Angela Jean drove, yes. Dale wanted to send the plane back, but I wasn't happy about the hurricane. It was getting quite wild out."

"You have a plane?"

"Yes, we just upgraded from a single prop to a Learjet 31A."

"I'm in the wrong business."

"A private jet doesn't maketh the man, Mr. Jones."

Neither did having to take your shoes off at airport security. "Where does it come in? PBI?"

"No, we have hangars at North Palm Beach County Airport."

I gave my impressed face. This NASCAR lark looked like a good business to be in.

"So I assume you want to chat with Angela Jean. Her office is at the other end of the house, next to the server room. I'll show you."

As we walked out of the kitchen, I asked, "Why would Angie handle the delivery of the F-88?"

"She handles all of Dale's affairs. She's going to be taking over the running of the company."

"When?"

"Someday soon. Here we are."

Missy knocked on the door with a resounding thud that spoke of expensive old-growth hardwood and then opened the door.

"Angela Jean, Mr. Jones is here to see you."

Angie was seated at a desk that was plain white and utilitarian. It looked like an Ikea piece. She was frowning at a computer monitor like she needed to drop in on an optometrist, and she looked up as if she had been a million miles away.

"Oh, Mr. Jones."

"I'll leave you kids to it," said Missy, closing the door. It had been some time since I had been referred to as a kid, and Angie was no yearling.

"I'm sorry, Mr. Jones, I wasn't expecting you."

"It's Miami," I said once again. Mr. Jones didn't roll off her tongue the same way as it had with her mother. She was not the product of a Southern upbringing. No doubt she had been raised a little further south than the Deep South.

"Miami, of course. How can I help?"

"I was hoping to get a look at the security video from the garage."

"I showed it to Detective Ronzoni. There wasn't much to see."

"Still. If I could have a look all the same."

She glanced at her screen and then back at me. "Of course. It's just in the next room."

Angie tapped a button on her keyboard and then stood and strode out of the room. The next door along was built of similar heft. She pushed it open and we stepped inside. It was a small space, like a child's bedroom. There was another utilitarian desk with a couple computer monitors on it. A rack of computer servers hummed loudly and pushed considerable heat into the room.

Angie sat at a desk and took hold of a mouse and clicked her way to a screen that opened up as a picture of the faux-English pub in the garage building.

"Take a seat, Miami."

I did that and directed my attention to the screen.

"This is the video from that morning. There are three cameras: one on the front of the garage looking at the driveway, one in the pub and one in the main garage."

"Nothing in the secret garage?"

"No, sir. There's no way to get in there except through the main garage anyhow."

"Okay. Let's see."

Angie clicked a button and the picture flickered. The video camera was mounted on the far end of the pub, looking back toward the television on the wall beside the door from the deck. Nothing was happening. The space was dark. The lights were off and storm clouds had driven the daylight away, but I guessed the camera had some kind of infrared capability, so we could make out the booths and the bar and even some of the posters with surprising clarity.

Then the picture changed to a view of the driveway. The rain was coming down, heavy but nowhere near as heavy as it was going to get.

"What happened?" I asked.

"The video rotates automatically through the three cameras. Twenty seconds each shot. It saves on DVR space, I guess."

I said nothing. I was watching something slink its way up the driveway toward the garage. It looked like the backend of a trailer. Then the picture changed again to a view of the darkened garage. The shot was from above the bank of windows into the pub, looking back at the roller door at the end. I could make out the shapes of cars parked at angles, display style. In the darkness the white walls glowed. Then the video went back to the pub.

I waited for the shot to go back outside. A semitrailer was backing up to the roller door of the garage. It was an enclosed trailer, not one of those open ones I saw moving new cars covered in plastic up and down I-95. The rain bounced off the top of the trailer and red circles glowed from the rear. Then we were back inside the garage. The roller door began moving up. There was no sound with the video but I heard the noise in my head. The door opened a third of the way and someone stepped under wearing a rain slicker. The rain was already forming puddles on the gravel outside. Then the lights burst on.

Angie Beadman flipped the hood off her head in the video and looked across the garage. There were ten cars. They were all gleaming in the lights. I saw the black Model T, next to a blue sedan that looked like a seventies muscle car. On the other side, my eye was drawn to a red sports car that could be nothing but the work of Enzo Ferrari.

"Ferrari," I said.

"250 Testa Rossa."

"Testa Rossa. Wasn't that what Magnum PI drove? It doesn't look like his car."

Angie gave me a sideways glance. "Yes, but no. Magnum's car was a Testarossa, all one word. That was a large production model for Ferrari in the 1980s. Probably their most popular model ever. This is Testa Rossa, two words. It's a race car from the late fifties. Only thirty-four were ever built."

"You know a lot about cars."

"Occupational hazard."

The video went back to the bar, which was now bathed in light from the garage. Then back outside, where all I could see was the top of the truck trailer. We waited for the garage shot again. The back of the trailer was opening like a whale's mouth, creating a ramp down onto the pristine concrete. Water cascaded off it onto the floor. Then I saw another person appear at the rear of the truck, dripping wet. It was a man. He wore a cap rather than a hood, and the cap looked drenched. Then the video flicked to the outside view and we sat back to wait.

"What's the collection worth?" I asked.

"It's insured for thirty million."

I nearly fell off my chair, literally. I caught the back as I tipped and pulled myself up.

"You okay?" Angie asked.

"That's a lot of money."

"It's insurance value. What they'd sell for is anyone's guess. Values go up and down."

"And the F-88 is the most valuable?"

"No, not by a long shot."

"Really? So why is it so special?"

"It's the latest baby?" Angie shrugged. "My dad has a thing for domestic cars."

The video came back into the garage. The man in the cap stepped up onto the ramp and walked up into the guts of the trailer. It was too dark in there to see anything.

"Who's the guy?"

"Rex Jennings. He's one of Dad's truck drivers."

"So this is your dad's truck?"

"That's right. We have three. Two are for the main cars, 29 and 09. This one is used for the development engineers in Charlotte, and as backup in case one of the others breaks down."

The video switched again.

"So about the F-88—it's not the most expensive?"

"No. If it were insured, it would be covered for maybe four or five million."

"But it's not insured."

"No, it's not."

"Hence wanting it back so badly."

"It's not really the money. The insurance on the others would cover that loss, too, easily."

"Who insures the cars?"

"Great Southeast Permanent."

I knew the name. The same grandiosely titled outfit that covered my house, which was worth considerably less than Beadman's car collection.

"So which one is the most valuable?"

"You spotted it. The Testa Rossa. Dad found it in a dusty

shed in Italy. Got it for eight hundred thousand, years ago. They restored it at his workshop."

"What's it worth?"

"Last one I heard about sold at auction for sixteen million."

I was holding on to my chair this time. I'm rarely fooled twice.

"That's a tidy sum."

Angie nodded and the video returned to the garage.

The driver, Rex, strode down the ramp and across to the shelves on the wall. He pulled them apart to reveal the hidden room. Then he marched back up into the truck. We waited for the video to rotate and then saw Rex pushing a car down the ramp and into the garage. He had the driver's door cracked open and was using one hand to steer the vehicle down the middle of the space between the rows of cars on either side. There were six on the right wall as we looked at it and four on the left. The space on the left remained to access the hidden room, which was where Rex pushed the car. The video rotated again.

"That's the F-88?"

"Yes."

"It's covered up. How do you know?"

"Rex took the cover off once it was in place."

"But how did he verify it was the right car in the first place?"

"He didn't. Simon did that."

"Simon?"

"Simon Lees. Head engineer at the team workshop. He went to Lansing to handle the pick up and verify it all."

The video came back and Rex strode out of the hidden room with a large sheet rolled up under his arm. I assumed it was the car cover. He walked back out to the trailer and reappeared with a mop. The video rotated, and when it returned, Rex was mopping the residual water off the shiny floor. It was truly A-grade service. He worked his way back to the base of the ramp, where Angie stood waiting. They spoke. Then the video moved on.

"What did you discuss?"

"Nothing much. I told him to drive safe on the roads. It was raining and it was going to get worse. He said to say hi to Mom, and to make sure we got out of town ASAP."

We watched the video switch back. The driver, Rex, was working a control panel at the rear side of the truck to make the ramp lift back up. Angie flicked her hood up and dashed out into the rain.

"Where were you going now?" I asked.

"Back to the house. I had to lock everything up and then get the hell out of Dodge."

I watched as the ramp on the trailer closed up tight and then Rex took a phone out and made a quick call. Then he flicked the garage lights off. The space was plunged into darkness and I saw the shadow of the driver step out into the rain. He moved away from the truck and out of view. Then the roller door shuddered. I waited for the video to rotate through again, which was getting tiresome, and then it was back in time to see the roller door lower the last few feet until it shuddered to a close. It took the infrared sensors in the camera a few seconds to do their thing, but gradually the shapes of the cars formed in the darkness of the garage.

"What happens now?" I asked.

"Nothing," said Angie. "I mean, I haven't watched the whole thing, but we forwarded through it with Detective Ronzoni, and it just stays like this until the power cuts out."

"How long until that happens?"

"About twelve hours, I guess. There's no timestamp or anything on this video."

"Do you remember what time the truck arrived?"

"It was eleven. I remember Dad's grandfather clock chimed as I was getting my rain jacket on."

"So what did you do after you left the garage?"

"I went back to the house. We packed some things, made sure all the storm shutters were in place, and then we left."

"You and your mother."

"That's right."

"How long later?"

"About two hours, by the time we got everything ready."

"That's a while. The hurricane wasn't that big a surprise."

"My mother doesn't travel light."

I could see that. "And the truck was gone."

"Yes."

I watched the video loop through a couple more times. Nothing happened in the garage or the bar. Outside I saw the top of the trailer the next time around. The time after that the truck was gone. Rain was pelting down on the gravel, a portent of the flood to come.

"Anyone else still here when you left?"

"No. We sent everyone home the previous night. The groundsmen put the shutters up before they went. We told them not to come back until it was safe."

"Your mother told me you drove to Charlotte. How did you get off the island?"

"Flagler was closed, so we had to use Royal Park."

"It was still open?"

"Yes."

"And then I-95?"

"Yes. It was pretty slow, but it opened up after Port St. Lucie."

"Which car did you take?"

"Mine. The Camaro."

"Take long to get to Charlotte?"

She smiled a little. "Not that long. Not in my baby."

Apparently, the apple hadn't fallen far from the tree when it came to speed.

"Can I get a copy of the video?"

"All of it?"

"Sure."

"You're going to watch twelve hours of nothing happening?"

"Someone is."

"I can set up a user account. You can access it securely over the internet. You have internet access restored?"

I wasn't sure about that. I didn't have any power at my house at all, but then I didn't have any internet access, either. I knew we had it at the office, but whether it was up or down was between Lizzy and the cable company.

"I'll work something out. Set me up."

Angie tapped some keys and then scribbled something on a piece of DBR notepaper and tore off the page and handed it to me.

"You need anything else?" she asked.

"Not right now."

Angie walked me out to my car. Guys were raking the decomposed granite across the driveway and I think they were happy about me moving out of the way. I told Angie I'd be in touch and got in my car. I looked at the piece of paper in my hand and thought about the video. And how the hell someone had gotten eleven cars off an island during a hurricane.

CHAPTER SEVEN

I DROVE THE LONG WAY HOME. FIRST I WENT NORTH ALL the way to the top end of the island, which wasn't far from the Beadman estate. I stopped at the top end of North Ocean Boulevard. The road to the right was a sliver of a one-way street, not all that suitable for a vehicle transporter. A pier sat at the end of the island behind a waist-high gate that would let a couple people in side-by-side. There was a bicycle rack, and a woman in a white blouse stood on the end of the pier, letting the breeze blow across her face. I tested the gate and the fence. The fence was firm and the gate lay permanently open.

On further inspection, I realized that the gate opened on both sides from the middle. The open side was just one half. The other side was locked to the peg in the concrete. Neither the lock nor the peg looked recently disturbed. I stood back and assessed the width of the entrance. It was wide enough for a car. Not a truck or a Hummer or anything equally ridiculous, but certainly a sports car.

The paved path led onto the pier. A boat could quite easily pull up to the pier. I knew that because a boat came in and tied up as I watched. There was a slight breeze and small chop and the boat bobbled on the water. A guy in the boat offered a hand to the woman in the white blouse. She took it and stepped care-fully into the vessel. The boat wasn't rocking with any kind of violence, but I could see it doing so in the kind of wind that the hurricane had pushed down the coast. Then there was the storm surge. My backyard had a speedboat dumped sitting in it thanks to the surge. There was every chance that the pier I was looking at had been underwater for the majority of the storm. It didn't seem like any kind of smart way to get cars off the island.

I turned away and headed south, all the way down the east side of the island, past the debris-strewn beaches along South Ocean Boulevard. I headed past the Bonita Mar Club and down onto Southern Boulevard. I had an itch to scratch and I had a reasonable idea of how to do just that. I drove across Bingham Island and onto the mainland and pulled into a small lot in front of a low office building. There was a sign for a realty business out front, and palm fronds had fallen across the lawn. I had had occasion to visit the offices before, but the franchise had changed hands and a new company's decal was on the door.

The young guy at the reception desk was still the same, though. He was shuffling papers, trying to keep busy while waiting for the phone to ring or someone to need an emergency Starbucks run. The door creaked a little as I stepped in, and he looked up. I was happy to see that he remembered me.

"Not you again," he said.

"You've got the place in good shape, considering," I said.

"It took a lot of mopping if you must know. The water was everywhere."

"I'm sure."

"What do you want?"

"I notice you have a security camera over the front door."

"Yeah, what of it?"

"You record it or is it just for show?"

"Of course we record. It wouldn't be very secure if we didn't."

I shrugged. "I'd like to see it."

"I need to see a warrant or something."

"I'm not the cops, junior. I don't do warrants. So you gonna help me out, or am I going to cause trouble?"

He snarled at me. He knew my kind of trouble, and he didn't want any of it, clearly, because he pushed his chair out and stood with a huff. "You know our power went out, right?"

"I am aware," I said. "I want to see the morning before the hurricane, if you have it."

He led me into the back of the building, a corridor leading to small offices. Most looked used, but none had actual people in them. Real estate agents didn't make their dough sitting in the office. The kid led me into an office that looked like all the others except for the lack of paperwork lying around. There was a computer, which he brought to life, and he tapped and clicked and up came the video.

The shot showed the front of the offices, across the parking lot and onto the westbound lanes of Southern Boulevard. It was those lanes I was interested in. Unlike the video at the Beadman residence, this one had a time stamp. I got the kid to pull it up to when I wanted it. I figured it had been fifteen minutes to deliver the F-88 and then I allowed fifteen minutes' grace to get down to Southern. In reality, it would take longer, especially in storm conditions and with traffic trying to flee the island at the last minute, but I wanted to start watching too early, not too late.

I watched the traffic zoom by, looking for the truck. I didn't see it. I watched well past the time it could have possibly taken the truck to get there. The kid huffed and puffed as he waited. He had his ear out for the squeaking door in case a potential buyer wandered in, but the real estate business wasn't exactly humming directly after a hurricane. Except for my house. Folks seemed awfully interested in that.

When I had seen enough, I thanked the kid and walked out. I wasn't surprised I hadn't seen the truck. I was just covering my bases. Southern Boulevard was the most southerly crossing on this part of the island, and I knew for a fact that the middle of the three crossings was still open when the truck would have been leaving. That was my next stop.

The second stop would be easier. I jumped on the freeway and got off at Palm Beach Lakes Boulevard and then back-tracked on myself. The building I wanted overlooked the on-ramp for I-95 North at Okeechobee. I parked in the lot and wandered in. The building was an apartment complex for senior citizens, with lake views on one side and freeway views on the other. I knocked on the door to the office I wanted and was asked to come in. I did that.

The guy sitting at the desk was a good-looking black kid with a winning smile. He gave me the smile.

"Mr. Jones," he beamed.

"Leo, how's it going?"

"It's all good, sir, it's all good."

"How's the property management game?"

"Learning plenty, sir."

"You'll be a mogul before you're thirty, Leo."

"That's the plan. What can I do for you?"

"I need your eyes, Leo, I need your eyes."

Leo had been taken under the wing of my good friend, Sal Mondavi. Sal was a grumpy piece of work with a heart of gold, which he exhibited by giving kids with troubled backgrounds money to pay for college. Many of the kids did odd jobs for him in return, although he never asked for it. Leo had helped Sal with his computers and set up video surveillance in his pawn shop. Sal had ensured Leo graduated college without a mountain of debt.

I suspected the apartment building would have security cameras covering the parking lot that overlooked the freeway on-ramp, and within seconds, Leo had the video I wanted. The traffic was heavy on I-95 with folks trying to make a late break for it, but eventually, we saw the moving billboard that was Dale Beadman's transport truck. I saw the green truck with DBR on the door. Dale Beadman Racing. The truck crawled up onto I-95 and headed out of shot. I checked the time on the video. It had been a slow haul off the island. Lots of people had been caught out by the late call on the intensity of the hurricane. But the truck had made it onto the freeway and headed for Charlotte.

I thanked Leo for his time. I'd crossed the t's and all that and seen the delivery vehicle on its way. Now I needed to figure out how the cars that were left behind had come to disappear.

CHAPTER EIGHT

THE SHADOWS WERE GROWING LONG AS I HEADED BACK across Blue Heron and onto Singer Island. I had a mind to head straight for Longboard Kelly's, but something in my guts turned my sails for home. I decided what I needed was a run on the beach, just to clear the cobwebs. I'm not a natural runner, few pitchers are, but I enjoyed the sea breeze and the feeling of the endorphins that kicked in toward the end. I figured I'd call Danielle when I got home and see if she was up for it.

I stopped before I got to the front of the house. I saw the notice on the door and for a moment I thought FPL must have been letting me know they were doing repairs to the dead power cables or something. But FPL tended to stick their notices on doors with masking tape. This notice was tacked to my door with a nail. I wasn't impressed with the damage to my door, even though the thing was waterlogged and would have to be replaced. There was a principle involved. I pulled the notice from the door, leaving the nail in place.

The seal of the County of Palm Beach was at the top. I read the note and then I read it again. The notice was summed up in the bold type at the top of the paper: *Code Violation. Unfit for*

Habitation. Apparently, the county had made the determination that my home was so damaged by the hurricane that it was no longer appropriate for human life. It went on to say that all persons, I assumed including me, were to vacate the premises and not enter again until all violations had been rectified and subject to inspection by an officer of the Planning, Zoning and Building Department, County of Palm Beach. The letter was signed illegibly by someone called Peter Malloy, Enforcement Inspector.

I checked the time. The offices of said inspector would be closed. Lucky for him. I left the front door alone and strode around the back of the house. The speedboat was still there, lying at a jaunty angle as marooned boats tend to do. I pulled apart the plastic that we had stuck up where the sliding door used to be and stepped inside. It felt dark and damp but far from uninhabitable. I'd paid good money for worse hotel rooms. I threw the notice on the counter and went to the fridge and opened it to realize that I had no power. There wasn't a cold beer on the premises, which only served to further darken my mood.

The fix for a bad mood is a good run. It either improves my outlook or it delivers the mean reds in full fury. It's an each-way proposition. I grabbed a t-shirt and shorts from my SUV and changed in my bedroom as the carpet squelched beneath my feet. The street had an eerie calm to it as I ran down toward City Beach. There were no birds flapping around looking for their nightly perch, no warm lights from the windows of homes. I jogged past the closed-up shops and bars at Ocean Mall and through the dunes and out onto the beach. The ocean had pushed the sea debris up to the high tide mark. The vendors with their beach loungers and umbrellas and boogie boards were nowhere to be seen. The water looked serene, almost inviting, showing the other side of its considerable mood swings. I ran on the hard sand north past the hotels and high-rise condos, until the island thinned out. My pulse was up and the good hormones should have kicked in, but I still felt uneasy.

I turned and ran back before the sun disappeared and I lost my bearings completely. I almost missed the cut through the dunes back to the mall. I dropped my pace to a walk through the parking lot of the mall and wandered back home in junglelike darkness. The lights were glowing from across the Intracoastal and I figured there must be some kind of transformer still out of action, preventing power from making it back to Singer Island. I was okay with the dark. It suited my mood.

My mood, however, picked up as I reached my house and saw Danielle's truck parked out front. She was sitting in the cab reading something on her phone. I walked across the front of the truck so she could see me without being startled. I find it best practice not to spook firearm bearing law enforcement types, even the ones that love me. She picked up on the movement and buzzed the window down.

"You're even sweatier than you were this morning. How is this possible?"

"Went for a run."

"Uh-oh. What happened?"

"Come inside, I'll show you."

We went in through the front door this time, and I handed her the letter that I had left on my counter. She read it over and then read it again.

"How did they ascertain the house was unfit?"

"Your guess is as good as mine. I'm going to take a shower."

The power might have been out, but the water was running just fine. Underground pipes versus overhead wires. Go figure. The only downside was that I hadn't relit the pilot on my hot water heater, so the shower was frigid, but that cooled me down quicker. I got dressed and found Danielle sitting on the counter.

The furniture in the living room was damp or dead, so it was as good a place to sit as any. She had lit a camp light and was reading something on her phone.

"You know it's not really the county's job to enforce code violations here," she said.

"No?"

"No. Code violation in an incorporated area is a city thing. The county might do a preliminary damage assessment, but that's not what this is."

"So what are you saying?"

"I don't know. It's—"

There was a hefty knock at the door. It was no Mormon knock. Those boys tended to prefer doorbells anyway. This knock was serious and laced with intent. Danielle slipped off the counter onto the damp carpet. I went to the door.

It was a sheriff's deputy with a bright flashlight pointed at my face. The county seemed to have my number today. I couldn't see the deputy behind the beam, and he didn't recognize me.

"Deputy," I said, with my hands in front of my face. "How can I help you?"

"Sir, are you aware that this dwelling has been declared unfit for habitation?"

I was tempted to say no, but lying to law enforcement about easily proved facts never ended well, so I went with, "Is that so?"

"Yes, sir. You must vacate this property immediately."

His eyes and his flashlight beam drifted over my shoulder and then got wide.

"Danielle," he said.

"Todd," Danielle replied. "Won't you come in?"

He hesitated but came inside. We stepped to the counter so we could see each other by the camp light. The deputy pointed his flashlight down but didn't turn it off. I tried to blink away the purple splotches that now marred my vision.

"I didn't know this was your place," said the deputy to Danielle.

She nodded. "Have you met my fiancé? Miami Jones."

He looked at me but didn't offer to shake hands or anything. "I've heard of you."

"What's this about?" asked Danielle.

"Sheriff got a call about illegal use of a condemned structure. Possible looting."

"Do we look like we're looting?" I asked.

He didn't look at me. "The call came in to the sheriff himself. He put the call out. I don't think he knew it was your place, Danielle."

"Well, it is."

"Unfortunately, I don't think that matters now. Someone with the sheriff's personal number called it in. The dwelling has been condemned, apparently."

"Not condemned," said Danielle, picking up the notice on county letterhead. "Unfit for habitation. Whatever that means."

"Either way, you shouldn't be here."

"It's not unfit for habitation," I said.

"You an engineer?"

"No, but are you telling me an engineer crawled under the house to check the joists?"

"I have no idea, Miami. But the call is on the sheriff's radar, and that means trouble for you. I'll tell him it's your house, Danielle, but that'll cut you some grace to get out, not to stay. You got anywhere you can go tonight?"

Danielle looked at me. I nodded. I didn't want to make trouble for her. I sure wanted to stick it to the county, but Danielle had only recently resigned from the Palm Beach Sheriff's Office to join the Florida Department of Law Enforcement.

As the state's version of the FBI, it tended to hold a trump card over the PBSO, and it would not be a great way for her to start by being seen to be taunting her old boss. And the fact was we did have somewhere to stay.

"Give me a minute," I said, and I wandered out the back, through the plastic sheeting and onto the patio where the cell phone reception was better.

"Lucas," I said.

"Hey, Miami. How's the cleanup, mate?"

"So-so." I told him about the notice and the deputy. "Is your condo still available?"

"Of course, it's yours."

Lucas had offered us the use of his two-bed rental condo at PGA National. I never even knew he had an investment property, but there was plenty of stuff that I didn't know about Lucas. He was hardly overbooked anyway, he said. Every course in South Florida was currently oozing warm moisture like a wrestler's armpit. That's the thing about summer hurricanes. It really sorts the wheat from the chaff when it comes to diehard golfers.

"Just collect the keys from the property manager. I'll give them a call."

"I appreciate it, Lucas. Really."

"Anytime, mate."

"How are things in Miami?"

"We're right as rain, pardon the pun. It's a marina. The tide went up, the boats went up. The tide went down, the boats went down. It's all in where you tie them."

"Good to hear."

"Listen, Miami. I was thinking about going and checking on Lenny tomorrow."

"I was thinking about that, too."

"In the arvo, that okay?"

"Tomorrow afternoon, then. I'm buying. And thanks again."
I cut the call and went back inside.

Danielle and Todd were still chatting, but they both fell
silent when I came back in.

"We're all set. Lucas's condo."

Todd nodded. "Good. It's better that way. This place is a bit
of swamp, anyway. I'm sure you'll sort it all out tomorrow." He
nodded and turned for the door. "Sorry for the trouble," he said
as he turned his flashlight to the path and stepped outside.

We watched him walk back to his car from the doorway.
Danielle put her hand on my shoulder.

"Thanks, MJ," she said.

"For what?"

"I know you didn't want to go."

"Hey, I hear Lucas's condo has HBO."

"Since when do you care about television?"

"I don't. I've just never seen HBO, that's all."

We packed some clothes and toiletries and locked the front
door despite the rear being nothing more than plastic sheet. I
hoped the sheriff's office was as vigilant about real looters as
they were about the nonexistent ones.

We each got in our vehicles, and Danielle followed me away
to PGA National.

CHAPTER NINE

Lucas's condo was a lot more comfortable than the Singer Island swamp. It was a two-bed, two-bath two-story townhouse off the Avenue of the Masters. There was water and power and all the modern conveniences. I tried the television and found HBO. It just looked like regular TV to me, so I shut it off. The refrigerator worked, but there was nothing but bottled water in it, so we grabbed corn chips and a six-pack from Publix and sat in the small courtyard. There was no golf course view, but it was dark anyway, so I didn't see the point. It was a nice, if bland, condo. Pretty fancy for a guy who lived in a room above the office at the South Beach marina.

There were a handful of folks on the golf course when we left the following morning. Danielle headed away to help people whose homes had been declared unfit for habitation but didn't have friends with rental condos at the local golf course, and I headed into the office.

Clematis Street was not getting better. Seagulls were feasting on mounds of garbage, and the stench was reaching biblical proportions. The lot by my office had been cleared, so I parked and ran up the stairs. Ron and Lizzy were already there, sipping on coffee in my office.

"How is everyone?" I asked, taking the sofa since Ron was in my chair.

"Well," said Ron. "And you?"

"Homeless," I said. I explained what had happened and where we had ended up.

"So not exactly homeless, then," said Lizzy. "Homeless people live on the street. They don't even get to try HBO."

I wanted to fire back a witty retort but nothing came to mind, mainly because I knew she was right and I was being melodramatic. I was lucky I wasn't sleeping in a school gym.

"What do we know?" I asked.

Ron drummed his fingers on my desk. "Well, Mr. Beadman seems to have done rather well for himself."

"That's news?"

"Not really. But I mean his companies. He got into automotive engineering. His company, Beadman Automotive Engineering, develops vehicle technologies—fuel systems, antilock brakes, that sort of thing. He was already a successful driver, but his business was where the real money came from. They license the technology they develop to car manufacturers. Seems they've come up with a few systems that get used in most cars these days, and the residuals look pretty good."

"So he's rich."

"He is, but as you say, that's not news. It hasn't all been plain sailing. I was able to find a few lawsuits."

"Aha."

"Companies get sued, it happens. But two suits stuck out in particular." Ron shuffled through his papers as he sipped his coffee. Lizzy sipped her coffee while she waited for him to continue. I didn't have a coffee so I just waited.

"He was sued by former business partners over the development of a fuel injection system that he patented. Seems he and the partners, well, parted company, shortly before Beadman announced the new system. The partners claimed that he had developed the system while in partnership with them but had held it back until after he had bought them out, knowing the value of the company would skyrocket."

"And did it skyrocket?"

"Presumably. It's a private company, so they don't have to produce public financials."

"What happened with the lawsuit?"

"Settled out of court. The terms were undisclosed."

"So maybe a disgruntled former partner, all right. Do we know who the partner is?"

"Partners. Two guys. And, yes, we know who they are. They still work together and they run a rival NASCAR team out of Mooresville, North Carolina."

"Is that anywhere near Charlotte?"

"Just outside."

"So rivals with a beef? Okay, that's something."

"There's more."

"I could tell by the look in your eye."

Ron smiled. "Another lawsuit. A former engineer who worked for Beadman claimed that he had invented some kind of braking system that Beadman was claiming as his own. The guy lost."

"Lost?"

"The court ruled that since the engineer worked for Beadman Engineering, everything he produced was work product and belonged to the company. The fact that he was later dismissed was neither here nor there."

"Disgruntled former employee. Always worth a look. This guy in Charlotte, too?"

"No. Beadman's racing team is based in Charlotte, but the engineering company is on the Space Coast, just near Daytona. The ex-engineer still lives and works in the area. Apparently, he's crew chief on a third-tier racing team there."

"Score one, Florida."

"You did hear me say third-tier?"

"I take them where I can get them, Ron. So two lawsuits, anything else?"

"That's the sum of it so far."

I nodded and smiled at Lizzy.

"Anything, Lizzy, my dear?"

"That's not appropriate office language."

"Ron says it all the time."

"That's Ron."

"Well, I'm in a mood."

"You're always in a mood. So. . . Dale's personal life. He has been married to his wife, Missy, for forty years. I trawled the papers and the gossip columns and got no hint of any extramarital activities."

"So, happily married. Nice to see."

"Yes, it is, isn't it?" She pouted her lips and gave me a stare. I gave her my *I don't know what you're getting at* face. She shook her head like she was disappointed but not surprised and she continued.

"They have one child, a daughter, Angela Jean. She grew up in Palm Beach and went to college at Tulane."

"Mardi Gras U. Nice."

"I suppose. She then joined her father's engineering business and later his racing team and now is chief operating officer of the racing team and is on the board of the engineering business."

"Chief operating officer? So she runs the show?"

"The nuts-and-bolts, pardon the pun," said Ron.

"You're on a roll today, Ron."

He blushed. "The COO generally runs the day-to-day of the business, while the CEO—the chief executive officer—oversees the strategic direction of a business."

"What does that mean, in this case?"

"It means Angie keeps the ship afloat but Dale still steers it."

"Okay, I'd like to think that was a helpful analogy. I'll get back to you on it."

"It might mean nothing. Or it might mean that Dale doesn't think Angie can handle running the entire business. Or he might just not be able to let go. That happens a lot. When a person builds a business, they don't always know when it's time to move on. Sometimes they take the business down with them because of it."

"Any sign that's happening?"

"No. The race team is competitive and the engineering business has the residual royalties. No mass layoffs or anything like that."

"Plus he just bought a new car, for cash."

"Assuming it was his cash."

"Whose cash would it be?"

"The business's."

"Are you saying he might be embezzling from his own company?"

"It's not embezzling," said Ron. "It's his company, he can distribute funds pretty much however he wants. But when owners start taking money away from the companies, bad things often follow."

"Okay, anything else?"

"Nothing yet," said Ron. "We'll keep digging."

Lizzy stood and made her way to the door.

"And Lizzy," I said. "Sorry about the *my dear* thing. I didn't mean anything by it."

Lizzy looked at me for a moment, and then she winked and walked out. I turned to Ron, who just smiled. I had no idea what was going on, but I suspected I was being plucked like a banjo.

CHAPTER TEN

THE CORN CHIPS FROM THE PREVIOUS NIGHT ONLY HELD me until late morning, so I decided to see how things were faring down at Longboard Kelly's. Ron and I found the courtyard deserted. The plastic was still flapping over the outdoor bar. We wandered inside, where we never sat. Everything looked pretty much shipshape for an opening. We found Mick in the walk-in refrigerator, taking stock.

"You open?" I asked.

"Nup," said Mick. "City says the inspectors are going as fast as they can. Bradley's is already open, dammit."

Ron and I glanced at each other, both considering lunch overlooking the Intracoastal. We shook our heads at the same time.

"What's for lunch?" I asked.

"You not listening?"

"The county condemned my house," I said. "What you got to eat?"

Mick shrugged. "I got burger patties, I got buns. I got mayo."

"Well, fish them out, I'm cooking."

I fired up the grill in the kitchen and rubbed it with oil

despite it having a patina like a lubed-up sunbather. Mick brought some beef patties in and I tossed them on and then cut open the buns and sliced some onion. Mick found some mayo, some cheese and a head of lettuce on its last legs, and Ron poured three beers. We sat inside in case the health inspector turned up. Someone turned up, but it wasn't the health inspector.

I recognized the clothes before I saw the face. The weather was warming up but the guy was still in an expensive suit. His hair was still brushed back and he looked like he'd just stepped off the set of a Mexican beer commercial. Or maybe a high-end tequila.

The guy stood in the courtyard as if he expected me to materialize. So I did.

"My house isn't for sale, pal," I said as I stepped out into the sun.

"Everything is for sale, *amigo*," he said, his accent giving the sentence gravitas. He wasn't Cuban, at least I didn't think so. He could have been from any number of places south of the border. Hell, he could have been from Wisconsin and just been good at accents.

"I am prepared to increase my offer," he said.

"You didn't make an offer."

"No? Well, let me do that."

He gave me a number and I wasn't all that impressed. For the sharp suit and the electric car, I thought the number was going to be one of those hard-to-say-no-to kinds of numbers. It wasn't. It wouldn't have mattered if it was.

"Really, that's all?"

"It's a very reasonable offer, *señor*. Think about how much it will cost to rebuild. Do you have that kind of money?" He shrugged like he didn't know.

"That's what insurance is for."

"Insurance. It doesn't always cover things, no? Maybe your insurance says it's an act of God. Maybe you get nothing. And then maybe my buyer has moved on. Too late for you."

"Who's your buyer?"

"I am not a liberty to say, *amigo*."

"Well, I'm not at liberty to sell."

"Perhaps you need some time to consider." He nodded like this was the last word on it and walked out of the courtyard. I watched him get in the electric car and roll silently away. I liked the stealth of a car like that.

"Who was that?" asked Ron as I came back inside.

"The guy who tried to buy my house. Again."

"I know him from somewhere," said Mick.

"Where?"

Mick shrugged. "Somewhere."

"Helpful."

"I thought you said the county condemned your house?" asked Mick.

"I did. They did. I just don't know why. We get the carpet dry, it'll be fine."

"You should find the guy on the notice. Get his story."

"That's not a bad idea, Mick."

"It's a terrible idea," said Ron. "The bureaucracy doesn't take kindly to circumventing the process."

"I like circumventing the process," I said. "And I'm not much one for bureaucracies."

"Amen to that," said Mick.

We finished our burgers and helped Mick clean up. Ron washed the glasses and placed them on a rack to dry, humming the entire time. I wondered if he had missed his calling. He would have been a hell of a bartender, if he didn't drink the profits.

I left in a much better frame of mind than when I had

NO RIGHT TURN   75

arrived. Score one, Longboard's. But Mick's comment about clarifying the story on my house had given me an idea, and I was ready to float it. We headed back out in my Caddy SUV.

THE PALM BEACH COUNTY courthouse was part of a monolithic structure that consumed the entire block between Quadrille Boulevard and North Dixie Highway. I left Ron in the lot by our building and walked across to the section signed as Office of the State Attorney. I wasn't a regular visitor to the offices like I was to Longboard's, but I had to admit I found myself there more often than most non-criminals. The lovely young lady behind the reception desk smiled like she knew me. I couldn't place her. I found most of the women in that particular office to be somewhat homogenous. Young, bubbly, blond seemed to be the job description.

"Hi," said the receptionist, or whatever it was that Lizzy thought I was supposed to call the girl. She gave me a smile that would melt an eighteen-year-old heart but made me wonder how her parents had afforded the bill for such dental perfection.

"Back at ya," I said. "Eric in?"

"You don't have an appointment, do you?" She smiled again.

"Not usually."

"He's in his office."

"Thanks."

I winked for reasons I couldn't fathom and wandered into the hustle and bustle of the SA's office. There were a lot of well-dressed young people walking around, chatting as they went. It looked like an Aaron Sorkin television drama. I tapped on the door of the Office of the State Attorney for the 15th Judicial District and went straight in.

Eric Edwards was frowning at a computer screen and stroking his tie. If he had been breathing heavy, I would have turned and left without a word. He wasn't. He never did. He was long and lean and had that vaguely famished look of people who spend too much of their leisure time jogging. He looked up, clearly expecting to see a young coed intern, and it took him a second for his brain to process the dude in the cargo shorts.

"Jones, do you ever knock?"

"I did knock."

"Do you ever make an appointment?"

"You usually manage not to be here when I make an appointment."

"Wonder why. What do you want?"

"How'd you make it through the storm?" I asked.

He paused like he was wondering if it was a trick question.

"Yard got flooded but the house is fine, thanks for asking. How about you?"

"Got a county notice saying my house was unfit for habitation."

"That bad?"

"No, Eric. Not that bad at all. That's why I'm here. Why would the county be putting a notice on my door when they have no reason to believe the structure is in any way unfit?"

"They do an inspection?"

"Not with me."

"Did you evacuate? Maybe they thought it was abandoned."

"I was at The Mornington during the hurricane."

"Nice for some."

"And then I went home. Then I went to work, and then I came back to find a note saying I couldn't stay there."

"The inspector probably had his reasons."

"Why is the county doing inspections in the city of Riviera Beach? That's a city job, isn't it?"

"Do I look like I know or care about whose responsibility it is? Maybe the city called in help? Everyone's stretched here, Jones. Including me, so if you will close the door as you leave."

"You okay with Danielle being homeless?"

He lost all expression on his face. It was a hell of a poker face. But the stroking of the tie was a bit of a giveaway. It always got under his skin whenever I mentioned his ex-wife. My fiancée. I knew it was cruel and unusual. But he was always so damned smug.

"If she hung around with you long enough, that was bound to happen," he said.

"Classy, Eric. Classy."

"Right back at you, Jones."

I stepped to the door. He was watching me. He knew I'd stop before I left for one last quip. My Columbo moment. So I kept going.

"Jones," he said.

I stopped just outside his office but didn't turn around.

"Don't do anything stupid. The county takes harassment of its staff very seriously."

"What about its citizens?" I asked as I strode away.

CHAPTER ELEVEN

SALLY MONDAVI'S PAWNSHOP SAT IN A TIRED STRIP MALL on Okeechobee Boulevard. It was out on the wrong side of the turnpike, where the ocean breezes never blew and recessions really hit hard when they came.

I parked in front of his store. The Chinese restaurant next door seemed to be doing a roaring trade, and I wondered if there was an entire Chinese community without power somewhere. The restaurant looked packed even if the parking lot didn't. Chinese folks knew a thing or two about sharing resources, so carpooling was something that came naturally to them. If it had been an American sports bar, the pickups with one guy inside would have been lined up along the street looking for spots.

I pushed in through the door and the little bell jingled in a non-Christmassy fashion, hard and abrupt. There was a Latina girl sitting inside the Plexiglas check-cashing booth, filing her nail down to the first knuckle out of boredom. It wasn't payday, so things were slow. I left her be and wandered into the maze of shelves and along the glass-topped cabinet that ran parallel to the wall. I wasn't in the market for a secondhand wedding ring or a gold watch that had once been a retirement gift. The notion of such things depressed me.

Sal Mondavi was at the back as usual, unpacking small packets of something from a delivery box. His solitary wisp of hair hung over his forehead. He looked like a walnut with an attitude.

"How's them Jets?" I asked, louder than was necessary.

"I knew it was you," he said. "I knew I'd see you before you even woke up this morning."

"Yes, but do you know where I woke up?"

Sal stopped his moving like he was redirecting the blood flow to his brain so he could think on it.

"Not at home."

"Good guess."

"If it was some floozy, I've got a cabinet full of handguns here I'm happy to turn on you."

"No floozies, Sal."

"Good. You gotta make that girl your bride, you know? Even if she is a cop."

"It'll happen, Sal."

"So will death, my friend. Which one you want first?"

"You're in a cheery mood today."

"You come in here joking about my Jets and you expect me to be cheery for you?"

"I expect nothing less from you, Sal."

Sally grunted and dropped the packets in his hand back into the box.

"What's that?" I asked.

"Pokémon cards."

"Seriously?"

"No lie. A shipment came into my possession. The kids love these things. I don't see it myself, but then I don't get the designated hitter either, and that's a thing."

"You get a lot of kids here in the store?"

"What do you think? I'll take these down to the children's hospital. They'll get a kick out of them."

I just smiled.

"What do you want, anyway? You drive out here just to give me grief about the Jets?"

"It's a reason."

"Your time will come, Patriot boy."

"But it wasn't the only reason. Did you come through the storm okay?"

Sally shrugged. It was a slow-motion thing.

"Even storm surge doesn't visit this part of the state."

"No repairs you need done?"

"Thanks, kid. I'm good. A couple of the kids came around and helped clean up the yard, do a little fixing on the roof."

"I just saw one of the kids. Leo."

Sal smiled his crooked nicotine grin. "He's a good boy. Money smarts. Gets his numbers. How's he doing?"

"He's a guy in his early twenties working in an old folks' home."

"Don't knock it. Old folks has got lots to teach, if you care to listen."

"I do, Sal. I do. And so does Leo."

"When he leaves there he'll know everything about managing condos and he'll have a deposit to put down on his first apartment building."

"I don't doubt it."

"And what about your place?"

"It's a swamp."

"You got the flood insurance, like I told ya?"

"I did. I'm insured like the crown jewels. That's why I'm here. There's some water damage, the carpets are done for.

Maybe the floors, I don't know. I need to find a contractor but my insurance guy says good luck with that."

"Yeah, those boys will be as busy as a firecracker store on the Fourth of July."

"You know anyone?"

Sal thought about it for a moment and slowly began nodding. He had a mental Rolodex in his head, with more names and faces and numbers than a baseball statistician's notebook. At his age, it took a while to look the stuff up, but it was still there all right.

"Yeah, I know a guy. Good boy. I know his mother, from way back. The father wasn't such a swell fella. Got himself shot. I helped them get set up when they relocated from the Bronx."

"When was this?"

"About thirty-five years ago."

I said nothing.

"I'll give him a call. His name's Danny, Danny Rucci."

"Thanks, Sal."

"You look like you got something else on your mind."

"You're like an X-ray machine for thoughts, Sal."

"I read faces, is all. You seen as many faces as I seen, you learn to read 'em."

"You ever heard of the F-88?"

Sal pouted his lips. "What is it? Top Gun?"

"No, it's a car. Like one of those concept cars from a car show. Only this one is from the fifties."

"Okay."

"There was only thought to be one of them in existence. Then a second turned up. The history is a bit fuzzy on it."

"Provenance."

"Right. So maybe it's hot, or maybe it's not. Maybe someone else might try to lay claim to it."

"Could happen."

"How do you sell something like that?"

"Quietly."

"Right. My client was approached. He's known to collect cars like this one. He buys it, and the day it's delivered, or maybe the day after—during the hurricane in any case—it gets stolen."

"Inside job."

"Yeah, that's what I was thinking."

"Your client did it for the insurance money, or someone close to him did it for the money, or the seller stole it back."

"It wasn't insured, because he'd have had to declare its existence to the insurance company. And he says he doesn't know who the seller was, that he was approached by an intermediary."

"And he won't say who that is."

"Exactly."

"I know some guys, move stuff like that. They like to keep a low profile. I'll put some feelers out."

"Thanks, Sal."

"So you gonna tell me?"

"Tell you what?"

"Where you woke up this morning?"

"PGA National."

"Like on the fairway? What are you, back at college?"

"Not on the course, Sal. In a condo. You remember Lucas."

"I do. He's a serious individual."

"He is. Turns out he has an investment property at PGA National."

"See, I keep telling you. Buy some real estate, kid. They ain't making no more land. But why did you sleep at PGA National?"

"Someone from the county put a no habitation order on my house."

"Is it that bad?"

"No, it's not. And then when Danielle and I got back there last night and just went in, someone called the sheriff's office to rat us out."

"Who?"

"I don't know. But I know this. Some well-dressed Latino guy has dropped by twice now to offer to buy my house."

"What's he offering?"

"Not the point, Sal. I don't want to leave. I like it there. And I'll never afford to get anything like it again."

"Depends on his price."

"Lowball."

"Typical. You see it after every big blow. Lowlifes swoop in to take people's houses while they're at their lowest point. But here's a question. Why call the sheriff? Why not the local PD?"

"I don't know."

"I'll tell you why. Because someone is connected to the sheriff but not the Riviera Beach PD. Your guy isn't local. Maybe from Palm Beach, or further away, but not local to you."

"Good point."

"And how did they know you were home? You see any cars or vans watching your place."

"No. I went for a run just before. The street was empty of vehicles."

"And yet someone called the sheriff. Someone's watching your house."

I thought on that.

"Thanks, Sal. You've got wisdom beyond your years."

"I've got years beyond all knowledge of mankind, that's what I got."

I thanked him and went to leave, then I remembered something.

"Hey, Sal—you like music?"

"That's like asking if I like food. I like Deano, I don't like rap."

"Yeah, Deano. The crooners. Sammy Davis, Jr., Nat King Cole, that sort of thing."

"That's the stuff, kid."

"Buzz Weeks and his crew are doing a benefit show at Ted's in Lauderhill. Help some folks who lost their homes. Danielle and I were planning to go. I think you'd enjoy it."

"I don't go to clubs at my age."

"Don't get old on me, Sal."

"All right, kid. I haven't seen Buzz in too long. Thanks."

"No, thank you."

I left before he could get all terse about thanking him. He didn't take thanks well. Some folks are like that. I got back in my car. The restaurant was still going gangbusters, and I now had a hankering for egg rolls and fried rice. But I suppressed it. I had someone I wanted to see. Someone just back along Okeechobee Boulevard. Someone who might shed some light on who it was trying to weasel me out of my house.

CHAPTER TWELVE

The Planning, Zoning and Building Department for Palm Beach County sat on Jog Road just off Okeechobee, on Sally's side of the turnpike. It was in one of those ubiquitous Florida government buildings that were built to look like some grand pantheon from Europe but on a more budget-friendly scale and looked so new and polished it was less old Europe than new Disney World.

Inside it was old-fashioned bureaucracy. I found a woman at a desk whose sole purpose appeared to be to ignore customers at all costs. She focused hard on a computer screen in a way that suggested she was reading the same word over and over. Perhaps it was a tough word.

"Excuse me, ma'am," I said.

I got nothing in return. It must have been a really tough word.

"Excuse me, ma'am," I repeated.

"Take a number," she said without taking her eyes from the screen.

"Actually I don't need a number."

"You want to speak to anyone, you need a number."

"I just need to know if Peter Malloy is here."

"Not if you don't have a number."

"I can't take a number. The machine's broken."

This was a lie. We both knew it, but it put her in a difficult position. She dragged her eyes from the screen and gave a look of absolute and intense boredom, like she'd heard it all before.

"Just press the button."

"Did that."

"Do it again."

"That would be insanity."

"What?"

"Doing the same thing and expecting a different result is the definition of insanity."

I had no idea if that was true. I'd heard it somewhere, an urban legend. It certainly wasn't a clever way of going about things, but I wasn't sure it qualified as fully-fledged insanity.

The woman was a millisecond short of an eye roll. She hefted herself out of her chair and wandered away toward a door that separated them from us. She wandered out into the foyer with all the joy of a funeral march and headed for the ticket machine that dispensed the numbers that delineated who got to speak to whom and in what order.

She got to the machine ahead of a guy in paint-splattered bib and brace overalls. He waited without comment. I got the impression it wasn't his first time at this particular rodeo, and he knew pushing the bureaucracy was pointless. The woman made eye contact with me and then in slow motion punched the button on the machine. It gave a quiet hum as it printed a ticket and then it slowly ejected the square of paper. She left the ticket hanging from the machine like a tongue poking out of a mouth.

"I just need to know if Peter Malloy is here."

The woman didn't answer. She just ambled back to her post staring at the screen, ignoring all comers. The guy in the overalls hesitated. He wanted to take a number but my ticket still hung from the machine.

"It's all yours," I told him.

He nodded and pulled the paper out. "You looking for Malloy?"

"Yeah. You know him?"

"We've crossed swords. But you won't find him here. He'll be in the field." He put air quotes around *in the field*. "If I wanted to find him, I'd look at Bar Playa, west of PBI. You know it?"

"I know it."

"Look for the book guy."

I didn't know what that meant, but I figured I would when I needed to. I thanked the guy, got back in my SUV and headed down toward the airport. Just west of the airport was a run of strip malls—fast-food franchises, vehicle repair outlets and donut shops—that serviced the local community rather than the traveler that tended to congregate east of the airport, nearer the beach. At the rear of a strip mall sat a small Cuban bar that was popular with taxi drivers. There was a small indoor restaurant, but the main business was in the plastic picnic tables and chairs and the bar that sat under corrugated plastic roofing outside. The Buena Vista Social Club blared out of a tall black speaker and the scent of carnitas wafted on the air. A large sign above the bar said that rideshare drivers were not welcome.

The guy in the paint-splattered overalls had been on the money. All the men at the bar looked like tradesmen, enjoying a beer or a taco plate before heading home, and all the people sitting at the tables looked like taxi drivers, waiting on a fare or taking a break from a long shift. Except one guy. He was at a table alone, closer to the airport than the bar, sitting on a bottle of Modelo and chomping on a Cuban sandwich. He was small-framed and balding and wore thin glasses and a button-up shirt with no tie. He could have played a librarian on television.

I grabbed a cold beer from the young woman at the bar and wandered over and sat down opposite Malloy. He frowned and then looked around and then looked back at me. I could see him wondering who I was and why I had sat at his table when there were vacant tables available. I sipped my beer and glanced out at the taxis parked on the other side of the railing. Then I glanced back at Malloy. He squirmed in his seat.

"Hard day?" I asked.

"About normal," he said. He spoke quietly like a librarian, too.

"You normally inspect buildings from the comfort of a Cuban bar?"

"What?" His eyes tightened. "Who are you?"

"Me? Just a guy. Wondering how it is that a building inspector is able to slap a no habitation order on a house on Singer Island when he's got his bony backside in a chair in West Palm."

The penny dropped. Malloy sat back and crossed his arms over his chest. "You can't be here."

"Why? It's a bar."

"You got a problem, you need to go to the department offices."

"Did that. Got asked to take a number. I don't like to wait."

"You can't harass me in my private time. Union says so." He grinned like this was the last word on it.

"First, Pete, this isn't private time. It's still office hours. So you really shouldn't be drinking on the county's time. And second, it isn't harassment. After I've followed you for a month and taken video of every time you've taken a drink on the county dime, every time you've written an order on a building you haven't inspected to the letter of the law, maybe then you can call it harassment. And I'll call the State Attorney's office. Again."

"You can't intimidate me, whoever you are."

"How do you even inspect a house that you haven't been inside?"

"I know what I'm doing. I've been doing it for a long time."

"I can see that," I said, nodding at his beer bottle. "Did you even look inside?"

"Of course."

"How? The front door was locked and the front blinds were down."

"Rear windows. I can see what I need to see. And before you try to say trespass, I can go onto a property if I believe it is in a dangerous or derelict condition."

"How did you even see past all the sandbags?"

"I can step over sandbags."

We both knew he was lying. Danielle and Ron and I had removed the sandbags from the rear of the house and lined them up along the side of the backyard. Malloy could have stepped in through the plastic where the sliding door had been if he had really gone around the back of my house. But he didn't. I knew it and he knew it.

"And I don't need to explain myself to you," he continued.

"On the contrary. I pay your salary. I'm exactly the person you need to explain yourself to."

"If you don't leave, I will call the police."

"I'm sure that will make you very popular here." I stood and took a final swing of my beer. "Who paid you?" I asked.

Malloy snarled. "Get lost."

"Don't get comfortable," I said, and I strode away before I ran out of clever things to say.

CHAPTER THIRTEEN

I stopped at a store and grabbed a six-pack. Then I headed south and west and parked my vehicle next to the beat-up truck near the entrance to the South Florida National Cemetery. It had been a new facility the first time I had visited, ten years earlier, and now there were too many headstones to count. I took my six-pack and walked in. The cemetery looked as orderly as it always did. The VA had wasted no time in getting the grounds cleaned up, and coordinating the veterans who had descended on the place to help get it shipshape after the hurricane.

Lucas was wiping down Lenny's headstone as I walked over to him. I stopped and looked at it for a moment. It was simple. His name, Lenny Cox, and dates of birth and death. No inscription. No fuss. Just like Lenny.

"Am I late?" I asked Lucas.

"Nah, mate. Just got here."

Lucas took a seat on the moist grass on one side of Lenny and I sat on the other. I opened three beers and passed two to Lucas. He held them out and I clinked mine to them in a toast. I waited to take a sip as Lucas turned one of the bottles upside down and poured it into the grass over Lenny's plot. Then we each took a sip.

"You clean up okay in Miami?" I asked.

"No problems. We were up and running as soon the swell dropped. Not that many people are taking their yachts out right now."

"Slow?"

"Yeah. The boys have got it all under control. How about you? You sort the house thing out?"

I told him about my visit with the building inspector.

"Mongrel," he said.

"If you need your condo back, just let me know."

"It's no sweat, mate. Use it as long as you need." He took a sip and looked around the manicured lawns of the cemetery. I watched him. His skin was tanned and ageless, his hair cut short and dirty golden. He had to be north of sixty, but he was lean and wiry and looked like he might be immortal. Lenny hadn't been quite so wiry, but he had that same look about him, time-less like he might live forever. But he didn't live forever. I knew that for a fact.

"You workin'?" Lucas asked.

"Yeah. For a race car driver, would you believe?"

"Who's that?"

"Dale Beadman."

Lucas spun around. "Dale Beadman?"

"Yeah, you know him?"

"The NASCAR driver? Yeah, the man's a legend."

"I didn't realize you were into car racing."

"Sure. I grew up watching racing."

"NASCAR?"

"Nah. We call them touring cars in Australia, but it's the same idea. They used to be stock models but over the years became something that wore the same body shape as a regular car but had nothing in common underneath."

"Sounds like NASCAR."

"Yeah. Plus we had more Indy-style road courses than the super speedway tracks." Lucas took a sip of his beer. "I even drove a drag racer when I was a younger man."

"That right? The quarter mile?"

"Yep. Pedal to the metal. Hell of a thing, that much power under you. You ever done that?"

"No. Fastest I've been is Danielle driving on the turnpike."

Lucas smiled. "So what are you doing for old Dale Beadman?"

"He had a car collection stolen."

"No way."

"Yep. Actually thinking I might have to go up to Daytona and chat to some folks about it."

"Daytona? Isn't Beadman Racing in Charlotte?"

"Does everyone know that but me? Yeah, it is. Might have to go there, too. It's a bit of a drive."

Lucas sipped his beer again and nodded like a long drive was his idea of a good time. Not me. Driving was a means of getting from point A to point B. I didn't get the romance of it. Especially in Florida. There were miles and miles of nothing to look at on freeways in Florida. When I was a kid growing up in Connecticut, we used to drive along Merritt Parkway and see the fall foliage raining down on the road like embers. That was something to see. There's not much fall foliage in Florida. Then I got an idea.

"You want to come?"

He belched and then looked into middle distance like he was thinking about it. "Daytona and Charlotte?"

"Yeah."

"Never been to Charlotte."

"No?"

"Always wanted to go. See the speedway, maybe visit a workshop."

"I'm sure we can get the guided tour."

"Yeah?" He nodded and sipped his beer. "All right, why not? Things are slow at the marina, anyway."

I nodded and finished my drink and opened three more. "What do you know about Dale Beadman?" I asked.

"He won it all, or almost all of it. Multiple NASCAR trophies, he won the Daytona 500 three times, he won at the Brickyard, he won at Talladega. He became crew chief and won it all over again."

"You sound like a fan."

"Of 29? Sure, I'm a fan."

"29?"

"Dale's car number. In NASCAR you support the number as much as the driver. I guess it's a way of saying that only a great combination of driver and car can win. It's more of a team sport than people realize. A great driver makes all the difference, but without a great car there are no great drivers."

"I never really thought about it like that."

"That's how it is. See, racing's a tough game. As soon as a team starts winning, the racing bodies change the rules to even things up. NASCAR do it, F1 do it, Indy do it. They want the races close and the championships even closer. No one cares about a one-horse race, do they?"

Only the winners, I thought. Which made me think about the people who had lost to Dale Beadman, and not just those on the race track.

We finished our drinks and cleaned up around Lenny. We stood for a moment looking at his headstone. We always did. He was ten years gone and I still found myself turning to ask him things. I suspect Lucas did the same thing. Some people leave an impression like a child scrawling their initials in wet concrete, others leave no more than a gust of breeze. Lenny was concrete, all the way. He had a personality that stuck with you, in a good way for most people. He'd helped a lot of folks on his earthbound journey. I often wondered if I measured up to him that way. I didn't know. Perhaps it wasn't my place to say. But it lit an idea in my head. I was looking at all the people that Dale Beadman might have wronged. They were usually good for a motive for any crime. But thinking of Lenny made me consider the opposite option. Who was it that might have been helped by stealing the cars? I'd have to ruminate a bit on that one.

Lucas and I wandered back to the entrance to the cemetery. I ran my hand along the tailgate of his beat-up old truck, that had once been Lenny's old truck. It was a marvel of engineering that it was still going. It wasn't Lucas's regular ride, but he liked to drive it up when he came to visit Lenny. After a decade, it didn't smell like Lenny anymore, just like the collection of Lenny's shirts in my wardrobe. But his essence was still in there somewhere. I knew that thought to be baloney, but I went with it anyway because it helped me get through the day.

"Got a few things to do tomorrow," I said. "So probably day after for Daytona."

Lucas nodded and opened the door to his truck. "Sounds good. I gotta see a man about a dog tomorrow, anyway."

I nodded goodbye and got in my SUV. It was a sedan masquerading as something more. It wasn't anyone's idea of a Cadillac, but I supposed that nothing new really was. It gave me a vague sense of being a phony. I could neither comprehend nor pin the thought down, so I wrote it off to the melancholy associated with a visit to a cemetery.

I followed Lucas out and he turned right and I turned left, and I watched him disappear in my rearview. I needed some company of the best kind.

CHAPTER FOURTEEN

DANIELLE WAS IN THE SHOWER WHEN I GOT BACK TO THE PGA condo. I stepped into the steaming bathroom to let her know I was home. The frosted shower glass left just enough to the imagination, and I considered joining her, but she killed the water as I came in.

"How's your day?" I asked.

"MJ? It was okay. You know. A lot of folks lost their homes. Not great. Can you hand me a towel?"

I flopped a towel over the glass enclosure and leaned against the edge of the vanity. I watched her fuzzy silhouette drying off.

"How was your day?" she asked.

"Went and saw Lenny."

"How was it?"

"The cemetery was in pretty good condition, considering."

"How's Lenny?"

"Lenny's Lenny, you know."

She stepped out of the shower enclosure wrapped in a towel like a gorgeous burrito. Her hair was wet and dripping and darker because of the water. She gave me the half smile she always gave me. It was an all-purpose expression, good for whenever she was worried about me or thought I had done something stupid. Between the two, that covered a lot of territory.

"You okay? Really?" she asked.

"Our home is still standing even if we can't technically go inside it. And you're here. So I'm better than most."

Danielle looked me up and down the way law enforcement types do, like their eyes are X-ray machines at the airport and they can see what's going on inside a person just by looking at them. The scary part was she often could. She gave the half smile again and then disappeared underneath another towel to dry her hair.

"There's wine in the fridge," she said from inside the towels.

I nodded even though she wasn't looking and wandered out into the kitchen. The counters were granite and the appliances were new and the entire thing was as antiseptic as an operating theater. It wasn't Lucas at all. But then I figured he didn't live here and probably never planned to. He wasn't much of a golfer. I opened the bottle of New Zealand Sauvignon Blanc and was pouring the second glass when Danielle came out. She was in running shorts and a tight yoga top that did all kind of bad things for me. She was still drying her hair. I'd never had that much hair. I was scruffy enough without long hair. It looked like a lot of maintenance.

I offered Danielle a glass and we held them up and looked into each other's eyes. She held my gaze for longer than was necessary. Once again I noted how she smiled with her eyes, and I recalled Missy Beadman and her mouth-only smile. Perhaps that would mean Danielle would end up with all kinds of laugh lines when she was older. I liked the thought of that.

"Caesar salad for dinner?" she asked.

"Sure, if there isn't a burger going."

She tapped my belly as she slipped past. "There isn't. You want to sit on the patio?"

"Actually I was planning on watching something on television."

She stopped and frowned at me. We didn't own a television. Having one in Lucas's condo was a novelty.

"You want to catch up on *The West Wing*?" she asked.

"You're funny. No, I want to check out the security video from the Beadman place."

"You got a DVD?"

"No. Angie Beadman gave me access online. Just got to figure out how to get into it. We have internet access here, right?"

"There's Wi-Fi across the complex."

I pulled out a laptop computer that I had borrowed from Lizzy. Some people might find it odd that as owner of the business, I had to borrow equipment from my office manager, but not me, and certainly not Lizzy. We didn't work like that. Back in the day, when we had lost Lenny and then learned that he had gone and left the detective business to me, we had established pretty early on that we were a flat hierarchy office structure. I signed the checks, but I only signed the checks that Lizzy told me to sign. It was better that way. Looking after the minutiae was never my strong suit. Lizzy, on the other hand, always knew the state of things. Like where the equipment was, and who owed us money and the fact there were spare clothes in a closet in the second office. I'm a big believer in playing to your strengths. Sure, you needed to work on the odd weakness—like your knuckle ball or a penchant for peanuts—but mostly successful people focused on their strengths. Pitchers weren't lead-off hitters for a reason.

I sat at the coffee table and fired up the laptop and came to a complete stop. I turned to Danielle partly to see if she was watching my ham-fisted attempt at computing and partly for help. She was standing right behind me. I got the half smile again. All-purpose.

"You do the salad," she said. I nodded and let her take my seat and dropped the piece of paper that Angie Beadman had given me with the login details on it. I went into the kitchen. I'm better in a kitchen than I am with computers. It's not that I don't know how to use them, I just never really have cause to. I have Ron to do the web-based research for cases and Lizzy to plug the stuff in, and I don't have family on the other side of the country that want to chat online.

I dropped an egg, some olive oil, a few drops of Worcester-shire and a dollop of Dijon mustard into a blender. Recipes often make a big deal of emulsion as a science. I find a blender takes care of the science for me. I whizzed up a dressing and then set about frying some bacon pieces. There would be no croutons. Danielle had declared processed carbs my enemy. I suspected she had her eye on beer as the next battle, but that was going to be a fight to the death.

Danielle worked as I cut up the romaine lettuce. She pulled a cable out of the DVR below the television and stretched it across the room, plugged it into the laptop and then, hey presto, she made the computer's screen appear on the television. Then she found the site for the security video and logged in. There was a menu that allowed us to select six-hour chunks of time going back for two weeks. Danielle sat back with her wine and waited for me to join her.

I grated some Parmigiano Reggiano over the dressed salad and brought a plate in for Danielle. Then I returned for my own plate and my wine.

"What time do you want to look at?" Danielle asked.

I settled on the sofa with the plate in my lap. "Start the morning of the delivery."

Danielle clicked a link and then the television opened up the view of Dale Beadman's faux-English pub. It was the same scene I had viewed with Angie Beadman in their server room. There was light coming in from the window in the door beyond the bar, but not much. The weather was setting in as the hurricane drove its way up toward the Bahamas. As before, the picture stayed for twenty seconds and then rotated to show the driveway. The rain was hitting the gravel, but the rivulets were yet to form in it. Twenty seconds of nothing happened, and then the view switched to the garage interior. The original ten cars sat in dim light, all accounted for. Then the video returned to the pub view.

"Now I know why you don't own a television," Danielle said.

"It may not be guns and explosions, but there's a story in here somewhere."

"I like your idea of a good night in on the sofa." She smiled and stabbed a mound of lettuce. To an outsider, it might have sounded like sarcasm. But that's how you know you're sitting on a sofa with your soulmate. When watching a security video of nothing happening is truly a good night in as long as you're together.

We ate our salad and watched nothing happen. There was no sound with the video. Most security video was like that. That was partly because audio didn't add a whole lot, but it was also because, in most jurisdictions, recording audio of someone required their consent whereas video did not. I didn't know why that was the case, but I recalled Ronzoni mentioning it once. He was a wealth of useless information.

Danielle took our plates back into the kitchen and returned with the wine bottle. She poured two more glasses and then sat in tight against me, and I put my arm around her. It took an hour of viewing to see anything happen. Then we saw the truck backing up the driveway, and we saw the garage door open and the truck tailgate lower and the driver push the F-88 down the ramp and into the hidden room.

"What's with the secret room?" asked Danielle.

"He says it's for the vehicles he wants to enjoy alone."

"So it's stolen."

"The provenance is disputable."

"That's one way of putting it."

The driver cleaned up the floor and Angie Beadman ran away into the rain, and then the driver raised the roller door. Then the truck pulled away. One shot it was there, and the next time around, the outside shot showed nothing but wet gravel. Then regular programming resumed and nothing happened all over again.

"That's it?" asked Danielle.

"That's it. Then sometime later, all the cars disappear."

"But not on video?"

"Not according to Angie Beadman."

"But you're going to sit here all evening just to make sure."

"I am."

"We're going to need more wine."

"And that's why I love you."

We watched for hours. The sky got darker and the rain continued. Inside, nothing happened. The storm shutters on the garage blocked out the hurricane. The infrared on the outside camera showed nothing much of anything. There was rain but not much else. As darkness fell completely the outside shot became hard to discern.

"Nothing to see," said Danielle. "The infrared picks up shapes, movement. The driveway is just gravel. It just looks like a whiteboard."

The only external light making it inside was coming from the storm window in the French door to the pub. It was a code thing. At least one window or door had to be hurricane-proof. You couldn't put shutters on every window and door, not if you were inside the building. An external floodlight over the outside patio gave a tiny bit of light to the pub. In the reflection on the wall-mounted television, I could see the palapa outside, flapping in the wind like ribbons. It was the only thing moving in any of the video.

We got to the end of the six-hour segment and the vision ended and dropped us abruptly back to the menu screen. Danielle clicked the next segment and the video resumed. It was more of the same. My eyes stayed on the screen but my mind drifted. I was sure I was going to see what Angie Beadman had said I would see. Nothing. Right up until the power quit.

"The rain outside doesn't look so bad," said Danielle. "Was it?"

"It was. I was out in it more than I wanted to be and it was coming in sideways where I was. But the Beadman place is on the east side of the island and tucked behind a lot of trees. The hurricane made landfall at Fort Pierce, so the prevailing wind during the night was from north and northwest. Straight down the Intracoastal. They're pretty sheltered on their side."

She had her head nestled into my shoulder and she looked up at me. "I was worried. I wish I had been here."

"I was in a luxury hotel, remember?"

"On the roof, as I recall from Ron."

"Only briefly. I'm glad you were in Tallahassee."

"You were glad I was in Tallahassee?"

"Away from the storm, yes."

She edged around and looked at me. "What are we going to do?"

"About what?"

"About me being in Tallahassee."

"When do you have to go back?"

"A few days."

"You're not going to be there forever, though, are you?"

"Who knows?"

"I know. Your academy training is fourteen weeks, right?"

"And then I'll get posted somewhere. It isn't like working for the county. I won't get a position in West Palm, not first up."

"South Florida's not that big. We'll make it work."

"Might not be South Florida. I might have to stay in the Tallahassee office."

"Really?" I took my eyes off the video for the first time in hours. "Tallahassee?"

"Maybe," she said. "Could even be Pensacola. That's more than eight hours away."

"I never really thought about it."

"Maybe we need to think about it. If we're thinking about getting married."

"Thinking about it?"

"Isn't that what engagement is?"

"I thought it was more of a declaration of intention than a *think about it.*"

"I'm just saying, how does this work if I get a two-year posting far away?"

I sat up and tapped the computer to pause the video. "It'll work however we make it work, that's how. I don't know the particulars. Not yet. Maybe you do get posted to West Palm. Maybe you're in Miami. I don't know. I can't plan for what I don't know. There's no point worrying about what pitch I'm gonna throw until I know who the batter is."

"Baseball metaphor, really?"

"Sure. That's who I am. You know that. And you should know something else. You're my home. Not a waterlogged ranch house on the Intracoastal. You. So we'll work it out. You might end up far from West Palm, but you won't end up far from me. I guarantee it."

She frowned at me. I wasn't sure if she was considering my words or if she was x-raying my insides again. Then she nodded and settled back into my shoulder. I kissed the top of her head and glanced at the television as I made to press the key to start the video. Then I stopped. The shot was of the pub. Nothing was happening. There was no movement. I realized it wasn't just because the video was paused. I looked at the darkened reflection in the television on the wall. Nothing had been moving in the pub for hours. Except something had. The palapa outside Dale Beadman's pub room. It had been flapping in the wind, reflected in the television.

I hit the key and sank back into the sofa and let Danielle snuggle in and get comfortable. The video continued on, nothing followed by nothing, except for a palapa flapping in the breeze.

CHAPTER FIFTEEN

The guy looked like a builder, or even a guy dressed like a builder for Halloween. He wore pressed overalls and had a flat pencil tucked in behind his ear. His t-shirt bulged at thick biceps as he got out of his pickup. He was younger than I had expected him to be, and I wondered if maybe Sally had done him a favor when he was a kid.

"Miami?" he asked as he stepped up to my house.

"That's me," I said. "Thanks for coming. It's Rucci, right?"

"Rucci," he said. "Danny Rucci."

"You must be busy right now."

"If I could get more lumber and more workers I'd be busier."

"Let me show you the mess."

I ushered Rucci inside and he wandered around, looking at the bones of my house. He didn't seem to pay much attention to the damp floor, but he was awfully interested in the ceiling. He bounced up and down on the kitchen floor and then wandered out the back. He looked at the speedboat that still lay on the side of its hull on my back lawn.

"Your boat?" asked Rucci.

"No. No idea who owns it. I reported it to the cops, but no

one's called yet."

"Out-of-towner. Probably doesn't even know it's gone yet." He turned back to the house and looked at the roof. "How do you know Sal?" he asked as he frowned at the roof tiles.

"How does anyone know Sal? I did him a favor once, and ever since he's done a thousand for me."

"Sounds like Sal."

"How do you know him?"

Rucci shrugged like he didn't know. "He looked after my mom, after my old man ran out."

I nodded. There was a front-end loader full of subtext there, but I left it alone.

"Let me get my ladder and I'll take a quick look," he said, striding back through the house.

I didn't know my lintels from my lallies when it came to construction, so I left Rucci to his business. He climbed up on the roof and had a look, and then I heard him rooting around in the crawl space under the house. I was standing by the front door when the letter carrier zoomed to a stop in front of my house. He kicked the stand on his moped and ambled up the path. He looked hot under the helmet.

"Back at it already," I said.

"Not rain, nor sleet nor snow, and all that crap." He handed me a wad of mail bound by a rubber band and turned away.

"Thanks," I said, rifling through the mail. It was the usual junk, bills and such. I noted the logo of Great Southeast Permanent. I slipped their envelope out of the deck and tore it open with my finger. It was a single sheet. I flicked it open. It was a letter. Not from my local agent. It was signed by someone calling himself the senior vice president of claimant relations. It was a hell of a title. The letter spelled out, in much plainer English than my actual policy, that my claim for damages to my dwelling was being denied.

I read the letter a second time just to make sure I was getting it right. The reasoning for the denial was noncoverage. What that meant exactly was anyone's guess. There was a 1-800 number I could call should I have any questions.

I had questions. Quite a few as it turned out. I called the number and got three separate numbered menus that I needed to select from to ensure I was routed to the person most able to help me. I felt myself falling down the rabbit hole as I got deeper into the labyrinth of menus. After a battle of wills that lasted a good ten minutes, I finally got hold of a human. I asked for the senior vice president of claimant relations and was told he was not available, but the woman on the line assured me that she could be of service.

"I have a home and contents policy with you. Now that my house has been blown away it seems you're denying my claim."

"I'd be more than happy to help you with that," she said. I could hear the happiness bursting down the phone line. I heard the sound of tapping keys and a grunt or two.

"Yes, it seems your coverage doesn't cover this particular incident."

"My house was blown away. My coverage specifically covers hurricane damage."

"I'm looking here, and it seems that your house didn't blow away."

I glanced up my house. It was still there, mostly.

"Not entirely, maybe."

"Yes, that's the problem, you see."

"How is that the problem? My house has been half-demolished by a hurricane. That's the problem."

"Yes, I see. However, the hurricane didn't damage your home, sir."

"How do you figure that? The county has declared it unfit for habitation."

"I'm looking here and see that the damage was caused by flooding, not a hurricane."

"What do you think caused the flooding, lady?"

"I'm afraid I'm not a meteorologist, sir. I couldn't say."

"The hurricane caused the flooding. It was on television and everything."

"Well, I can't speak to the cause of the flooding, but I see here your home and contents insurance doesn't cover flooding."

"Of course it does. I have flood insurance."

"Not as part of the policy I see here, sir."

"Of course not. It's a separate policy. That's how flood insurance works."

"Is it?"

"Is it? You're the insurance agent and you're asking me *is it?*"

"Sir, I'm just looking at your home and contents policy here, and I can confirm that you are not covered for losses by flood or similar act of God."

"Then how about you look at my flood policy?"

"I'm afraid that's a different department, sir."

"Of course it is. Can you put me through to the right department?"

"I'd be happy to help you, sir."

"Great, thanks."

"Unfortunately we're not connected to that department, telephonically speaking."

"So how do I get hold of them, telephonically speaking?"

"We have a 1-800 number." She recited the number to me.

"That's the number I used to call you."

"Of course."

"So when I called just now, there was no option for flood insurance, specifically."

"Is there anything else I can help you with?"

"As far I can count, you haven't actually helped me with anything yet."

"Of course, sir. Thank you for allowing Great Southeast Permanent to serve you. Have a nice day."

The sound of silence rang hollow in my ear. I looked at my phone as if it was faulty somehow and wondered if this was the kind of service Angie Beadman was getting with her claim. I resolved to ask Ron about it. He had worked in insurance, and if anyone could penetrate their wall of babble and misdirection, it was him.

"You're sinking into the ocean." I turned to see Rucci the builder standing before me, dusting his hands off like he'd just been baking.

"I'm what?"

"Your foundation. It's no good. The flooding damaged your posts. The back half of your house is sinking."

"That doesn't sound good."

He shrugged. I loved the way that guys like that reacted to things. What sounded like the end of the world to me was water off the backs of guys like Rucci. I guess he wasn't so confident throwing a fastball at a batter averaging .400.

"You need to replace them, is all."

"Okay. So what am I looking at?"

He shrugged again. "Fix the foundation, you'll have to redo most of the subfloor. I can put in new engineered floorboards or tile, fix up your roof damage. Probably eighty thousand. But since you know Sal, let's say fifty grand."

I gave him my pouty face of consideration. I had no doubt that a friend of Sal's wasn't going to cheat me on price. Hell hath no fury like Sally Mondavi when someone let him down.

"Of course, your insurance might just write the whole house off. Then I could knock it down and build you something like that," he said, nodding toward the wedding cake that I had to live beside. "Probably do that for two hundred, nice concrete slab and all."

"You can't save the carpet?" I asked.

Rucci looked at me like I should be happy to be rid of the orange shag. "It's done for. Better to get it out sooner than later. It's a breeding ground for mold."

I thanked Rucci for his time and told him I would be out of town for a few days but would let him know which way I wanted to go as soon as I got back. He left me with a card and the thought that he could really do something with the lot I had. I didn't doubt it. The problem was, I didn't want to really do something with the lot. I liked it how it was. I liked the thick shag pile and the Formica counters. I liked the paved patio out back that overlooked the Intracoastal. It was my home, just the way it was.

Then I thought about Danielle and about what I had said the previous night. How she was my home. So how did this waterlogged structure before me fit into that definition? I never felt more at ease than when Danielle and I ended a day by laying on our loungers and watching the sun fall beyond Riviera Beach. Suddenly I wasn't sure what part of that equation was the home part. Or was it all of it? And if it really was all of it, then what happened if Danielle was no longer in Palm Beach?

It was too much to think of. I pulled the front door closed and stuffed my mail in the glove compartment. I started my SUV and looked around the plastic interior. It was new, it smelled good and it drove easy. But all of a sudden, even my vehicle didn't feel like mine. I didn't give my house another glance. I didn't know which direction I would drive if I did. And I needed to drive to my office. That was where some of the answers lay.

At least I hoped so.

CHAPTER SIXTEEN

I handed the laptop back to Lizzy as I came in the office. I was surprised she hadn't made me pay a deposit to take it, and she looked equally surprised that I had returned it in one piece. I wandered into my office and found Ron at my desk, clicking away at something or other on the screen. I flopped down on the sofa.

"That good, huh?" asked Ron.

I let out a huff. "The insurance company is denying my claim."

Ron nodded like this was the most natural thing in the world. "That used to always be the opening gambit. Deny and hope they go away. If the client pressed a little more, they'd often get their claim. It's not done so much anymore. A new insurance policy is but a click away." He held up the computer mouse he had in his hand. "Did they send something?"

I rolled off the sofa and tossed the letter on the desk and then flopped back down. Ron took the letter and read, nodding like he'd seen it all before.

"Not all that surprising," he said.

"Not to you, maybe. I figured if I paid my premiums I'd get looked after, you know, after a hurricane or something."

"You'd hope, wouldn't you? No, I mean it's not surprising from what I hear about this company, Great Southeast Permanent."

"What are you hearing?"

"The CEO is a real go-getter. One of these entrepreneurial types. You know the ones. Get the product to market and work out the kinks later."

"Isn't insurance more regulated than that?"

"It is. Sort of. But a storm like this one can take down a smaller insurance company if they hold too much paper in the one location."

"Too much paper?"

"Too many policies. See, from an actuarial point of view, it is always better to spread your risk. Across different sectors, different products, different geographies. Then if something happens in one of them, you still have others paying their premiums to keep your bottom line healthy."

"So?"

"So I heard on the grapevine that Kent—that's the CEO, Kent Fulsome—was pushing hard in this market to buoy his chances of getting the okay to do business in New York. See, he's New York people but he went to college at Florida. Word is he wants pretty bad to get into the right circles in the Empire State, so he's been aggressive with his growth strategy here."

"You know, Ron, some days I have no idea what the words coming out of your mouth mean."

"If he's taken on too much coverage in one location—say, South Florida—and a natural disaster hits that location—say, a hurricane—then he might not have enough cookies to refill the jar."

"You know a lot about this guy."

"Like I say, he's making some noise in the market. And you know, he just joined the club."

"Which club?"

"My club. South Lakes Country Club."

"The golf club?"

"Yes. So did you speak to Sally's guy?"

"Yeah, I did. He says he can fix the house for fifty thousand."

"Could be worse."

"Yeah, Great Southeast Permanent could go broke."

"I'm not saying that's going to happen. I just mean that might explain using an old-school denial of coverage technique."

"They seem to have the technique down pat. They even passed me off to a department they couldn't contact themselves."

"That is old-school. The next trick is to deny the hurricane policy because it doesn't cover flood, and deny the flood policy because it doesn't cover a hurricane."

"They're gonna love getting the claim from Dale Beadman."

"They hold the paper on Dale Beadman's collection?"

"They do. For thirty million."

"Ouch."

"So if they get nailed by that claim, I might be toast. And I don't have fifty grand to fix my place."

"You know, I just had a thought."

"Better you than me."

"You might be able to negotiate a bounty."

"A bounty? What am I, a bail bondsman?"

"No. Insurance companies sometimes offer bounties to find stolen or missing property. It can be cheaper to pay out ten percent of the value of a claim than the claim itself."

"You're saying if I get the cars back and save them the claim, I could get ten percent?"

"Not every company does it and not in every case, but for a thirty-million-dollar payout? That might be the difference between GSEP's financial viability or not."

"How would I get hold of this guy? I can't even call the department I need to process a claim."

"Let me put the feelers out at the club. Maybe he's due for a tee time."

"Thanks, Ron. Do that."

We heard the front office door open and Lizzy squeal.

"Lucas," she said.

If there was one person Lizzy had a soft spot for, other than Lenny Cox, it was Lucas. Perhaps she too thought them to be two halves of the same fortune cookie.

"How are ya, darl?" I heard him say. I wasn't sure what that meant but I was certain that it would have earned me a slap.

We waited for them to do whatever it was they were going to do, and then Lizzy poked her head in through the door.

"Lucas is here," she said, beaming like a child on Christmas Day. It was an interesting look given her otherwise gothic appearance. Lucas stepped in past her.

"G'day, all," he said.

"Don't leave without saying goodbye," said Lizzy, stepping back. Lucas shot her a wink and I thought she was going to burst.

Lucas stood before us, all sinew and tanned hide, a canvas backpack hanging off his shoulder.

"How are you, Lucas?" Ron asked, half-standing and shaking hands.

"Still tickin', Ronnie. You?"

"I'm well."

"How's that filly of yours?"

"Cassandra? She's very well. Cleaning up after the storm."

"Yeah, it was a good blow." Lucas smiled at me. "How are you, champ?"

"You ever have one of those weeks where you just shouldn't get out of bed?"

"Nup. Every day's a good day if you consider the other option."

"What's the other option?"

"Dead, mate. Dead."

I nodded. It was a reasonable point. The other option did put my troubles into perspective.

"So, we going to Daytona, or are we just gonna stand around here like a bunch of galahs?"

Once again I had no idea what Lucas was saying, but I got the point.

"No, let's get out of here. Ron, will you check up on that Southeast Permanent guy?"

"Kent Fulsome. Will do."

"Lucas, shall we?"

"Let's blow this popsicle stand."

CHAPTER SEVENTEEN

Daytona Beach was a nice three-hour zoom up the coast along I-95 from West Palm Beach. It was an easy run and the traffic really thinned out in Martin County. A guy could make great time in the right car. A Cadillac SUV is not the right car. It's a very nice vehicle for the discerning family. It is not Daytona-approved. Lucas made this point several times on the ride up. On the plus side, the state troopers could be rather vigilant north of the Titusville turnoff, and we drove by a number of Daytona-approved muscle cars and convertibles pulled over to receive speeding tickets.

Route 92 peels off the freeway and heads past Daytona International Speedway—which itself is nestled into the armpit of Daytona Airport—and on toward the beach, where it is imaginatively known as International Speedway Boulevard. We passed the usual assortment of chain restaurants and bars on the left before the stadium stands of the race track showed themselves on our right. Lucas wore a face like a kid at the carnival as we drove by the speedway, the flags of various car brands fluttering in the breeze. He craned his neck as I continued past the track and under the *Welcome to Daytona Beach* emblazoned on the walkway overpass, and then turned left.

"Who is this guy again?" Lucas asked as he lost sight of the racetrack behind us.

"Travis Zanchuk. He was an engineer with Dale Beadman's automotive engineering company. According to Ron, he was fired by Beadman for attempting to steal trade secrets. Zanchuk, on the other hand, claimed that he had invented some kind of braking system that made Beadman a bundle, so he sued him."

"I feel like it didn't go well for old Travis," said Lucas.

"What makes you say that?"

"Look around."

I was looking. We had left the new hotels and the Bob Evans and the wide, freshly paved boulevards of tourist poster Florida for the other Florida. The one where the roads had been baked so hard by the sun they'd gone a powdery gray and cracked like a forsaken mirror. The one where the grass was thirsty yellow not lush green and the buildings looked like they had photographic filters applied to them to make them look like they were something from the sixties. But there were no filters. The buildings were just from the sixties, and had not been painted or had siding replaced since then. The whole area felt run-down and forgotten and was in stark contrast to the commercialism and shiny new look of the area surrounding the speedway. Yet we had only driven a couple miles.

I followed my GPS to a complex that looked like a storage facility that no one visited anymore. There were rows of buildings, more like large sheds, each with a roller door. Most of the doors were closed. I took my foot from the accelerator and rolled through. It was like some kind of ghost town. I had to turn at the end and roll down a second row to make any sense of the numbering system for the units. There really didn't seem to be one.

"I think that might be what you're looking for," said Lucas.

He pointed at one of the sheds that had the door rolled up. It looked like a down-at-heel automotive workshop. There was a car out front with its hood up, and inside we could see a second car up on a hydraulic automotive lift. I didn't pull in. There didn't seem to be any point. I just stopped the Caddy in the middle of the driveway and we got out.

There was a small plate affixed to the wall that told us we were visiting Harder Uniforms Racing. I noted that the car with its hood up had no engine inside. The workshop smelled like oil. There was a tall rack unit holding boxes and boxes of car parts. None of the boxes looked new, but the inventory was orderly. A radio echoed AM talkback around the space. We wandered toward the vehicle lift and the whistling that was emanating from within. It sounded like a tune I couldn't quite place. I glanced at Lucas.

"Kenny Rogers," he said. "*Ruby, Don't Take Your Love to Town.*"

I nodded like that was useful information.

"Hello," I called out.

The whistling stopped but the AM radio didn't. Those guys could talk and talk. We waited as a man withdrew himself from the innards of the car on the lift. He was skinny and had thin hair and the kind of reading glasses that people spent their entire time peering over the top of. He wore blue coveralls that looked like they might have been used by the guy who stoked the coals on the continental railway.

"Help you?" he asked. He wiped his hands on a rag despite the dirty overalls. He didn't come out from underneath the car.

"Travis Zanchuk?" I asked.

"Who's asking?"

"Miami Jones."

"Miami Jones?"

"Yes, sir."

"*The* Miami Jones."

Lucas raised his eyebrows. It happened from time to time. I was—in the small-time version of the word—famous. I had played professional minor league baseball and there were fans of that particular genre that remembered players, even those like me who had made it to the big leagues but never thrown a pitch in anger. I had, however, played four years in Modesto, California, before my brief stint with the Oakland A's. After that, I had spent two years plying my trade with the St. Lucie Mets. I had been to Jackie Robinson Ballpark in Daytona once or twice. I had pitched there, I had won there. Some folks remembered stuff like that. Not many, but some. So I got recognized here and there. Less than Derek Jeter on Fifth Avenue but more than some late-night cable reality television people.

The guy under the car stepped out. He was still wiping his hands on the rag. The color of oil appeared to be tattooed into his skin.

"It is you," he said. "Miami Jones. I saw you pitch."

"You have a good memory."

"Yeah, I do. I saw you throw a one-walk, no-hitter here against the Cubs."

"I remember that game."

"Yeah, me too. You could have had a perfect game, but then Jessie Heskie did a Babe Ruth on you and pointed out to the bleachers like he was going to smack you out of the park."

"I remember."

"Did your pitch break his arm?"

I shook my head. "No. He had a couple games on the disabled list, but there was no break."

"Bet he never did that again."

"It's a reasonable assumption."

"So what brings you to my workshop?"

I took a breath. In through the nose and out through the mouth. Our pleasant chat was about to take a turn. Travis wasn't likely to be such a Miami Jones fan within the next ten seconds.

"Dale Beadman," I said.

Zanchuk frowned. He had deep furrows in his forehead. I have the same, but mine are from too much time in the sun. Travis just looked like a worrier.

"What about him?"

"You have much to do with him these days?"

"I have nothing to do with him, period."

"But you have history."

"What's this about?"

"I'm an investigator now, Travis. I'm undertaking an investigation."

"Investigator? Seriously? I would have figured you for a bar owner."

I had the same thought on a fairly regular basis.

Lucas wandered over to the lift and looked up into the guts of the car. "Chevy," he said.

Travis doubled down on his frown. "Yeah, what of it?"

"You race these cars?" asked Lucas.

"Yes. What of it?"

Lucas shrugged. "You drive?"

"No. I'm a crew chief and head engineer."

I looked around the workshop and decided that Zanchuk's title was like my lawn guy calling himself head groundskeeper.

Lucas continued. "Where do you race?"

"On the All-American Series."

"New Smyrna Speedway?"

"Yes, sometimes."

"How do you go?"

"We go okay. Could be better, could be worse. Listen, what's this about?"

"I'm led to understand that you sued Dale Beadman," I said.

"That's old news."

"Why?"

"Why's it old news?"

"Why did you sue him?"

"If you're here asking the question, then you know." Zanchuk wandered over to a work table by the wall and tossed his rag onto it.

I said, "I know what the lawsuit claimed. But that doesn't tell me anything."

Zanchuk turned and leaned back against the work table. "It tells you he won. It tells you I got fired and no team would touch me. It tells you I ended up running a third-string team for beer money instead of being a crew chief for a cup team in Charlotte."

"Yeah, that's what I don't get, Travis. You had to know that was all going to happen. You knew you couldn't win the suit."

"Did I?"

"Of course. I've known you for five minutes and I can tell you're a smart guy. Smarter than me, by the length of the straight. And even I could see you'd lose. You worked for Beadman Engineering. You were an employee. You knew that anything you developed was work product. The company owned it. That's what they paid you for. So you couldn't win a claim that you owned the right to the braking system. There's no legal basis for it. You know that now, you knew it then. So why?"

Zanchuk shuffled his feet. I waited. I don't feel the need to talk when no talking is required. Lucas was even better at it than I was. Lenny had been, too. He could be mute for days, if the mood took him. But Zanchuk couldn't. He had things to say.

"I invented the damned system. I did. Not him."

"I don't think that's in dispute, Travis."

"You don't, huh? Well, the great Dale Beadman went around telling everyone he invented it. Like it was his baby and we were all there just to clean up after his genius. I was ten times the engineer he was."

"But wasn't that his job? He was the figurehead for the company. Like Steve Jobs invented the iPhone. He didn't really invent it. I'm sure tens, hundreds, hell, maybe thousands of people played a role. But it was his company. He was *the man.* That's how it works."

"I should have been crew chief. But he couldn't stand aside. He couldn't abide someone else having the spotlight."

"You were head engineer. That's pretty good."

"It's not enough!" screamed Zanchuk. He clenched his jaw and took a few deep breaths to calm himself. "I should have been crew chief."

Lucas spoke from under the Chevy. "And now you are."

"Yeah," said Zanchuk with a laugh. "Head honcho on a team on the local circuit racing against kids who don't even have driver's licenses yet. Our lead sponsor is the local hospitality uniform company, and I have to moonlight doing up Subarus for rich kids just to make ends meet. Yeah, this is the life."

"Money's tight," I said.

"Look around."

"Did you ever see Dale Beadman's car collection?"

"No," he said a little too quickly. "Well, maybe a couple of them. Some of them came through the workshop for some restoration. I remember a Testa Rossa. We fixed that one up for him. But I never saw the collection. Not together. Why?"

"Just curious."

"Curious? Why?" asked Zanchuk. "What happened to his cars? They get stolen or something?"

I said nothing.

"If they did, I say fantastic. I hope they were broken down

and sold for parts. But if you're trying to suggest I had something to do with it, ask yourself this. If I stole his cars, would I be standing in this workshop right now?"

It wasn't the final word on the subject, but it was a good point. I thanked Zanchuk for his time, and he shrugged like he had time to kill. I turned to leave. Lucas stopped by Zanchuk. He looked around the workshop like he was a Catholic in the Sistine Chapel.

"I sure do love racing," Lucas said. "You?"

Zanchuk nodded. "Since I ran go-karts as a kid."

"You ever wanted to do anything else?"

"Never."

Lucas nodded and patted Zanchuk on the shoulder.

"A man who wakes up every day to do what he loves is a lucky man," he said, and then he nodded and walked out of the workshop, and I followed him, wondering who it was exactly that he had been talking to.

CHAPTER EIGHTEEN

It was late afternoon by the time we left Travis Zanchuk, but Lucas decided to take the wheel and make time while the going was good. It was a six-hour drive through to Charlotte. Lucas took us through to a Cracker Barrel country store just south of Savannah, where we ate chicken and waffles and apple pie, and then I took the wheel again into Charlotte. We stopped at a Motel 6 and I asked Lucas if he minded splitting a room or preferred his own. He said he had spent more nights in his life bunking with other men in the room than he hadn't, so sharing a room was fine with him. We grabbed a six-pack, lay on our twin beds and watched *SportsCenter* until sleep called.

Lucas woke early. He was like a kid who had just been told they were off to visit Disney World. We ate breakfast at another Cracker Barrel because they were good, well-priced and right off every freeway we drove along. We were in Statesville before the office workers had gotten to their desks in Charlotte.

WinLobe Racing was the polar opposite of Travis Zanchuk's workshop. It was huge, over a hundred thousand square feet. The lobby was larger than Zanchuk's entire space.

It looked like an office complex, and there wasn't a hint of oil on the air. One thing about NASCAR folks. They're early birds. The workshop at WinLobe Racing was in full swing when we arrived. Unfortunately the office wasn't, so we milled around in the lobby looking at memorabilia, waiting for someone to make it into the office.

That someone was a nice young lady who told us that without an appointment, it would not be possible to see either Mr. Lobe or Mr. Gifford today. I'm not a fan of appointments. I find them too easily broken. I'm more a *just turn up and see what happens* kind of guy. So I told her that I was a private investigator and I was working for Dale Beadman, and if either Mr. Lobe or Mr. Gifford didn't want to see me, then I completely understood and we'd let the chips fall where they may. The private investigator bit worried a lot of people. It held no legal weight whatsoever, but it did open a few doors. But I found the really tough doors were opened by the mentioning of chips falling where they may. It really meant nothing but conjured up all kinds of chaos in the minds of people who were worried about how the chips might affect them.

We found ourselves in a boardroom overlooking one section of the racing team workshop. We were offered coffee, which we declined, and water, which we accepted. We'd had our fill of coffee at Cracker Barrel, and nothing killed the momentum of an investigation like having to excuse yourself from interviewing a suspect for a tinkle.

We waited about ten minutes, which I thought was more than acceptable given our lack of an invitation. Rory Lobe and Winton Gifford were what my mother would have called good old boys. They were tall and wore cowboy hats, even inside. They also drank water. There were a lot of men of a certain age in the room. If it came down to a pissing contest, no one wanted to be the first to have to go.

"Rory Lobe," said the white hat. His accent dripped the South like honey. His hair was short and gray at the sides and he was in good shape.

"Winton Gifford," said the black hat. They were like a county music duo. Gifford sported a mustache and a belly with a large buckle on it like a headlight. "What can we do for you gentlemen?" said Gifford.

I said, "We had some questions about your relationship with Dale Beadman."

Lobe sipped his water. "May I ask what this is regarding?"

"A criminal matter," I said.

Lobe smiled. "Do I need to lawyer up?"

"I don't know, sir. Do you?"

"Son, we're busy men. You got questions, you best ask them."

"You were partners with Beadman, once upon a time."

"Yes, sir."

"But it didn't end well."

"I wouldn't say that."

"It ended in court."

"Well, that's not strictly speaking true."

"So how did it end, then?"

"Dale bought us out. This story has done the rounds, son. You don't know it?"

"No, sir, I don't."

"I do," said Lucas. "He bought you out. He wanted to focus just on cars and you gentlemen wanted to expand into aircraft engineering. So you went your separate ways."

"Yep, that's the story," said Gifford.

"So how did it end up in court?" I asked.

"Business, son," said Lobe. "Business. All that our Australian friend here has said is accurate, to a point. But it also turned out that Dale had been holding out on us some. The company had developed a fuel management system that is currently used in about forty percent of vehicles on the road. He neglected to mention this fact when we negotiated our separation agreement. We simply rectified that."

"Are you saying you bear no ill will toward Mr. Beadman?" I asked.

Gifford leaned back in his chair, perhaps to better show off his belt buckle. "Only on the racetrack. On the speedway we're enemies. Nothing less. Off it, we're former business associates. That's all."

I said nothing. Mainly because I had nothing to say. The duo had a good patter, but they also seemed genuine. Despite my better judgment, I liked them. Which gave me a problem, because I had also liked the idea that Beadman's former partners were out for revenge. It was trite, but it was also true more often than not. So I threw a Hail Mary.

"Do you gentlemen happen to collect cars?"

"I think we both have a number of cars in garages, son, but I don't know you'd call either of us collectors. Would you say that's right, Win?"

"I would. I have six or seven. But personally, I prefer to collect wine."

My impression of Winton Gifford took a little dip. I never understood people who collected wine. Surely that was for drinking.

"But I know Dale does collect," said Lobe. "He has a thing for domestic cars in particular, I believe."

"Have you seen this collection?"

"No, son, I have not. As you inferred, we are not as close with Dale as we once were. But that does not go as far as bearing him any ill will. Now, may I ask a question of you?"

"Yes, sir."

"Why is it you have come all this way to ask us about long-forgotten business? What exactly are you investigating?"

"Something that belonged to Mr. Beadman was stolen. I have been tasked with finding it."

"A car, I assume. And you think we stole this car?"

"No, sir. As much as anything, an investigation is a process of eliminating suspects."

"So you're looking to eliminate us?" Lobe offered a mischievous smile.

"Not quite how I'd phrase it, sir, but. . ."

"And can I ask why the police are not asking these questions?"

"They have a few protocols to go through, especially when it comes to crossing state lines. And there are budgets they have to consider."

Lobe smiled again. "Palm Beach budgets?"

I shrugged. "Can you think of anyone who might want to harm or embarrass Mr. Beadman?"

Gifford took the baton. "If you're in business as long as we've been, you get your share of people who feel they've been wronged."

"Anyone stick out in your mind?"

Gifford shook his head.

"Rivals?" I asked. "Other than yourselves, of course."

"We were never Dale's biggest rivals, son," said Lobe. "That mantle surely goes to Brasher."

"Brasher?"

"I'm sure your friend here can inform you," said Lobe. "He seems to know his racing." The way he said it was not so much a plaudit for Lucas as a condemnation of me.

"Now if you'll excuse us, gentlemen, we have a race to prepare for." The two men stood together, the white hat and the black hat. They each shook our hands.

"Good luck on Sunday," said Lucas.

"Thank you, sir," said Lobe.

The two of them shuffled out of the conference room.

"What's happening on Sunday?" I said.

Lucas frowned. "You're not into NASCAR at all, are you?"

"I don't own a television."

"And yet you can recite baseball stats up the yin-yang. Sunday is race day in NASCAR."

"Okay. Where is it?"

"This week? Darlington, I think. About two hours from here. South Carolina."

The young lady who had ushered us in came to usher us out. We stood for a moment in the parking lot.

"So who is this Brasher they were talking about?"

"Ansel Brasher. He was a driver. More open-wheelers than NASCAR, though. He drove Formula One for a while, Indy too."

"So why do they think he was a rival? Or are they blowing smoke?"

"I can't recall." He seemed to think about it but said nothing.

"What do you think?" I asked.

"Nothing," he said.

"Helpful, thanks. I mean those two. You think they could have done it?"

"Of course they could have. Means, motive and opportunity, isn't that what they say on the telly?"

I didn't know if that was what they said on the telly. I didn't have a television. It was starting to feel like a character flaw.

"So you do think they might have done it?" I asked.

"Nup. I don't think they did any such thing."

"I don't either."

"But there's no such thing as reading people. Some folks are great liars."

"Helpful."

"So I recall something about a tour of a workshop?"

I nodded. "Let's go."

Lucas got in, and put his belt on and smiled. "Are we actually expected this time?"

CHAPTER NINETEEN

IF WINLOBE RACING WAS DISNEY WORLD TO LUCAS, THEN Dale Beadman Racing, aka DBR, was like rolling all the amusement parks in the country into one. We took the short drive down to Mooresville and found the workshop without problem. Workshop was an understatement. We saw it from a mile away. Surrounded by lush trees and plenty of open space, the two-hundred-thousand-foot facility looked like an aircraft factory. It was crisp lines and lots of reflecting windows and chrome. There was a loading dock where two big rigs sat patiently. Each wore the livery for the cars that they transported—29 and 09—and were covered in sponsors' logos. The rear of the trailers were open to the inside of the facility and were as busy as the business end of a beehive. People were coming and going, not ambling but striding, no time to waste.

We headed for the lobby. It turned out to be more than a lobby. It was a museum. A fully-fledged curated space honoring the achievements of Dale Beadman. I wondered if that accounted for the additional size of the facility or whether that was some kind of *mine is bigger than yours* thing with the folks at WinLobe.

I left Lucas to wander around the museum and went to the reception desk to let Dale Beadman know we were there. The young guy behind the desk made a call and told me that Dale was in a race review meeting and would be available shortly, so he invited me to visit the museum while I waited.

I found Lucas reading an old newspaper article that was posted beside a full body suit that itself was plastered with sponsors' logos.

"His first championship," said Lucas.

I ambled through the dimly lit space. I supposed the dark room put emphasis on the spotlit artifacts, but I always felt one step from tripping over. There were a number of drivers' suits, and there were trophies of all sizes. Probably every trophy that Dale had ever won. At either end, there was a car in its own roped off area. They were both Chevrolet-badged but didn't look like any Chevy I'd seen on the street. The one near the entrance looked like a prototype for the Corvette. I walked over to the one at the far end. It was Dale Beadman green and numbered 29. The shape clearly marked it as an old iteration, but it was so shiny it might have just rolled out of the workshop. I wondered how they got it so shiny. Perhaps they had a full-time waxer and buffer. Maybe two guys.

There were three men standing before the 29 car. They were each adorned in Beadman green. Various versions of caps and t-shirts and jackets celebrating the team. They each wore blue jeans and stood with a kind of muted awe at the car. It was a semireligious experience, if the looks on their faces were anything to go by. One of them glanced at me and I offered him a nod, which he returned with a grin, as if we were sharing in something that we would remember for the rest of our lives.

I turned away and left them to it. I'm not much one for glory days. I had a fair few trinkets myself, baseball and football trophies, pennants and posters of me pitching, old playing uniforms and t-shirts and such. I didn't have a room or a man cave where they were displayed. Right now they were in a box in the spare room of Lucas's condo. It's not that I don't admire achievement or understand why people celebrate it. I get the team mentality as much as anyone. I bought right into it for the longest time. I still do. We're social beasts, us humans. We need our tribe. Be it family or friends or church or sports teams, we need somewhere to belong. I just found that a lot of people wasted a lot of time lingering over days gone and ended up missing out on the present. Sure, I had thrown a mean fastball in my day. I was a decent quarterback, good enough for a scholarship to college but not good enough to play regularly once there. We won a college baseball world series. I remembered those times as some of the best of my life. But I never dwelled on them. Because right now I was the happiest I had ever been. I had the affection of a woman my superior in almost every way, I had good friends and people to depend on. I had a watering hole with a wooden barstool that had the shape of my butt worn into the seat. I had my tribe.

Dale Beadman found me standing in the lobby looking out at the Florida morning sun. He shook my hand, and I went and found Lucas and introduced him. Dale welcomed him like an old friend. Lucas played it pretty cool. I knew he was a fan, but Lucas had a way of seeing a man as a man and not as a hero. Maybe that was how you saw the world when you had been a real hero yourself. Lenny had hinted more than once that Lucas had performed more than his fair share of heroics in their younger days. He had never elaborated, but I had never doubted the subtext.

"I'm not sure what you expect to find up here, Miami," said Beadman.

"Me either, Dale. But that's how this works. I talk to people.

I learn things. Something that wasn't important becomes important. I never know where that will come from."

"You're the doctor," he said. "How can I help."

"Perhaps you can give us the ten-cent tour?"

So he did. Dale Beadman wandered around his domain, the king of all he surveyed. We walked through a large open workshop that wasn't that different from his garage at home. The floor was polished and clean, the walls were white and tools were laid out in an orderly manner, ready for use at a moment's notice. Dale pointed out various teams and what they did, how they related to the performance of the cars. Everyone wore polo shirts with sponsor logos on the breast or coveralls with the same. There was no AM talkback or whistling, just the hum of diagnostic computers and the soft chatter of people looking for that winning edge.

We left the workshop and walked through a corridor that had photos of the cars on various racetracks along its length. Then we came out into another workshop, a duplicate of the last. Except for the color. The Beadman green was replaced with red. The sponsors' logos were different but everything else was the same.

"This is the 09 team," Dale said.

"And the other workshop was 29?" I asked.

"That's right."

"They feel pretty separate."

"For a reason. They're both my teams, but they are separate teams. Separate cars, drivers, crew chiefs, mechanics, pit crews. A bit of internal competition goes a long way."

"So they don't cooperate at all?"

"Sure they do, at the top level. The crew chiefs sit in on the cross-team meetings with me and Simon—he's the head engineer. So we share at that top level, but we give the crew chiefs a fair bit of latitude to run their teams."

"Where are the drivers?" I asked.

"At home. Spending time with the family. They'll be in later. We've got a good week this week. Sunday is at Darlington, so we're only a couple hours away. It means everyone gets a little more home time."

"How many days a week do you all work?"

"All of them," said Dale, without a hint of irony.

We walked into another workshop that held no vehicles. Guys were working machines that looked like lathes.

"This is our fabrication workshop. We can make almost any part we can't source. Anything else can be fabricated at the shop in Daytona."

"Impressive," said Lucas.

As we walked through the space, I was struck by one thing more than any other. It was the seamless way Dale moved through the facility. No one was in awe of him, no one stopped or stared or got busy because the boss was walking through. They just went about their business. If they had a question for him, they asked it. If he had a question for them, they quietly explained what they were doing and why. It was very collaborative, like the best football teams.

Again I was reminded of what Lucas had told me. He didn't just support the driver, he supported the car. It wasn't Dale's team. It was the 29 car. And like a great football team, the quarterback was crucial. Without a great quarterback, a team rarely found success at the top level. But without a great offensive line, a great quarterback got smashed regularly. And without a great defense, teams gave up too many points to win. And so it was here. Dale was the coach and the drivers were the QBs. They had the posters and the adulation. They signed the hero cards and the caps and the body parts flashed at them. But without the crew, each and every one at the top of their game, the team just wouldn't cut it.

"Tell me about Travis Zanchuk," I said as we watched the team work.

"Travis?" Dale asked, surprised. "He was a great engineer. Had a great feel for what made cars go fast."

"He's not that big a fan of you."

"You spoke to Travis?"

"In Daytona."

"Why?"

"We're investigating your stolen cars. People who don't like you are called suspects."

Dale shook his head slowly. "Travis wasn't a team player. He wanted it to be all about him."

"And that didn't work for you?"

"No, it didn't. It's never about any one of us. It's about all of us, or it's about none of us. That's the way it works."

"So you cut him loose."

"Had to. Only takes one guy like that to bring everyone else down."

"What about Lobe and Gifford?"

"You've been digging through my past?"

"I have. That's what you're paying me for, even if you don't know it."

"We were partners, that's all it was."

"But they sued you."

"Just business."

"That's what they said."

"You spoke to Rory and Win, too?"

I nodded. "Did you rip them off?"

"I don't see it that way. They wanted to go another way with the business, and I wanted to focus on cars. So I bought them out."

"Without mentioning the fuel management system that was going to make you millions."

"But it hadn't when I bought them out. I didn't see why I should pay them for something that hadn't happened."

"They disagreed?"

"They did. We came to an agreement."

"You think they hold any grudges about it?"

"Those old boys? That's ancient history."

Dale finished our tour in a small anteroom off one of the workshops. It had tall windows that looked out onto the workshop. He said he needed to get back to it but his head engineer would be in to chat with us. We waited in silence. Lucas stood at the window and watched. I sat back in a chair like I was waiting at the Jiffy Lube.

The guy who came in to us was as old as Dale and every bit as energetic but lacked Beadman's charisma. He shook our hands and told us his name was Simon Lees. He offered us a seat and a beverage. We took the seat but not the beverage.

"I can't believe what happened with Dale's collection," he said. He had thick black hair and wore a blue polo with the sponsors' logos on it.

"You know about that?" I asked.

"Of course."

"I didn't think Dale was making it common knowledge."

"He's not. But Dale and I have known each other a long time."

"Is that right?"

Lucas said, "You were crew chief of 09 when he was crew chief of 29."

"That's right. And his lead mechanic before that, when he was driving all those years."

"So you're a crew chief?" I asked.

"Not anymore." He smiled. "It's a younger man's game. I'm now chief engineer."

"What does that mean, exactly?"

"It means I oversee this workshop. I oversee our research and development. See, NASCAR likes to tinker with the rules. Constantly. As soon as one team finds an edge, a quarter second per lap, they'll change it up to even the playing field. It's my job to be on top of those changes and to make modifications."

"So you test the race cars?"

"Not so much the 29 and the 09. See, there's rules on that, too. NASCAR only allows certain sanctioned testing days at certain tracks for the team cars. Again, it's about evening up the field." He waved in the direction of the workshop. "We're obviously a big team. We have the sponsors and personnel to test. We can hire tracks when we need to. But some smaller teams could never afford that. So NASCAR says teams only get to test the actual race cars at certain fixed times. But outside those, we can develop products. They can't stop that."

"Develop products?"

"We build engines, fuel management systems, things like that. For smaller teams."

"You build their engines?"

"Sure. About a quarter of the teams run a car with one of our engines in it."

"That seems a bit strange. What's the incentive for you to give them an engine as good as yours?"

Lees shrugged. He had broad shoulders and it was quite a mannerism. "What's the incentive anytime? Money. It costs around a quarter million dollars for a high-performance engine. If they don't run, teams don't buy them. We're not the only game in town."

"You ever get beat by one of your own engines?" asked Lucas.

"Sure. It happens. But not often. See, the engine is built to race specs as set out by NASCAR. Ours is the same as theirs. A good car—that is, a fast car—is in the incremental things you do around that engine. How do you trim the engine, how durable are your parts, how much does everything weigh? Different tracks run differently. Every week we get back here from whatever race we were at last Sunday and we have to rejig the cars for the next track."

"Tracks all look the same to me," I said. "Round and round. No right turn."

"That's the old gag," said Lees. "But it's not accurate. See, some tracks have longer straights, some have tighter turns. The angle on the banks is different. Some speedways have a more abrasive asphalt that wears tires, others are cleaner and more about fuel management. We're not talking about seconds per lap, we're talking about tenths or hundredths of a second per lap. We're talking about being able to stay lower on the turns and cover less mileage, or greater straight-line speed so our cars can make the most of the slipstreams."

"It's a game of inches," I said.

"Fractions of inches. At a hundred eighty miles per hour."

I saw the smile on Lucas's face. He was nodding vigorously. I figured he liked the idea of those kinds of margins at that kind of speed.

Our attention was drawn by the roller door going up at the far end of the workshop.

"Boys are heading out," he said. "Come see."

We walked out into the workshop but stayed out of the way. The roller door was raised to the top. The ceiling was high enough to fit a space shuttle inside. One of the semitrailers had moved from the loading dock to the workshop door. Like at Dale Beadman's garage the rear of the trailer was down, forming a ramp. Six guys got around the 29 car and pushed it up into the bowels of the trailer.

"Where's it going?" I asked.

"Darlington," said Lees.

"This early?"

"This is not early. This is late. Normally the trucks are out by Tuesday night, Wednesday morning latest. But Darlington's close by."

"How many cars go in there?" I said, looking into the trailer.

"Two. Race car and backup."

"Two? It's a big trailer for two cars."

"Size-wise you could fit a dozen cars, top and bottom. But most of the space is equipment. It's like a mobile workshop. Scratch that. It is a mobile workshop. And there's a meeting space and drivers' quarters at the front. Somewhere for the guys to relax after their work is done."

The word *guys* made me think. "You don't have any women drivers?"

"Not on our team," Lees said matter-of-factly. "There's a couple with teams at the top level and a couple more on the series one step down."

"Why so few?"

Lees shrugged. "You know any girls who like cars?"

"That's a bit sexist, isn't it?"

"Sure it is. But tell me I'm wrong."

I couldn't. I didn't know any.

"Don't get me wrong. There's no reason at all women can't succeed in racing. But it's traditionally a male thing. The speed, the smell. Men stuff. I've seen girls at the kart level, even local races doing pretty well. But by the time they get into their late teens, they've usually dropped out. Could racing be more welcoming for women? Sure. Could there be more female-only races to get girls interested? You bet. But it's chicken and egg. Do you put the effort in to encourage kids who aren't showing interest, or do you focus your limited time and money and energy on the kids who want to be there? The kids who will turn up just to watch and learn. I've only got twenty-four hours in a day. I know where my energy's going.

And those kids tend to be boys. I hope it changes, I really do. And maybe with some of the women winning at the top level, it will."

"You could have a woman as your CEO," I said.

Lees nodded slowly. "Angie. Yep, you're right there. Her time will come."

"Why isn't her time now? From what I hear, she's more than capable."

"You're right about that. She already takes care of everything that's worth taking care of."

"She not capable of the step up?"

"No, that's not it at all." Lees looked at me like my father used to do when he thought he had something really important to say. "Dale Beadman's one of the best there's ever been. Up there with Petty, Earnhardt, Gordon, Waltrip. The greats. Racing has been his life. Everything good that happened to him happened because of racing."

"Some might say his family gets in there somewhere."

"Of course. Top of the list. But he met Missy at a race meet. And young Angie? She was conceived in a team RV."

It was more information than I needed, and I think my expression conveyed that fact.

"What I'm saying is, when something has been your life's work, it's hard to give it up. What's he supposed to do? Take up gardening?"

"He had a pretty nice car collection to tinker with."

Lees nodded. "All's I'm saying is, Angie's time will come. Yes, if you want to hear it, she should already be running everything here. She's earned it. People respect her. The teams love her. She's the best of her daddy and her momma all wrapped up in one, that's for sure. But it ain't about her being a woman. It's about how hard it is for an old man to let go of all that defines him."

We watched the 29 car get covered up inside the trailer. It was treated with kid gloves. It reminded me of the delivery of Dale Beadman's latest toy.

"What do you know about the F-88?" I asked Lees.

He looked around to see if anyone was listening. They were too busy to care. "Everything."

"You saw it, right?"

"Twice. Once when I went to Michigan with Dale to view it, and then to inspect it before it was loaded onto the transport down to Palm Beach."

"You saw it being loaded?"

"Of course."

"Dale wasn't there."

"No. Just me and Rex."

"Rex, the truck driver."

"That's right."

"Why you?"

"I'm Dale's head engineer. I've inspected every one of his cars before he bought them."

"Why wasn't he there?"

"He had a race meet."

"And you didn't."

"No. I don't go to many races, anymore. I'm not part of one of the teams. My role is here, in the workshop."

"So you went to Michigan?"

"I did. Flew in, drove up to the barn, watched it get loaded, watched the escrow happen and then watched Rex drive away. Then I drove back to the airport and flew back here. All in a day."

"How about this guy, Rex? You trust him?"

"You suggesting Rex took the car?"

"I'm canvassing every possibility."

"Dale said there's video of Rex delivering the car to his garage."

"There's video of Rex delivering a car."

"It's a pretty distinctive vehicle."

That was true. It was a one-off. Or maybe a two-off.

"Rex didn't take the car," said Lees.

"How do you know?"

"He's been with us since the beginning."

"Crimes are often perpetrated by people close to the victim."

"I mean he's been with us since right at the beginning. He's been with Dale and Missy before they were anything."

"So why's he just a truck driver?"

Lees suddenly looked uncomfortable. I felt like I'd hit a nerve, which in my business was a good thing to do.

"Look, Rex was a driver, back in the day. A teammate. But some guys are cut out for that side of things and some guys are not. He loved to drive, though. Hell, he even raced trucks at one point. So he took on the job of moving the cars from track to track. He had a perfect record. Never missed a deadline, never missed a meet. No speeding tickets, no fines, no nothing. He's one of us. He wouldn't do anything to hurt Dale and Missy. I personally guarantee it."

"So he's driving this truck here?" I nodded at the truck that was closing up before us.

"No. He doesn't do the races anymore."

"Why not?"

"Like I said, Mr. Jones. It's a young man's game. Rex now handles local work. He's on my team. He gets the development vehicles to where I need them to be. We're moving them today, as it happens."

"Moving them where?"

"To the speedway. In Charlotte. We've rented track time.

The development team will be down there after the race teams are away."

Lees looked at me and then at Lucas.

"You boys want to come for a ride in a stock car?"

Lucas nearly had a heart attack.

CHAPTER TWENTY

WE LET SIMON LEES GO AND DO HIS JOB AND WE WATCHED the two team trucks gobble up the cars and close up and pull out, destined for Darlington. I wasn't sure why they were leaving so early, but there was plenty I didn't know about this stuff. After the frantic action of the trucks, the workshop fell back into its quiet rhythm. Guys tinkered with engines and fabricated parts. A guy Lucas recognized as one of the team drivers arrived. There was no fanfare. A few nods and greetings, but otherwise he was just one of the guys. He was in the same polo shirt as everyone else. He climbed the steps to an upstairs room, where we were told he was going to be analyzing video of past Darlington races with his crew chief. I could relate to that. I'd watched my fair share of tape. Analyzing the opposition, figuring out how to stop them, how they were going to try to stop us. Searching for that elusive edge.

An hour later Simon Lees found us and directed us outside. A third semitrailer was at a workshop door, this one on the far end of the building. I noted the billboard-like side of the trailer, a giant promotion for Dale Beadman Racing and a soda that I never drank. A couple race cars were loaded into the trailer and then the development team got into a series of pickups and headed away. Lees offered Lucas and me a ride to the track.

"Is that Rex?" I asked Lees, gesturing at the driver closing up the vehicle transporter.

"Yup, that's him."

"Maybe I'll take a ride with him. Does he know about the cars going missing?"

"Like I told you, Mr. Jones, he's been with us forever. He knows."

I left Lucas and Simon Lees and jogged across the lot to the big rig. Rex Jennings was striding around the trailer doing checks of some kind to make sure everything was squared away. I usually just patted my pockets to make sure I had my keys.

"Rex Jennings," I said.

"That's me," he said.

"Miami Jones," I said. "I'm helping Dale with, you know. . ."

"I know who you are." His voice was deep like a baritone and he had the shaven haircut of a drill sergeant.

"Mind if I get a ride with you to the track? Mr. Lees said we could come along."

"Sure, no problem. Jump on up."

We climbed up into the cabin and Rex fired up the truck. The entire thing shuddered and then let out a horrendous groan and hiss, and then we started moving. I was convinced we were going to take out every pole, streetlight and canvas awning that we turned past. But Rex wound us out onto the freeway with practiced ease.

"I hear you've known Dale for a long time."

"That I have. We drove karts together when we were young 'uns."

"You didn't get into the NASCAR thing?"

"What do you think I do for a living, Miami?"

"I mean the driving."

"Same question."

He was a sharp tack. "Race driving."

He closed his eyes like a tired cat and then slowly opened them again. "I raced for a while. But not everyone's made to be a champion. You know what I mean?"

"Sure."

"Dale has gifts that I never had. He's fearless."

"Not you?"

"Not most people. Most of us care too much. About what other people think, about what might happen if we do this or do that. So we don't do anything, all out of fear. You know what I mean?"

"Yeah, I do. So you've always been part of the development side?"

"No," he said. Rex clunked down hard on the gear stick and pushed the truck up to fifty-five. "I drove the rig for Dale for years. When he was a driver and then when he was crew chief."

"So you carried 29 from track to track."

"That's right."

"A lot of miles."

"Millions."

"You enjoy it?"

"Loved it. Mostly."

"So tell me, why did the trucks leave so early? The rest of the crew didn't look in any hurry to get to Darlington."

"That's not early, it's late. I'd normally have been hell and gone by now. But Darlington's close. See, it's the rig driver's job to get to the track first. I'd get there, unload some of the equipment, get the truck set up so the crew could just come in and get to work. Then when it's done, we'd pack her up and I'd head out Sunday night. Depending on the race, I'd get back here in Charlotte late Monday, early Tuesday. Late Tuesday if I was coming from California."

"You drove to California? Aren't there like laws on how long you can drive for?"

"Oh, yeah. They're real serious about that, too. The Cali trips we'd split rig. I'd drive halfway with a co-driver and meet another rig in Oklahoma City, and we'd swap the trailer and he'd take her out to Cali. We'd wait in OKC until they came back. Some years we'd even head from there straight to Michigan."

"That's some serious driving."

"Yup. Even the good weeks we'd be home late Monday and gone Wednesday."

"But you don't do that anymore?"

"No. Winning comes at a cost, you know? For everybody. I spent a lot of time away. I got to be part of a great team of guys and gals. We won races, we won championships. Hell of a life. But there's always a cost. For everyone."

I waited for him to say something more, but he focused on the road.

"Why did you give it up?" I asked, although I already knew.

"You hear what I'm saying? You know what you lose when you got a family you never see? A daughter who don't know you? A son who you never see play baseball?"

I shook my head. But I knew.

"You lose 'em. Plain and simple."

"I'm sorry."

Rex shrugged. "Ain't your fault."

"I didn't mean that."

"It's my fault. I made my choice. You know? Ain't no one ever held a gun to my head. Sometimes wish someone hadda." He glanced at me. "You got a wife?"

"No," I said. "I'm engaged."

"Love of your life or you just tired of being alone?"

"Excuse me?"

"I don't mean nothing by it. Either reason's an okay reason to be with someone, far as I can tell."

"Love of my life. No doubt."

He nodded. "Me, too. Two loves. The road and my wife. Until one hit the other." He snorted. "Sounds like a damned country song, don't it?"

I said nothing.

"Winning has a price," he said again, but I didn't think he was talking to me this time. "For me, for Dale, for everybody. You, too."

I waited a couple miles before I spoke again. "So now you stay local?"

He nodded. "Yup. Gave up the long haul when my wife told me she was leaving for Boulder. We tried for a while, but even though she was here, she was already gone. And now I'm an old guy, you know? My back don't take too kindly to sleeping in cheap motels or the back of the rig. So Dale said I should drive for the development team."

"Doesn't seem so bad."

"It's fine. They're good boys. And I've known Simon forever, too."

"But you picked up the F-88 in Detroit?"

"Outside of Lansing."

"Right. That's a long drive."

"Just a favor for Dale. He wanted someone with his best interests at heart."

"So what happened? You collected the car in a barn?"

He stayed silent as he pulled the rig onto the off-ramp from I-85. Across the freeway, I could see Charlotte Motor Speedway. It was in the middle of open fields and there was nothing around it. It looked as big as Palm Beach International Airport.

"Yeah, in a damned barn. Simon was there, he checked it all

over, and then we wheeled her up into the trailer and that was that."

"You didn't open it again until you got to Palm Beach?"

"Nope. I unlocked her at Dale and Missy's place and rolled the car into its little room, and then I left."

"Before the hurricane."

"Yep. No desire to hang out in a hurricane."

"How did you get off the island?"

He looked like he was thinking about this. "The one bridge was out. So the next bridge. Got on I-95 and got going."

"Straight through? Long drive."

"If I recall, I got gas leaving West Palm Beach and then stopped outside of Savannah for a coffee."

"Cracker Barrel?"

"Nah. Fuelex. Always Fuelex."

Rex pulled the truck in through the gates to the racetrack. The guard at the gate waved and Rex waved back through his open window.

"You're an expert on moving cars, Rex. If it were you, how would you move eleven cars out of Dale's garage and off an island during a hurricane?"

"If I was into grand theft auto, Miami, I'd be the getaway driver, not the brains behind the operation."

I smiled. "Me, too."

"Then my suggestion to you is to go home to the brains behind your operation and never let her go."

CHAPTER TWENTY-ONE

THE CREW WAS ALREADY IN PLACE AS WE PULLED INTO the garage area. Rex killed the engine with a sound like a dragon sighing and jumped down from the cabin. He unlocked the trailer like he'd done it a thousand times, which I realized might literally have been true. Then he took the same controls I'd seen him use in the security video and he dropped the rear of the truck into a ramp. The crew strode up into the trailer and unhitched the cars and rolled them down into the garage. It was then that I noticed the big difference between these cars and those that had been taken away to Darlington. They were the same basic size and the same basic shape. They were Beadman green and had the logo for the soda I didn't drink on the hood. But neither car had a number on them. Not on the hood, not on the door. The sides of both vehicles were covered by the DBR logo and the word Chevrolet.

Lucas was standing with Simon Lees under a popup shade. Lees was setting up a computer and another guy was working with a two-way radio.

"How's your truck driver?" Lucas asked.

"Let's just say that truck drivers are a lot more emotionally aware than they were when I was a boy."

"Did he do it?"

"Not unless he's a better actor than he is a trucker."

"Cary Grant was a truck driver, did you know that?"

"I did not."

"And he was a good actor."

"I don't think Rex is Cary Grant."

I watched the crew moving around the cars like there was a race about to start. "They're getting busy," I said.

"Time is money," said Lees. "Renting a race track isn't cheap."

"Why do it?"

"NASCAR rules don't allow for much in the way of telemetry. That's computer systems that send diagnostic information back from the car. They like to keep it basic. Man-and-car type stuff. Most telemetry you see on TV is exactly that, there for the networks, not for us. So off-circuit testing allows us to use telemetry to track incremental changes in our engine designs. So, you guys ready to ride?"

Lucas was born ready. I wasn't so sure. "I thought NASCARs only had one seat."

"They do, in race config. But these are development cars. We also use them for sponsor events. We can put a passenger seat in there nice and easy."

"Don't go to any trouble," I said.

"Ready to go, boss," called one of the crew.

"No trouble," said Lees. "It's ready. Now if you'll go in the truck, the guys will get you suited up."

Lucas practically ran up into the truck. I took my time. We stripped down and then put on fireproof suits and balaclavas. I was given a pair of boots that were a touch too big and a pair of gloves that were a touch too small.

I was led out to one of the cars, where a similarly dressed guy stood waiting. He was chisel-jawed and had movie star stubble.

"Mike Walters," he said.

"Miami Jones. You driving?"

"Unless *y-y-you* want a go."

"No, you're the pro."

"Smart choice. First time?" he asked, nodding at the car.

"Yep."

"It's loud so feel free to scream."

That was what I wanted to hear.

"Let's get in," he said.

Mike climbed in through where the window should have been. My side was a little more conventional. One of the crew put his arm in through the window space and opened the door from the outside, and I realized there were no latches on the outside. Probably an aerodynamic thing. The guy told me to keep my helmet off until they were finished setting up the telemetry. I squeezed myself into the seat. It was roomy enough. There was no dashboard to speak of, no glove compartment. There was no leather interior or stereo system. There were thick roll bars and a bare steel floor. The seat was contoured and wrapped around me like a bear hug. The crew guy strapped me in so tight I thought I was ready for an Apollo mission. Which made me think of Apollo 13. Which made me swallow hard.

"I didn't know we had sponsors today," said Mike. He choked a little on the word *sponsors*.

I turned to him and noticed that there was no steering wheel in front him. "I'm not a sponsor. I'm doing some work for Dale."

"That explains it. You know Dale well?" he asked.

"Not really, you?"

"Twen-twenty-five years."

"You always driven for him?"

He nodded. "Used to race."

"Tough game."

"Ye-yep. The sponsor bit was th-the bit I hated."

"I imagine that would be my downfall, too. A lot of shaking hands and kissing babies."

He nodded. "Constant. No sponsors, no team. And th-the drivers are the faces of the teams. You spend less time driving than y-y-you do doing appearances."

"Everybody wants their piece of you."

"And appearances weren't really m-m-my thing."

"Me either. So you started doing testing?"

He nodded again. "Thanks to Dale."

"How so?"

"Most teams would have dum-dumped me. Not Dale. He found me a job where I still get to go fast. Not racing, but still g-g-good."

A guy leaned in and fixed the steering wheel to the column, and I realized once it was there that there was no way Mike was getting into the car with the wheel in place.

"So he's a good guy to work for, Dale?"

Mike shook his head. "Without Dale, I'd be stack-acking shelves at the Piggly-Wiggly."

"Folks sure seem to like him around here."

"He's one of the goo-good ones."

"Everyone can't like him. He have any rivals or enemies?"

Mike frowned underneath his balaclava. "What do you do for Dale?"

"I protect him."

Mike nodded and thought about it.

"What about WinLobe?"

Mike shook his head. "Rivals, yes. But they're old school. Keep it on th-th-the track."

"He must have made some enemies over the years."

Mike shrugged. "There's always Brasher."

There was that name again. Before I got a chance to ask about it, a guy pulled a helmet down over my head. It was like having my head stuck inside a watermelon. He tugged on the restraints again and then clipped the webbing across where the window was supposed to be.

Mike flicked a switch and the engine burst to life. I had owned a Mustang once upon a time, and I'd thought that was a pretty throaty engine. It was a pussy cat's meow compared to this thing. It was a beastly roar, like a waking tiger. A crew guy gave Mike the thumbs-up and he returned the gesture. He pulled the car out onto the pit lane, and I could already feel the pull at my restraints even though we were doing barely more than walking pace. He increased speed some along the pit lane.

"Okay?" he said, and I realized I had some kind of radio in my helmet.

I nodded in return.

"We'll take the first one easy," he said, and his eyes gave away the smile hidden behind his helmet.

Then we took off.

I left my colon in Albuquerque.

The car accelerated at a rate that I had not previously thought possible outside of a fighter jet. I was pressed deep into my seat and I had to force my head to the left to confirm that Mike still had his hands on the steering wheel. Then I heard the yelling.

"Whooooooo!" screamed Lucas through my helmet radio. He was somewhere behind us having the time of his life. He was clearly on a different ride from me. Mike hit the bank hard and the physics of it all pushed us up toward the wall. I thought for a moment I was going to end up as goo on the outside wall, but at the last moment Mike held the car steady and we cruised around the bank what felt like only inches from the wall.

Then in one swift motion, Mike yanked hard on the wheel and we dropped like a rock down the slope. The bank ended and then we were on the flat and the other car fired past us like a bullet on the low side.

"Miamiiiiii!" was all I could hear over the sound of the engine and my heart pounding out of my chest. We sped down the back straight, and Mike pulled in behind the front car. What we were doing was illegal in all fifty states and most countries. Probably not Germany with their crazy autobahns. We were tailgating at about six inches. The whine of the engine grew higher and higher, like a soprano building up to explode glassware with her voice. It was penetrating my brain pan.

Mike braked and I was pinned by my restraints, and then he shifted down the gears and we cut down low as the bank rose above us again. He hit the gas and we drifted up the bank until I realized we were door to door with the other car. I looked right and the other driver took his hand off the wheel to wave to me. I looked away. I really didn't want to encourage him. As we hit the main straight, I heard Mike speak.

"Okay, let's open her up."

I wasn't sure what he meant. Had we been going slow? Had we been doing the NASCAR version of old-timer-in-a-Cadillac? He hit the pedal and I was planted back in my seat as we took off. We went faster. I didn't think it was possible, but I was wrong. The funny thing was, it didn't feel faster. Relative to what we had just done, it just didn't feel that much faster. Like boiling a frog. The vibration of the car was intense. It drove right up through my legs, into my guts and my lungs and my eyes.

We did three laps. It was the longest three minutes of my life. Mike spoke into his radio to Simon Lees as we screamed around the track, but their conversation was unintelligible to me. We cruised back into the pit lane and dropped the speed. It felt like standing still.

"Okay?" he asked.

"How fast was that?" I yelled despite the fact that we had slowed down.

"I don't know," he said. "Maybe one fifty at the top."

"You don't know? You don't pay any attention to your speedometer."

"There is no speedometer."

I craned my neck to see the gauges. There was nothing complicated. Just analog dials in a steel panel. A tachometer to measure the RPMs of the engine, fuel pressure, electrics. No speedometer.

"How can there be no speedometer? Isn't the whole point of NASCAR speed?"

"No. The point of NASCAR is to win. And you win by beating the other guy and not killing your car or yourself. So we use the tachometer instead. It tells us how hard the engine is working. Run it too hard for too long, you'll blow it up."

"What about pit stops? Aren't there speed limits in the pits?"

"There are. In each race, a pace car leads the field around at the speed allowed in the pit lane. The drivers check their tachos to know what revs they should be at when they go in to pit."

Which is where we went. Mike pulled the car into where Simon Lees was sitting under his canvas shade. A crew member opened my door, unstrapped me and then helped peel me out of the seat.

Lucas had his helmet and balaclava off and was beaming like the Florida sun. I pulled my helmet off, nearly removing my ears in the process, and then I ripped off the balaclava and breathed like it was the first time.

"Awesome," said Lucas. "Just bloody awesome."

I nodded. I had the feeling that speaking might bring forth my breakfast. I sat against the pit wall and watched the crew remove the seat I had been sitting in from the car. Then Mike pulled back out onto the track while the other car remained in the pit area.

"How fast was that?" asked Lucas.

"On the straight you topped out at about one fifty-five," said Lees.

Lucas nodded like that was good but he'd done faster. "What's the track record here?"

"NASCAR qualifying, about twenty-seven seconds, average speed about two hundred mph."

Lucas smiled like that was more like it.

"You guys mind waiting around while we test here?"

"No," said Lucas. "Do what you gotta do, mate."

Lucas and I stayed in our fireproof outfits and sat in camp chairs by the pit wall. I slugged a quart of water. The car zoomed around and around on a permanent left turn. The sound wasn't the same as in the car itself but it was still tremendous.

Lucas watched with rapt fascination. I wandered over to the truck, reminded of what a pantomime professional sports were. What we saw on television was never real. The colors were bolder and the camera lens saturated the light. Football fields were never perfectly flat. The batter's box in baseball wasn't either. It was torn up by guys digging in their cleats. Bullpens were hot and sweaty. Change rooms ran out of hot water in the showers and cold water to drink. There was nothing glamorous about long bus trips to play minor league ball games in front of a hundred people. Nothing glamorous about Travis Zanchuk's workshop. Racing was no different. It was loud, and it produced an oily stench that became part of your DNA. The suits were hot and uncomfortable and the cars were as utilitarian as they could possibly be.

And I could see why someone would want to give up everything to do it. Whatever the cost. I heard the cough-cough of Mike's car returning to the pit area and watched the second car head out. Mike spoke with Simon Lees and then came over to the truck to grab some water from a cooler.

"Enjoy that?" he asked.

"Sure. You?"

"Love it," he said, slugging back his water.

"Driving like that is harder than it looks."

He nodded. "Every fan can drive, so they th-think it's like cruising in their air-conditioned Silverado."

"You guys are athletes. No doubts about it."

He nodded and smiled.

We sat on the ramp up to the trailer and watched the second car zooming around the track.

"In the car before, you mentioned a guy called Brasher," I said.

"Ansel Brasher. You know him?"

"He's a driver, right?"

"Was. Now he d-does the commentary for NASCAR on Fox."

I nodded. Now I could place the guy. He looked like a Persian prince in a blue blazer.

"So what was his deal with Dale?"

"You don't know?"

I shook my head.

"Brasher was more an open-wheeler. You know, Indy, F1. He ran a couple seasons in NASCAR and Dale beat him. He didn't take it well. He said Dale was too chicken to race him in open-wheels."

"Let me guess where this is going."

"Do you know the Triple Crown?"

"Like Secretariat?"

"Not horses. Motorsports. NASCAR has one—Daytona, Talladega, Charlotte—but the more famous Triple Crown outside the US is the Indianapolis 500, the Le Mans twenty-four-hour and the Monaco F1. Some people replace the Monaco race with the F1 world championship now because Indy and Monaco are now on the same weekend, but it doesn't matter because only one guy has ever done it either way. Graham Hill. English dude, back in the sixties."

"Okay."

"So in the early nineties, I think it was, Brasher won the Le Mans in a Porsche. At Monaco, he raced for Ferrari and won. He said there that he was going to win the Triple Crown on his home turf in Indianapolis."

"He's from Indiana?"

"No. The States. He meant the States."

"Okay."

"So it turns out that Dale was visiting the Monaco race as a guest of his sponsors. I think he was trying to move from driver to owner about then. Was kissing the babies, like you called it. Get sponsors. And someone says to Brasher at the after-party that Dale's a way better driver."

"Red rag to a bull."

"Yeah, whatever. So Brasher says Dale doesn't have the guts to race him at Indy. Of course, it's only two weeks between Monaco and Indy back then, so there's no time for Dale to get a drive. Except then this guy, can't remember his name—he owns like a massive cigarette company—he says he has a backup car and Dale can have it, and a crew."

"I can see where this is going."

"You know the rest."

"No, I don't. Go on, Mike."

"Well, they race. And Brasher's leading the whole thing. From pole to the last lap. And you know what happens?"

"Dale wins."

"No. Dale's into second place. Second last turn, he goes to pass on the inside and they smash wheels."

"So who won?"

"I don't know. Some guy. But you know what the open wheels are like. Axels like toothpicks. Both Dale and Brasher crash out."

"They crash out?"

"Yeah. So Brasher doesn't win the Indy. And he never did. He retired, like, soon after. He never wins the Triple Crown."

"That's got to hurt."

"You're telling me. But I haven't told you the worst part."

"It gets worse?"

"Yeah. Everyone—the commentators, the press, the other drivers—they all say that Dale's drive was one of the best ever at Indy. Maybe the best ever not to have won."

"Why?"

"He's a NASCAR driver. He hadn't driven an open-wheeler since he raced karts as a kid. So with two weeks' prep, a second-choice car and a hand-me-down crew, he nearly won the Indy 500."

"That is pretty impressive."

"Yeah, you bet it is. And a lot of people say he had the racing line on that turn, too. Brasher should have let him through."

"I suspect Brasher doesn't agree."

"Nah. He called Dale a cheat, which wasn't cool. Dale's a good man."

"So why the animosity? Why did this Brasher have it in for Dale in the first place? Just because he beat him in NASCAR?"

Mike shrugged. "I don't know this for sure. It was before my time, right? But I heard that Brasher had been stepping out with Missy before she met Dale."

"Stepping out?" I hadn't heard that phrase since I'd listened to my grandfather's stories as a kid.

"Dating, maybe," said Mike.

I thought back to when I had met Missy Beadman. She had said that a suitor had taken her to the race track where she had met Dale. If Brasher had been that suitor, I could see how that might rankle a guy. Men did very stupid things for much less.

The second car came into the pits and the crew started packing up. We moved off the ramp so Mike's test car could be rolled up into the truck.

"Thanks, Mike. Appreciate the story."

"You're welcome."

"I couldn't help but notice. The stutter."

"Yeah."

"It disappeared once you started driving."

"Yeah. It d-does. If I don't think about it."

"You got any idea if this Brasher will be at Darlington this weekend?"

"Probably not. I think the meet's only on cable. He's on Fox. Network TV."

"Worth a shot."

"But he lives in Lake Norman."

"Which is where?"

"Here in Mooresville."

I thanked Mike again for the info and the terrifying ride. Lucas hugged Simon Lees. Lees drove us back to the workshop. I asked Lees about Ansel Brasher and he confirmed there was a good bit of history between Brasher and Dale. I asked Lees if he knew where Brasher lived, and he said he had been to his home once or twice for charity functions.

The sun was dropping low in the sky and the air was a good

deal cooler than in West Palm. I'd go as far as to say it was pleasant. I was exhausted. My adrenaline had bounced around like a toddler on a trampoline. I hadn't eaten since breakfast. Lucas looked like he was coming down off his high. I could see some beers in my future.

But first I had one last thing to check.

CHAPTER TWENTY-TWO

DESPITE MY BETTER EFFORTS, IT FELT AS THOUGH I WASN'T getting very far. It was a familiar feeling. Cases, like baseball seasons, have a momentum all of their own. You can try but you can't force it. You just have to keep showing up, doing your best work and making sure when the momentum turns in your favor you hang on like hell.

It seemed like Dale Beadman was a regular Ray Romano. Everyone loved the guy. And even those that didn't love him, like Rory Lobe and Winton Gifford, didn't exactly hate him, either. Of course, it was entirely possible they had sold me a bridge. Time would tell. And even the one guy who did hate him, Travis Zanchuk, didn't seem to fit the profile. He just didn't have the energy to pull off a heist of this magnitude. Once again, I could be wrong. It wouldn't have been the first time.

Mike Walters had given me an inkling of momentum. It wasn't much, but even a ground ball to shortstop can become an error that changes things your way. This Ansel Brasher guy sounded like a likely customer. And when it came to crime, the most likely customer was most often the guilty one. The guy who looked like he did it usually did.

I just had one itch to scratch before we were done at DBR. Simon Lees wandered back into the workshop to study his diagnostics or telemetry or whatever the hell it was. Lucas went for a final walk around the museum. I went upstairs to find Dale Beadman's assistant.

"How was the track, Mr. Jones?"

"It was an education. Say, is Dale still here?"

"No. He has a dinner with some sponsors. Can I help?"

"Perhaps. Do you have GPS on your vehicles?"

"I don't know. You mean like maps?"

"No, like a locator. For tracking purposes."

"No, I don't think we have anything like that."

"Just a thought. What about gas?"

"Gas?"

"As in gas purchases. Do you do expenses with receipts, or how does that work?"

"For which vehicles?"

"I was thinking about the rigs that carry the race cars."

"No, I think they use fuel cards. It's all done electronically. You'd have to talk to Sydney."

"Can I? Talk to Sydney?"

"She wasn't in earlier. But we could drop in on her office and see."

Dale's assistant walked me to another section of the offices, where we found Sydney. She was six-two, thin as a bean and as gorgeous as a supermodel. That was just the superficial analysis. Dale's assistant told me Sydney handled the team accounts, which made me think of Missy Beadman, back in the day, and confirmed that Sydney was also smart. Which made me wonder about the law of averages, and whether somewhere, Sydney's opposite twin was a short, ugly, stupid person. And whether that person was Detective Ronzoni.

"Take a seat, please, Mr. Jones," said Sydney. "Now, how can I help?"

I find talking to extremely attractive people disconcerting. It's like dealing with another species. They're generally pretty hard work. They have to be. It's a defense mechanism. Getting hit on once in a while is good for the confidence and for the soul. So are Brussels sprouts. But like sprouts, there's such a concept as too much of a good thing. Getting hit on all the time would grow tiresome quickly. I had seen it with Danielle. Guys hit on her right in front of me, and I'm no wallflower. I could once throw a fastball at near a hundred miles an hour, and I've got the shoulders to prove it. But some guys just don't care. Danielle's way around it was to wear a weapon. A gun hanging off her belt was a good deterrent to most jackasses. I'm not saying it was why she got into law enforcement, but it was food for thought.

"Can you tell me how your drivers pay for gas?"

She frowned. It was stunning.

"They don't."

"They don't? How does that work?"

"It's a NASCAR race, Mr. Jones. The fuel is part of the race. It's supplied by the fuel sponsor. The drivers don't pay for it."

"I'm sorry. I'm not making myself clear. I don't mean the race car drivers. I mean the guys who drive the vehicle transports."

She nodded. "I see. Well, in that case, each driver carries a gas card, like a credit card."

"I know what a gas card is."

"I'm glad."

"So can they use the card anywhere, or how does that work?"

"No, they can't use it anywhere. It isn't actually a credit card."

"I get that."

"I mean our transports can't stop just anywhere. It's part of the sponsor's agreement. East of the Mississippi, the trucks can only use Fuelex gas stations and truck stops."

"So you have a record of where the trucks stop?"

"I have a record of where they buy gas."

I reconfirmed my theory about attractive people being hard work.

"Could you tell where the test car transport fueled up on the day of the hurricane?"

"The test car transport? You mean Rex's truck?"

"That's the one."

"He stays local." She tapped the keys on her computer keyboard.

"He did a delivery for Dale. I just want to confirm his route home."

She looked at her screen. "The day of the hurricane. Okay. Yes, I see a transaction here. Palm Beach Gardens. I don't know where that is."

"It's in Palm Beach. Hence the name." Score one for being painful and hard work, Jones.

"It says the Fuelex station on PGA Boulevard."

"Okay, anything after that?"

"Hmm. No. No stops until he checks into the workshop about. . . ten hours later."

I thought about the timing. Ten hours wasn't an unreasonable amount of time to drive from Palm Beach Gardens to Charlotte. The traffic was heavy-ish with folks fleeing the storm. We'd done it quicker in my Cadillac, and Angie Beadman had done it quicker still in her Camaro. And the logic didn't fit, either. If Rex had somehow taken the cars from Dale Beadman's garage, which video proved he didn't, he wouldn't have stopped to fuel up minutes later. He'd do it before or he'd do it well after. You don't stop the getaway car for gas a block from the bank.

"Ten hours," I said softly.

"That's pretty much straight through from Palm Beach to Charlotte."

"I thought you didn't know where Palm Beach Gardens was?"

"I just put it into Google Maps," she said, pointing at her computer screen.

"Oh. Well. Good for you. But he could have stopped and hit the gas hard after."

"You mean drive above the speed limit? No."

"No? Why not? People do speed."

"Often, Mr. Jones. Always for some. But not our trucks."

"Why?"

"Have you seen those trucks, Mr. Jones?"

"I have."

"And what is their defining characteristic, as far as vehicles of that type go?"

"You've got me."

"They are billboards, Mr. Jones. Massive rolling advertisements for Dale Beadman Racing, for our sponsors and for NASCAR. An organization built around the idea of driving cars very, very fast. Can you imagine what would happen if one of our trucks got caught speeding on a public road? Could you imagine the controversy? Sponsors would be running for the door. No, the trucks cannot speed, Mr. Jones. Above all else, they must obey the speed limit on all roads. And they are speed-limited to sixty-five on the freeways. So ten hours is a straight-through run."

I nodded. She made sense. She was beautiful, and she made a sound argument. It didn't improve my impression.

"Okay. Palm Beach Gardens, straight to Charlotte. Good."

It was good. I liked Rex. He was a bit sensitive for a trucker to suit my tastes, but then I didn't have a lot of experience in the area of truckers. Perhaps my impressions were based upon false tropes in movies and such. I didn't know. Either way, it made sense. He'd dropped off the F-88 and fled the hurricane, as any sane man would. How the cars had gotten off the island was still a mystery to me. But I was eliminating possibilities, and that was half the battle.

I stood. "Thanks, Miss, uh, Sydney."

"Of course." She nodded but kept her eyes on her screen, like I had already left. I got it. This was the worst part for attractive people. I was about to leave, and it was my last chance to throw her a line, ask her to dinner, wow her with my wit and charm. Except I had no intention of doing anything of the sort. I had a beautiful woman waiting for me at home. One that turned rain clouds into sunshine just by giving me a half smile. I wanted to tell Sydney that, but there was no point. It would sound like I just didn't have the confidence to make my move. And weakness like that was the worst thing of all in the eyes of the truly beautiful.

"Enjoy your evening," I said and I walked out.

I was in the corridor when I heard her speak.

"Mr. Jones," she called.

I stopped and took a deep breath. I turned and stepped back to her door.

"Yes?"

"Mr. Jones, I owe you an apology."

"I can't possibly think what for."

"I was curt with you. I'm sorry."

"I didn't notice." If I didn't notice, I must have been deaf and blind.

"It's just. . ." She took a deep breath. In through the nose, out through the mouth. Like an athlete or a yoga practitioner.

"My cat died this afternoon."

"Your what?"

"My cat. He died. I was at the vet all afternoon. And I came back to the office and I probably shouldn't have, and I acted appallingly to you."

My heart sank into my shoes. If there was anyone who had acted appallingly, it was me. Score negative one, Jones. Now I took the deep breath.

"You were fine. Don't worry about it. I'm sorry about your cat."

She nodded, and a tear rolled down her cheek. She even looked good crying and I hated myself for thinking that.

"Go home, Sydney. Drink some wine, toast your kitty."

She smiled a smile that I suspected she wasn't going to be able to hold. The dam walls were about to break.

So I walked away. I knew it was going to keep me awake at night. There were a lot better ways to behave when a fellow human being was hurting. I walked down the stairs and out through the main lobby. It was twilight out. Crickets chirped and the breeze wafted by. Lucas wasn't there. I figured he was still in the museum. Which meant I had to go back inside.

So I did. I ran. I ran right back up the stairs and down the corridor and into Sydney's office. She was facing away from the door, so she spun around in her chair toward me. Her face was red and wet and puffy. I stepped around her desk, and she stood and she plunged her head into my chest despite being an inch taller than me. She wept like a baby. A very sad baby that had lost her kitty. I held her as her tears soaked my shirt. She was a stranger to me and would remain so. But she was a human in need of a little humanity, and I was a human with some to spare.

I was just glad I had stopped long enough to wonder what Lenny would have done.

CHAPTER TWENTY-THREE

LAKE NORMAN WAS A MAN-MADE LAKE JUST ON THE OTHER side of I-77 from Mooresville. The lake was surrounded by houses worth more than most entire inner-city suburbs. The house we were looking for sat in an enclave called The Point, a peninsula of land that jutted out into the lake and was home to a Trump National Golf course and homes with values closer to ten million than to one. It looked like a regular suburb except the homes were like mini-castles and were mostly waterfront.

The Lake Norman area was a popular home for many of the NASCAR drivers, which made sense given its proximity to the team headquarters that dotted the landscape surrounding Charlotte. It also made sense that it would be popular with former drivers as well. Which was exactly what Ansel Brasher was. Simon Lees had given me the address with some trepidation. I wasn't sure what he thought I was going to do there, but I had promised to be on my best behavior.

Brasher's house was an enormous Mediterranean hidden from the street by old-growth oaks. The driveway was the size of a parking lot at Walmart, and it was full of cars whose owners got no closer to Walmart than opening their stock certificates.

There must have twenty cars, and most of them looked new and shiny and worthy of Dale Beadman's collection. I saw a Bugatti and an Aston Martin and a Ferrari. There were two Teslas. We parked on the street, which seemed to be against the rules, but there were no signs, so I went with it. Besides, the guys doing the valeting in the driveway didn't say I couldn't.

We strode past a five-car garage around the side of the house. I find walking with a purpose makes most people believe you belong where you are. This despite the fact that both Lucas and I were wearing shorts and I had a shirt that had just had a gallon of tears poured on it. Plus we had helmet head. I was surprised security didn't jump out of the trees and take us down. We walked around the side of the house because all the sound seemed to be coming from the rear of the property.

We stopped in the shadows just short of the paved patio. It was a space the size of three basketball courts. There were tiki lamps and cocktail tables and well-dressed folks sipping champagne. To my left was a buffet table where a guy in a white apron was cooking steaks on a massive grill. I could see a pool glistening with blue light, a small waterfall cascading into it for effect. Beyond the pool lay the calm water of the lake. I glanced at Lucas's attire and he at mine. I couldn't help but feel everyone else was overdressed for a barbecue.

I strode into the light. The first few people who saw me did double takes. Was this Ansel's errant son come home to beg for more money? I don't know if that was what they were thinking. I didn't even know if Ansel Brasher had a son. But that was the facial expression I got. I walked up to a short guy in a Brooks Brothers shirt and asked him if he had seen Ansel. The guy recoiled like I had sneezed on him.

"I have not," he spluttered.

I shrugged and kept moving. The secret is to keep moving. If you stop, you're fair game. I walked toward the house. Inside I saw more people. Through floor-to-ceiling windows, I noted a large fireplace that sat idle. I got as far as the concertina doors, where I ran into a young guy who looked like an Abercrombie ad. His hair was lush and silky and he wore a sweater tied around his shoulders. I had no idea people still did that, but I hadn't visited Cape Cod in the summer for many years.

"Can I help you?" he asked.

"Only if you're Ansel Brasher, and I'm guessing no plastic surgery is that good."

"This is a private residence. Mr. Brasher does not see fans here. You can contact him via the Fox Sports office in New York City."

"You're suggesting I go to New York?"

"I'm suggesting you call."

"But I'm here already, Junior." I went to step past the kid, but he shifted his weight and our shoulders connected. I still had pitcher's shoulders, but the kid was built pretty well, too.

"I would prefer not to have to call the police."

"So we agree on something. But now you're wasting my time. I need Ansel Brasher and you're not him."

"I am Mr. Brasher's personal secretary. You don't see him unless I say so."

I took a good look at the kid and thought about his choice of phrase. I was sure there was a time and place that he would never have referred to himself as a secretary. Even secretaries didn't like the word anymore. My secretary, Lizzy, preferred office manager. In her case, it was a reasonable summation of her role. She managed everything. Perhaps *everything manager* would have been more fitting. But some people actually were secretaries. They generally preferred to be called administrative assistants or some equally banal title. Somewhere along the line, secretary had become a derogatory word. I had no idea why. Being a secretary was as good a job as any other, and it wasn't made any better or worse by changing the title. But using the word *personal* changed everything. Like it made this guy important somehow. But he was still a gatekeeper, and I needed to get through the gate.

"All right, Junior. Tell Brasher that I'm here about Missy Beadman."

"What?"

"Just tell him. Or I'll tell his wife."

The guy flexed his pec muscle and his shirt rippled. He was in good shape.

"Not here. Go to the guesthouse."

"Where's the guesthouse?"

The kid pointed further down the lakefront. "Down there. It'll be open." He turned away and walked inside.

I made sure Lucas was on my six and I strode along the windows and across the patio to the far side. In the darkness across a wide expanse of lawn, I saw the silhouette of a house. As I got closer, I wondered if I had gone the wrong way and wandered into a neighbor's yard. The house was much smaller than the main house but was still way bigger than my house in Singer Island. There was a keypad on the front door. I pulled the latch and found the door open. Maybe it was operated by one of those smartphone applications. I had no idea.

Lights came on as we walked inside. The foyer gave way to a great room with a lounge suite and a granite kitchen and a view of the darkened lake beyond. I couldn't imagine inviting guests to stay in such a house. They would never want to leave.

"What's the deal with Missy Beadman?" Lucas asked.

"The guy who drove me round the track today, Mike? He said he thought there might have been some history there."

"Brasher and Dale's wife?"

I nodded. "Before they met. So I took a punt. Now I'm not so sure it was after they met."

We waited for twenty minutes. I figured it would take the kid about one minute to locate Brasher. I figured he would always have a pretty good bead on his location. It was about a one-minute walk across the lawn to the guesthouse for a guy who knew his way. So the other eighteen minutes were for show. Telling us exactly who was in charge. I leaned against the counter that led to the kitchen. I thought about turning the television on, but I couldn't find a remote, and televisions these days don't seem to have buttons anywhere that I can find.

Brasher arrived alone. That was bold. Sure we were relatively harmless in the grand scheme of things, but he couldn't know that for sure. We could have been crazed fans, or even fans of someone else. Dale Beadman fans, crazy enough to wander onto his property, so crazy enough to do him harm. There seemed to be more and more of those people around. But he strode into the room alone like he owned it, which of course, he did. He was taller than most race car drivers I had seen. He still looked fit despite being in his seventies. He had the strong jaw and complete hairline that television loved.

"Who the hell are you?" he said.

"Miami Jones," I said. "And that's Lucas."

Lucas nodded his hello.

"Why are you interrupting my barbecue?"

"You a car collector, Mr. Brasher?"

"A what?"

"A car collector."

"I have a few cars. What's your point?"

"You have any domestic cars?"

"Domestic? You mean American?"

"Yes."

"I have some."

"You got an F-88?"

He frowned. "A what?"

"F-88 Oldsmobile."

"No. I don't have an Oldsmobile here. Listen, who the hell are you? Grantley told me you said Missy Beadman sent you."

Grantley. Some people fit their names perfectly.

"I said I was here about Missy Beadman."

"What about her?"

"You know her."

"Of course I know her."

"Back in the day, I hear you were sweethearts."

"Who the hell told you that?"

"It's the word on the street."

"It's complete baloney, is what it is."

"Does your wife know? About Missy?"

"There's nothing to know, you maggot. My wife and I have no secrets."

"Is Missy the reason you've had a bug up your butt about Dale Beadman for forty years?"

"Dale Beadman is a cheat and a loser. He doesn't deserve a fine woman like Missy. But I'll tell you this. There was nothing between Missy and me. We were friends, before he came along. That's it. And if you so much as besmirch her name I will break you apart."

I doubted that. He was tall and fit, but there wasn't a lot to him. "I'm trying to save Missy's good name."

"What did you say your name was?"

"Miami Jones," I said again.

He looked at me like old guys do when they can't recall where they left their keys. Then he remembered. "You're that guy. You worked for BJ Baker that time."

I shrugged. I was fascinated that Brasher would connect me through the same guy that Dale Beadman had. Like Brasher, BJ was a television sportscaster, only his game was football.

Between the two of them, they really didn't give sportscasters a great name.

"He told me you were a maggot. Now I see for myself it's true."

He waited for his words to sink in. They didn't. What people like Ansel Brasher never got about me was that I truly didn't give a damn what they thought of me. I cared what plenty of people thought. Danielle, Ron, Lucas, Sally. I had cared more about what my father had thought than I ever admitted to myself. But I really didn't give the time of day to Brasher. And he would never have understood that, because he believed the sun revolved around him.

"When was the last time you saw Dale Beadman?" I asked.

"I don't see Beadman."

"Is that an eye complaint thing, or do you actually believe him to be invisible?"

"What? Not literally, you maggot."

He really needed a new curse word.

"I see him at the track," he spat.

"Were you at the track the day the hurricane hit Palm Beach?"

"Yes, I was."

"Why? There was no racing."

"We're making a film."

"A film? Like a movie?"

"Yes. I'm an executive producer." He didn't raise his chin as he said that, but I knew he wanted to.

"What's the movie about?"

"What do you think? NASCAR."

I nodded. I recalled that Dale Beadman said he had been delayed in Charlotte because of some filming and had not gotten back to Palm Beach for the delivery of his beloved F-88.

"Is Dale Beadman in your movie?"

"Not if I can help it. That's what editing is for."

"But you filmed him. That day."

"I don't work the camera, pal."

"Of course not."

"Listen, I don't know what you think you're getting at, but I've got friends here and I'm not wasting any more time on you. Get off my property or I will call the police."

"That would be fun for your guests."

"No, it wouldn't. That's the only reason I'm giving you a chance to leave. But I'll do it. I give a lot of money to our fine police department, and I'm sure they'd be happy to host you for a day or two in their cells."

My guess was that he was bluffing, but I also knew a little about how police departments functioned in areas where rich people lived. Palm Beach was my turf. And I didn't like the idea of a day or two in the local lockup. I glanced at Lucas, and he shrugged like it was time to go. We walked out and Brasher closed the door behind us and then followed us across the lawn. He herded us toward the side of the house, away from his party.

"Don't come back," he said.

"Tell me one thing," I said. "That race at Indy. Dale Beadman had the racing line, right?"

"Get lost," said Brasher, and he turned and marched away toward his patio. I saw his personal secretary standing in the light of a tiki lamp, watching me. So I walked away into the shadows.

"Nice guy," said Lucas. "Seemed to like you."

"I thought so."

"You see how he hesitated when you asked about the F-88?"

"I did. And he's involved in this movie, which was what kept Dale from being at the delivery. Convenient if you wanted to steal it."

A valet was standing on the road when we walked across the front lawn.

"You can't park there," he said. "It'll get towed."

"We're leaving," I said.

We got in and I started the engine but didn't put it in drive.

"What ya thinkin'?" Lucas asked.

"I'm thinking I'm tired of talking to people who don't want to talk to me. What about you?"

"I'm thinking those steaks looked pretty good. We haven't eaten since brekky."

I started the engine and pulled away from Ansel Brasher's house. Away from the peninsula. I put *beer* into my GPS and was directed south into Charlotte to the periphery of the downtown area. It looked like a theater district. We stopped at a place that called itself VBGB, with a large beer garden out back and a list of beers as long as my arm. Lucas had a Narragansett Lager that made me think of my high school days in New England, and I stayed local with something called a Red Oak. The place was hopping both inside and out. People played giant chess, and we shared a long table with two guys with lumberjack beards who played Connect Four all night. We watched the crowd around us but didn't say much. Lucas ate a burger and I had a pork brat that was so good I had another.

I was better for the meal, but I felt my spirits dragging. I wanted to get home. But Lucas was as fatigued as I was, and after a few beers, we decided that the smart play was to stay local. I found a business hotel on my phone, and we left the lights and the energy of the beer garden and my vehicle in the lot and walked around the train line and cut through the adjacent cemetery. Our room was a star or four better than our digs the previous night, but it was essentially two beds and a television, and I wondered what the extra dimes bought us. I didn't care. They weren't my dimes. They were Dale Beadman's dimes, and he seemed to have plenty to spare. We flicked on *SportsCenter* but Lucas was snoring before I even got my head comfortable on the pillow. I lay in the light coming from the parking lot, watching headlights play on the ceiling, and I fell asleep thinking about fast cars and movies and ladies with kitties that were no longer of this world.

CHAPTER TWENTY-FOUR

ONE OF THE BENEFITS OF SHARING A MOTEL WITH A GUY who snores is that there is plenty of incentive to get an early start. We left Charlotte, North Carolina, at four a.m., got drive-through coffee in South Carolina and crab sandwiches in Georgia, and I pulled into the lot beside by my office in West Palm a tick before one in the afternoon.

I thanked Lucas for coming, and he thanked me for taking him. We made a date to visit Lenny in a few weeks. Lucas got in his truck and pulled away toward Miami. I hoped he didn't get pulled over for speeding. I didn't go into the office. I didn't get out of the car. I hadn't showered in a couple days, and in between I had sweated a few gallons inside a racing suit, so I headed back up 95 toward Lucas's condo at PGA.

I didn't get there. I found myself veering off the freeway at Blue Heron Boulevard as if my SUV was a homing pigeon. I stopped in front of my house. It looked weathered but not beaten, and certainly not uninhabitable. I got out and wandered around the side to check if someone had collected the speedboat yet.

They had not. It lay sadly marooned on its side where it

had been before. It was proving to be a bit of an obstacle to the men working in my backyard. Two Hispanic guys were holding opposite ends of a long measuring tape and were trying to get it to hold a straight line over the top of the speedboat.

"You guys checking your yardage?" I asked.

The two guys looked up at me and the one in the straw hat said, "*Cómo?*"

"The hole is a solid nine iron from here, if that helps."

"*Qué?*"

"What are you boys doing?"

"Measuring."

Ask a stupid question. . .

"Why are you measuring?"

"To dig the hole."

"What hole are you planning to dig?"

He looked at me like it was more than a lost in translation thing. He genuinely thought I was insane.

"For the pool."

I was going to say *what pool?* but I could see this conversation continuing for hours the way we were going, so I said, "I didn't order a pool."

"No?"

"No."

"No pool?"

"No pool." It wasn't that I had anything against a pool. It was just that my house was currently unfit for habitation according to the county and I didn't have the bankroll to fix that, let alone dig a pool. Then the thought popped into my head that maybe I wasn't the one ordering the pool.

"Who told you to put in a pool?"

"The boss," he said.

"Which boss?"

The guy nodded across the fence at the wedding cake that I had to live next to.

"They ordered the pool?"

"Si. I thought you leave."

I shook my head. "No. I didn't leave."

"You sell house?"

"No."

"Oh." He gave me a look that said that kind of stuff happened all the time, and he fired off a flow of Spanish at his buddy, who smiled. They wound up their tape measure.

"The boss around now?" I asked the guy in the straw hat.

"Si."

"Is he always there?"

"Si."

Suddenly I felt like I knew how the sheriff had found out that Danielle and I were in the house after I got the no habitation order, and how the deputy had turned up so quickly. Someone was watching, and they weren't sitting in a car on the street doing it. They were inside the house next door. Maybe they were fixing some stuff, or maybe they were house-sitting, or maybe they were just getting fifty bucks a day to watch out for me.

"Tell your boss I want to sell."

The poor guy looked thoroughly confused.

"You want to sell?"

"Si. I want to sell. Tell your boss to get his man to call me."

"Okay. I tell him."

The two guys walked back around the side of my house to the street and turned to the house next door. They were shrugging their shoulders the whole way.

I went over to the back door that still hadn't been replaced. The plastic flapped in the breeze. I had a good deal of stuff inside, but I wasn't worried about those guys stealing anything.

They weren't criminals. They were just guys doing a job. In some respects it was good they were around. It kept the real criminals away from my house while it was open to the world.

I was standing on my back patio, looking up at the house next door, wondering if the boss was up there watching me, when my phone rang. I didn't know the number.

But I knew the voice.

"I hear you're ready to sell, *amigo*," said the Latino guy with the sharp suit and the faded movie star looks.

"For the right offer," I said.

"Your house is not in such good shape, *amigo*. What kind of offer do you have in mind?"

"Let's talk about it. Meet me tonight."

"You want to meet? Okay."

"You know a club called Ted's? In Lauderhill?"

"No."

I knew he wouldn't. That was more or less the point.

"Ask around. You'll find it. Tonight at eight."

"All right, *señor*. I'll bring the paperwork."

"You do that."

I hung up without further pleasantries. I saw no movement in the wedding cake, but I knew someone was in there. I was having a hard time getting my head around the idea that whoever owned the house wanted a pool so badly that they would instigate a campaign to kick me out of my house. This wasn't Palm Beach real estate. Don't get me wrong, the market had gone up and my plot was right on the water. But how badly could you want a pool? Especially in a house that you were never in. I had never seen anyone in there other than cleaners and garden and other maintenance guys. The whole thing just didn't seem real.

We'd see how real it got in Lauderhill.

CHAPTER TWENTY-FIVE

I wasn't anyone's idea of a pleasant aroma, so I headed back to the condo to freshen up. Danielle had stocked the fridge in my absence, so I tossed a banana and some frozen berries and a dollop of good old Florida OJ into the blender and whizzed up a smoothie after my shower. Then I cruised on back to the island.

The gate to the Beadman residence stood open, and a small army of guys was sweeping the new decomposed granite driveway. They stood aside to let me in and I gave them a wave of thanks and pulled around in front of the house. The black Camaro was sitting askew in front of me.

I let myself in. It's generally impolite, but in certain circumstances it was worth being considered such a beast. The house was quiet downstairs. Upstairs I could hear the faint whine of a vacuum cleaner. Probably a maid. Angie and Missy didn't grab me as vacuuming types. I knew fellow vacuum allergy sufferers when I saw them.

I walked down the corridor toward Angie's office. All the office doors were closed. I stopped for a moment outside the room with the computer server in it, where I had seen the security video. I opened the door. The computers were humming away and the room was uncomfortably warm. I closed the door and knocked on Angie's office.

"Come in," called Angie and I opened the door. "Miami," she said. "Did we have an appointment?"

"No, I was in the neighborhood."

"You were?"

"Sure."

"How can I help?"

"Let's take a walk."

She looked at her computer as if it was too important to leave and then looked at me and must have concluded I wasn't going to take no for an answer. She gave a sigh like a walk was hard labor and stood from her desk.

We walked out through the great room onto a spacious deck that I hadn't seen before. There was a dining setting under an umbrella, a stone fire pit and another outdoor kitchen to match the one outside Dale's faux-English pub.

"What's on your mind?" asked Angie as we stepped down onto the lawn.

"I was up in Charlotte yesterday."

She stopped and then started walking again. "Really? Do you think my dad's cars are there?"

"I don't have any idea. I'm just learning the lay of the land."

"And what did you learn?"

"I learned that a lot of people think your dad's a pretty great guy."

"Why shouldn't they?"

"No reason at all. There are also a lot of people up there who think pretty highly of you."

"That's not for me to say."

"I know, it's for me to say, and I'm saying it."

"Okay. What's your point?"

"Why aren't you running DBR?"

"I'm the COO."

"Exactly. There's an E missing in there."

"I do my part."

"No one's saying otherwise. But the question is, why are you sitting in a disused bedroom down here in Palm Beach instead of being in a big glass-fronted office in Charlotte?"

She said nothing. She didn't shrug and she didn't make any kind of facial expression that conveyed anything. With a lot of people, I would have been waiting for them to come up with a story, to create a narrative that answered the question to some level of satisfaction. Angie was smart enough to have already come up with a story. I suspected she had to tell herself something on a regular basis. So the pause wasn't to create the narrative. That was already there somewhere. So I didn't know what the pause was for.

We walked down onto the beach. The sea debris had been removed. No kelp and jellyfish left here. The water winked brightly like a woman who had hurt me badly before but whose charms I could never deny. I kicked off my shoes and stepped into the sand. Angie wore jeans and Keds, so getting her shoes off took a little more effort. She pulled her shoes off from the heels and peeled off the little socks she had underneath. Then she rolled her jeans halfway up her calves.

We resumed walking along the beach but Angie didn't feel the need to fill the air with an answer to my question. I liked people who didn't feel the need to hear their own voices all the time, but I also liked answers. But silence was its own response.

"I met Rex," I said.

Angie nodded.

"He's a nice guy."

She nodded again. "Yes, he is."

"A little on the sad side for Florida."

"He lives in North Carolina."

Maybe that was why. I couldn't say. I'd never lived in either of the Carolinas. I had visited here and there. I found the people to be very hospitable.

"He's known your mom and dad a long time."

"Since the very beginning."

"I don't think he was involved."

"Why would you think Rex was involved?"

"I have to eliminate everyone. He had a big truck. He was here."

"Rex would take a bullet for my mom and dad."

"Like I say, he wasn't involved. I met someone else who knew your parents back at the beginning."

"Did you?"

"I did. Ansel Brasher."

Angie stopped on the hard wet sand. "Ansel Brasher. How did you meet Ansel Brasher?"

"I went to his house."

"You went to his house? In Lake Norman?"

"Yep. You been there?"

"I have. Once, for a NASCAR charity event."

"Nice place."

"If you like that sort of grotesque architecture and waste of space."

I was liking Angie even more.

"Yeah, especially then."

"Why did you visit with Brasher?"

"His name came up."

"In what context?"

"In the context of being a rival to your dad. In the context of someone who might have a long-running beef that itself might have led to the theft of eleven cars. Or one car."

"What do you mean, one car?"

"I mentioned the F-88 to him. He didn't say as much, but I got the distinct impression he was more than aware of it."

"I'm sure there are plenty of car fanatics who are aware of it."

"Aware enough to steal it?"

"You think Ansel stole the F-88?"

"Maybe."

"That's crazy."

"Is it?"

"Yes. He and Dad have had their moments, I grant you that, but I don't think Brasher would stoop to something like that."

"How can you know? You've only met him once."

"I've only been to his house on Lake Norman once."

"But you've met him on other occasions?"

"He's a race car driver. He was even in NASCAR for a couple years. Of course I met him. But if you think he stole the Oldsmobile, what about the other ten cars?"

"Smokescreen, maybe."

"Smokescreen?"

"Yeah. Steal them all to hide the fact that you only ever wanted the one. The cops, people like me, anyone trying to figure out what happened, we're all looking at a case of eleven cars. Lots of directions those cars could go, lots of leads to manage. Harder than just thinking about the one car."

"But you are thinking about the one car. Dad said he only cared about you finding the F-88."

"Exactly. But Brasher doesn't necessarily know that."

"I don't know, Miami. I don't think this has anything to do with Ansel Brasher."

"Why?"

"Just feels wrong."

Which was the most emotional assessment I had heard the

analytical woman provide so far. So I decided to throw some more emotion into the mix.

"I heard that Brasher had a thing for your mom."

"What?"

"That's what I heard. Were they dating when she met Dale?"

"No."

"How do you know?"

"They're my parents."

I let that hang in the breeze for a while. In my experience, children never knew their parents' backstories. Not completely. It was like the textbooks from school. All history is revisionist history because it's always written by the victor. We often get the sanitized version of our parents' lives before we became part of them. I had no reason to suspect the Beadmans were any different.

We walked a little ways along and then, for no particular reason and at no particular marker, we turned around.

"Did you get the police report from Ronzoni?" I asked.

"Yes. He's very conscientious."

"He is that. Did you get it to the insurance company?"

"Not yet."

"Do it."

"I will."

"I mean do it ASAP. It's Great Southeast Permanent, right?"

"Yes."

"Well, I hear their CEO's writing checks the company might not be able to cash."

"What does that mean?"

"It's a metaphor."

"I'm sure, but what does it mean?"

"They might be overexposed to the South Florida market. Lots of claims all at one time."

"I see."

"So get yours moving. You don't want to be left holding a worthless thirty-million-dollar policy."

She nodded but said nothing.

"You have filed the claim, right?"

She looked out at the ocean. It winked back.

"You haven't put in the claim yet?"

"I wanted to see how far you got first."

"Don't wait for me. I might not get the cars back. And even if I do, you can always cancel the claim. Hell, if they've paid up, you can always give the money back. But you can't get blood from a dead stone."

"A dead stone?"

"Or any other kind of stone. Point is, if they don't go broke, they'll probably try to weasel out of it anyway, and anytime you waste getting the claim will be time they can use against you."

"How?"

"I have no idea. I'm not the world's expert on weaseling out of things. But take it from me, they'll do it." I didn't add they had done it to me. It didn't feel relevant.

We walked back along the beach and up onto the lawn. The gardeners had gotten the place looking good. I wondered if the folks in the Bahamas were so lucky. The palapa was back in place over the little outside deck area behind the faux-English pub. The guys had done a good job. I wondered if I could convince them to drop by Longboard Kelly's and do some work. I suspected there was plenty of work on offer. South Florida has more than its share of palapas, and a good number of those had blown away in the hurricane. I didn't recall seeing the palapa having blown off on the security video, but I'd had a good fill of wine by that point in the long video. Then I recalled what Mick had said about palapas and why he didn't want to replace his. Which gave me something else to think about. Something I would have to check on the way back to the office.

As we stepped back inside the house, I told Angie to get the insurance paperwork.

"Why?"

"I'm going to see them. I'll drop it off for you."

She nodded and went back to her office. She pulled some papers from an in-tray or an out-tray, I couldn't tell the difference. The police report was paper-clipped to the insurance paperwork. Angie signed and dated it and handed it to me.

"Thank you," she said.

"All part of the service."

CHAPTER TWENTY-SIX

The Mornington was one of Palm Beach's finest hotels. It was glamorous in a very old-fashioned way. It didn't feature the sprawling grounds of The Breakers, but it did have a certain charm that spoke of Prohibition and rich folks escaping New York winters. And it was well built.

I knew that for a fact because it was where I had spent the hurricane. I hadn't intended to do so, but that was just how the dice had rolled, and when the dice dropped such that you spent a hurricane in a luxury hotel, it was best not to complain.

The grounds staff at The Mornington had been as busy as those at the Beadman compound. Detective Ronzoni, whose company I had enjoyed for the duration of the storm, had left the hotel the morning after in a Coast Guard tender that had cut straight across where the driveway should have been. I had left a few hours later in my Caddy in tire-high water. But now the water was gone. The lawn looked dark and damp and was putting out all kinds of humidity but was in surprisingly good shape.

I parked in the front lot, where I had stopped prior to the hurricane, and stepped up past the doorman.

"You're back in business?"

He smiled and tipped his little hat. "The Mornington never closed, sir."

I guess that was technically true. Paying guests had stayed during the hurricane, and the bar had stayed open.

He pulled the door open for me and I nodded my thanks. There wasn't a lot of activity in the lobby. It felt strange to be back. Like visiting your high school for the twenty-year reunion. Familiar, but only in a very distant sense. I felt like I had no business being there. I looked over to the door to the bar and heard the sound of clinking china, and then I looked straight ahead across the marble floors and through the large glass windows that showed off the oceanfront location. The storm shutters that had covered most of the windows were long gone, tucked away in some hidden part of the hotel.

I turned to the reception desk to my right. There was no one checking in and no one checking out. The Mornington was open, but trade was not brisk. Lots of tourists had canceled vacations in the aftermath of the storm. They'd be back, sooner than later. I stepped up to the young woman behind the desk. She wore a tailored jacket and long blond hair that fell stylishly but was just conservative enough for The Mornington. She was tapping on a computer keyboard and heard my footsteps and looked up with an impish grin. She had one of those Florida faces that shone as bright as the sun.

"Look what the cat dragged in," she said.

"Miss Taylor," I said.

"Mr. Jones, I didn't expect to see you."

"I didn't expect to be here."

"Well, decorum is out the window." She stepped out from behind the reception desk and around to me and wrapped her arms around me in a big hug. I returned the hug, just a little softer. She was built like a little bird. She pulled away but left her hands on my biceps.

"We survived a hurricane together, Miami. We're beyond handshakes, don't you think?"

"Why not? Although there are harder places to survive a hurricane than The Mornington."

"It wasn't the hurricane I was worried about. I can't tell you how glad I was you were here. And now you're here again."

"I am."

"I'd love to believe you just wanted to see me."

"It's a benefit, Emery, but there is another reason."

"What can I do for you?"

"Are you busy?"

She waved her hands around the lobby. "It's picking up, but slowly. I have time."

"I'd like to check the security video."

"I thought you solved that crime?"

"Actually, it's for another case."

"You have another case already?"

"The weather didn't blow away the bad guys."

She put her palm on my chest. "Or the good guys. Come on."

Emery led me back past the reception desk and into the small office behind it. It was the office of the general manager but also housed the security video system. I had become familiar with it, but I let Emery drive. She was better at it than me anyway.

"Take a seat," she said. "Would you like a coffee?"

"Sure."

She picked up the phone and asked whoever answered if they wouldn't mind bringing two coffees over to the GM's office. Then she fired up the video system.

"How did your place get through?" she asked.

"Underwater, unfortunately."

She looked genuinely shocked. "You're homeless?"

"No. I'm using a friend's rental condo."

"Okay. There's always room at the inn, if you need it."

"Not sure I can accommodate the nightly rate."

She smiled. It was a winning smile. "Bah. We have ways of taking care of that."

A woman arrived with a silver tray that held a carafe of coffee, two cups and assorted cookies. I thanked her and poured the coffee while Emery found the right file.

She sipped her coffee and said, "So what did you want to see?"

"The power going out."

"Really?"

"I remember your video having a time stamp."

"Yes, it does. Which camera?"

"Any. Let's go with the lobby."

She brought up the vision. It was a shot from high at the north end of the lobby, looking back toward the check-in desk, where I had just found Emery, and then further up the lobby toward a darkened corridor that I recalled led to a gym and out to the pool. Emery fast-forwarded the video and we saw various people come in and out of shot, moving like Olympic speed walkers. I wasn't interested in who they were or where they went. I knew all that.

"I think it was about eleven, wasn't it?"

"Somewhere around there."

She sipped her coffee and let the video flash ahead. I sipped my coffee. It was rich and dark and better than Cracker Barrel's, but Cracker Barrel's cost pennies on the dollar in comparison.

"The police didn't take this video as evidence?" I asked as we watched it speed by.

"They did. They took the whole drive. I suspected they

might, so I made a backup before they came."

"Clever."

She beamed like I had when I was a kid and I threw a strike, and my coach had slapped my back and said well done.

Emery put her coffee down and held her finger over the computer mouse, and then the video disappeared and the screen turned to snow.

"That's it," she said, and she clicked and slowly wound the picture back until the lobby reappeared. Then she started the video at regular pace, and we watched for few seconds before it turned to snow again. Emery repeated the process, took the video back just a touch until the second the lobby reappeared and then she paused it.

"There you go," she said.

I looked at the timestamp on the video. 11:02 p.m.

"I thought it was about eleven," she said.

"You were on the money," I said.

"Is that what you wanted?" she asked.

"Exactly what I wanted."

She turned to me. I got the scent of coffee and roses.

"Does it help?"

I smiled. "It does." I wanted her to believe that it did. Sometimes people needed encouragement, even the confident ones. Maybe the confident ones needed it more. And sometimes I found I was the one they looked to for such encouragement. There's often no rationale about where we seek approval. Some people seek it from everyone they meet, like it's oxygen. Some people seek it from fathers who should be sitting in the bleachers but aren't. And some seek it from scruffy private investigators. There's just no telling. But when I find myself the source, I try to remember all that. Because you never know which seed might be the one that grows into the oak.

But the fact was, I didn't know if it was of help. I had no

idea what it meant. I had no idea why I even needed to know. I just had a memory that kept nagging at me. A memory of crouching on the roof of this very hotel in the middle of a hurricane, trying to get the generator to go, and looking across the island at a blanket of darkness. Absolute, primal darkness.

We finished our coffees and I thanked Emery for her time, and she told me not to be a stranger and to come for dinner sometime soon.

"Bring your fiancée," she said. "When there are no hurricanes, the patio's pretty romantic."

I thanked her again and she hugged me once more and I gave a little more in return. She was one of those people. A bright light in a dark tunnel.

The doorman was chatting with a guest, so I opened the lobby door for myself. I'm okay with that. Fact is, I prefer it. I've never grown comfortable with having the door opened for me. Unless I'm carrying something heavy. It seems like something that belongs to the Queen of England, not to Miami Jones.

I got in the car and called Ron.

"Can you text me the address of Great Southeast Permanent? I need to have a chat with the CEO. What's his name?"

"Kent Fulsome. And he won't be at the office."

"How do you know that?"

"Because I just got a call from Natalie at the country club. Fulsome had a tee time this afternoon."

"That so? At South Lakes?"

"Yes. If you're leaving now, he'll probably be on the eighth hole by the time you get there."

"Awesome. Thanks, Ron."

"Miami. Don't do anything stupid."

"Me? Stupid?"

"Anything too stupid."

"Roger that."

CHAPTER TWENTY-SEVEN

South Lakes Country Club sat west of Lake Worth in an area that had once been the middle of the middle of nowhere in Palm Beach County but was now the middle of suburbia. I pulled in through the gate and found a spot in the lot far away from the clubhouse. I like to park far away from places. It's one of a million little things that keep the muffin top at bay. Plus it reduces my stress. No one is ever fighting for the furthest space from the front door.

I wandered across the lot past a wider selection of cars than one might expect to find at a country club. There were obvious Bimmers and Mercs, but there were pickups and Civics and a VW Beetle with more miles on the clock than me. The hostess at the front desk offered me a Florida smile. It wasn't quite Emery Taylor, but it was full of the good tidings that people who live in a place that they really want to be tend to have. Even after a hurricane. Maybe especially after a hurricane.

"Just heading to the pro shop," I said, and she upped the amps on her smile and told me to enjoy my round.

I strode out through the restaurant and onto the patio overlooking the eighteenth green. The course looked in reasonable shape. The biggest giveaway that a storm had swept through was the lack of leaves on many of the trees. South Florida golf courses are like the canary in the coal mine. They're a fair barometer of the mood of the country. When the economy is down, so are the number of rounds of golf. Some folks can't afford the green fees, and those who can feel like they need to be in the office doing the hard yards, not zipping around the fairways on an electric cart. But when times are good, the courses in South Florida are booking weeks or months in advance. I looked across the course. There were a good number of players out despite the softness underfoot, and I suspected it wouldn't be long before normal service was resumed after the lull from the hurricane.

The pro shop sat to the side of the clubhouse. A battalion of golf carts stood in rows outside like tanks ready for battle. A sign said I could get off-brand balls for a dollar. I didn't know if that was value or not. I went inside and asked the guy behind the counter where Kent Fulsome would be on the course. He looked me over to check if I was some kind of urban terrorist.

"You're Ron's friend?"

"That's right."

He nodded like that made all the difference and then he looked down at his tee time book.

"His group should be on the ninth by now. I expect you'll see them stop in at the clubhouse for a drink before they turn for the back nine."

I thanked him and walked out to the ninth green. It was on the other side of the clubhouse. There's a small store there that supplied drinks and sandwiches and candy bars to the players moving straight through to the tenth tee, and tables with umbrellas for those that wanted to stop for a quick pitstop.

A group was walking off the green, and another group was further down the fairway waiting to play. I approached one of the guys coming off the green. He was an older guy with Popeye arms and a yellow visor on his head.

"Kent Fulsome?" I asked.

He looked at me like I was a debt collector.

"Jackass," he said.

"Sorry?"

"Fulsome. Played right into us. Twice."

I took that to mean Fulsome had hit his ball into where the guy's group had been standing, which as I understood it was bad form. Doing it twice was clearly not an improvement on the situation.

"Which one is he?"

The guy turned to the fairway and spat.

"In the pink."

He stormed away to get a Gatorade or a Valium or something. I walked down onto the fairway. Fulsome's group was hitting onto the green, and I got the impression they weren't that happy about me walking into their space. But I was watching and I wasn't about to get hit by a ball. I just strode toward them, four guys and two electric carts.

"What the hell are you doing, you moron?" said a guy in a Jack Nicklaus polo who didn't look like he had been born the last time the Golden Bear had won the Masters.

"Shut it, Junior," I said. "The grownups need to talk."

I strode right by him looking like I was paying him no attention. But I was paying attention. The first idiot in a group to mouth off was usually the hothead, and the hothead was always the first one that needed to be shut down. But they were also the most likely to do something dumb like swing a golf club at my head.

He didn't. He was still processing someone having the temerity to talk to him like his father probably should have but clearly hadn't.

I headed for the guy in pink. He looked like a golfer. Tanned arms, polo shirt and a Miami Dolphins ball cap.

"Fulsome," I said.

"What?"

"What the hell do you think you're doing?"

"What?"

He was a confident-looking son of a gun, but even confident guys could get flustered when they had no idea what was going on.

"Your good-for-nothing company is about to go under and you're out playing golf?"

"What?" he spluttered a third time.

"You've got tens of millions in claims you can't pay and you're playing games."

He started to regain his composure. "Are you an investor? Look, I can assure you we can cover all legitimate claims. We know what we're doing."

"You're committing fraud, that's what you're doing."

"Look, pal, you better watch your mouth."

"I have a claim. Totally legit. You denied that."

"You're a claimant?"

"And then you tried to send me off on a wild goose chase to find someone to do something about it. Have you instructed your staff to deny all claims resulting from the hurricane? Because that would be highly illegal, Kent."

He started marching toward the green. He had completely forgotten he had arrived in a golf cart. "Let me give you some advice, pal. Keep your mouth shut. I hear any more from you and I'll sue you for defamation. I'll take everything you own."

"You're already doing that, Kent. It's called systematic denial of claims."

He stopped in the middle of the fairway. "Prove it."

"I intend to. You can't tell me I'm not covered by hurricane insurance because it was a flood and then I'm not covered by flood insurance because it was a hurricane."

"Actually, I can." He got a great big smug look on his face. "It's called concurrent risk. And you should have read your policy."

"Is that how you're going to handle Dale Beadman, too?"

"Who?"

"Dale Beadman, the NASCAR driver. One of your more high-profile customers, I'd guess."

"I know who Dale Beadman is. And his property wasn't damaged. I checked."

"Nice that you're so on top of your Palm Beach clientele."

He smiled. I thought about Ron and doing stupid things. I really didn't think punching out all his teeth was such a stupid thing, but I held back anyway. I just slapped Angie Beadman's insurance claim into his chest. His grin turned rapidly into a frown.

"What the hell? What's this?"

"That's a claim. From Dale Beadman. His car collection was stolen. Not a hurricane. Not a flood. Not a concurrent anything. Theft. Lucky for him, it's insured. By you, you ingrate. For thirty million bucks."

Fulsome frowned at the papers but said nothing. His tan seemed to leave his skin and was replaced by a sickly pallor that I couldn't help but enjoy.

"How's your bottom line now, Kent?"

I strode away. I wasn't sure what I had achieved. Maybe nothing. Maybe I'd learned that my claim was up a creek without a paddle. But at least I knew why. And I had delivered the documents as promised. I looked forward to seeing Kent deny that claim.

I got about fifty yards up the fairway before I turned around.

"And Kent? Just so you know. I don't give up. Ask around the club here. I don't give up. Ever."

I turned and left him there. I strode back around the green full of adrenaline and fury. Big guys holding it over little guys offended my sense of fair play. And it wasn't just about me. There were going to be hundreds, maybe thousands of folks in worse places than I was who were going to be ruined by Kent Fulsome and his semantics. It was true, though. I was likely to be one of them. I didn't have the money to fix my place. I might have to sell to my mystery buyer. I had a business. I had Ron and Lizzy to think about. But I wouldn't give up. Not easily, anyway.

I paced toward the clubhouse, and the guy in the yellow visor who had pointed Kent Fulsome out for me stepped into my path. I really wasn't in the mood. He handed me a card.

"I'm a lawyer," he said. "You want to fight that guy, I'm in. And I don't give up, either."

I nodded and waved the card in thanks, and he stepped out of my way and let me march away.

CHAPTER TWENTY-EIGHT

TED'S JAZZ AND SOCIAL CLUB WAS A NONDESCRIPT PLACE behind a strip mall in Lauderhill. Lauderhill was one of those pockets of humanity in South Florida that had become an enclave for a particular group of people. Another name for it could have been Little Jamaica. The Jamaican flag hung from store windows, and the smell of allspice and jerk chicken permeated the air. There was even a cricket ground down the road.

Danielle, Sally and I parked in front of a nail salon in the strip mall and walked down the alley between two stores. As usual, there were two old guys sitting on a sofa outside the club, chattering away at the passing wildlife. Both of them directed their attention toward Danielle. Sal and I could have been invisible.

"Welcome, young lady," said the one guy with the salt-and-pepper hair. He wore a pork pie hat and had a touch of the Morgan Freemans about him.

"Thank you," Danielle said, always humble before a compliment, even delivered by an octogenarian.

"All the fine ladies come to Ted's. Has always been so," said the other guy. He had no hair at all but wore thick frames that must have had similar magnification to a microscope.

"Buzz here?" I asked.

"Oh, yeah. He's in the back."

We stepped into the club. It was a sparse open space with bare floorboards and folding chairs set up around small wooden tables, with a bar at the back and a dark stage at the front. The stage was empty but for a small drum kit and a lone microphone.

I ushered Sally in before me. He looked around like he had been transported to a place a long time ago in a city far, far away. I could see the memories were pleasant ones. He wasn't remotely flustered by the fact that, other than Danielle and I, he was the only white guy in the room. Hell, maybe in the suburb. Color was not a big thing with Sal.

Color was a big thing behind the bar. The bartender was concocting all manner of beverages in all the colors of the rainbow. Sal didn't look quite so sure about that.

"Miss Danielle," called a woman in a red dress that made me think of the words *bee bop*. She floated over and offered Danielle an air-kiss.

"Gabrielle, nice to see you," Danielle said, before she was swept away to the bar. Gabrielle spoke over her shoulder as she went.

"Buzz be in the back, honey."

I nodded and walked around the small gathering near the bar. I held up two fingers to the guy behind the bar and he passed me two bottles of Red Stripe. I handed one of the beers to Sally.

"I thought you were gonna make me drink one of them fruity drinks," he said.

We clinked bottles and I led him down the side of the room to a door beside the stage. I pushed through into a corridor that led to another door. I pushed through the second door into a room that looked like the living room in a frat house. There were guys sitting on chairs and laying on sofas and leaning against the walls. They all had musical instruments of one breed or another. A guy kicked back on the sofa with a trumpet gave me a wide toothy grin as I stepped in.

"Sax man," he yelled, and he started laughing to himself.

"Hey, brother," I said. I looked at his sharp suit. "You're dressed well tonight."

He nodded and looked over my chinos and palm tree print shirt. "And you got the big boy pants on." He slapped a high five with the guy next to him. "You look like a man, brother."

I got various other welcomes and hi's and such. Then a guy with a saxophone attached to a sling around his neck waved to me. "Miami, good to see you, man."

"You too, Buzz." I stepped into the room, and Buzz saw Sal come in behind me.

"Sally!" he yelled. Buzz dashed around the sofa and embraced Sally. "I can't believe it, man. I haven't seen you in forever."

Sally looked a little taken aback by the hug. "It's good to see you, too, Buzz."

"Man, I can't believe you're here." Buzz looked at me. "I can't believe you got him here."

"He loves the crooners."

Buzz turned to the room. "Boys, I want you all to know Sally Mondavi. He's my, well, he's a . . . hell, I owe this man my life."

The guys all welcomed Sally, and he looked more and more uncomfortable in the spotlight. Buzz slapped Sal on the shoulder and looked to me. "I ever tell you what this man did for me?"

He hadn't, and I had a good inkling that Sally didn't want to hear it recounted now. But I didn't need the specifics. Whatever it was, it was something similar to what Sal had done for me, and plenty of others besides.

"I been there," I said.

Buzz caught my meaning and let it go. "You been practicing?" he asked me.

"I have. Before the storm, anyway. I've been working on that Billy Joel solo."

The guy on the sofa let out a howl. "Billy Joel. He's a fine black man."

"Billy Joel's a black man?"

"Of course, brother. Just look at the cat's eyes."

"Isn't Joel a Jewish name?"

"Black ain't just here, brother," he said, touching the skin on his hand. "It's in here." He pointed to his temple.

I nodded. I could see what he was saying. It didn't explain *Uptown Girl*.

We were chatting with Buzz when a young guy in a black suit popped his head into the room. "There's a guy here says he's looking for Mr. Miami."

I glanced at Sally and then at the young guy. "Can you send him back?"

"Trouble?" asked Buzz.

"No. Just a little chat."

We waited for the guy representing my mystery buyer to come through the door. When he did he wasn't wearing the same confident look he had when he'd turned up at Longboard Kelly's. He looked like a guy who wasn't in Kansas anymore. And I doubted this guy had ever been to Kansas. But he was a Latino living in South Florida. He could probably go months not seeing another person who wasn't Latino if he wanted. Permanently swimming among fish just like him. Only now the fish weren't just like him. I didn't blame the guy; it was learned behavior. We're taught to fear that which is different from us. We're not born with it. As a boy, I had played Pop Warner football with Irish, Italians, Greeks, Africans, and Hispanics. There was even a kid who came from California. We were boys, we all loved football. That's all I knew. They were my teammates, my brothers. We got into trouble at school together and we ran around the field in pads too big for us together. It wasn't until later that I learned we were different. That my friend Robert wasn't just American, he was African American. And that made him different in some kind of important way that my father could never explain. And then later still, they tried to tell me that his difference was something I should fear. They could never explain that to me, either. Why was it that I should fear a kid who was now a judge for the United States District of Massachusetts? I hadn't gotten it then and I didn't get it now. But I knew it was learned behavior and that I could use it to put this guy off kilter. That and other methods.

"I never got your name?"

He looked uneasily around the room. Lots of black faces. And Sally. He tried mightily to regain his composure, get himself back into character.

"What do names matter?"

"They matter on a contract of sale."

The guy shrugged, or maybe he had ants crawling on his neck.

"I know you," said Sally.

I was surprised, but I shouldn't have been. Sally knew most of the lowlifes around the traps.

Sally took a step toward the guy. "You're an actor."

I scrunched my brow at Sal. "An actor?"

"Yeah, I've seen him. In Mexican soaps."

"Are you kidding me, Sal? When do you see Mexican soaps?"

"Some of the girls in the check-cashing booth watch them. It's not the most exciting job in the world." He turned to the guy. "I've seen you, haven't I? Telenovelas?"

The guy tried to shrug humbly, but it came off as a spasm. I had pegged him as having movie star looks at our first meeting, and I patted myself on the back for my perception and insight.

"I was in some shows. Did you see *El Camino Secreto*?"

"I said I'd seen you," said Sal. "I didn't say I was a lifelong fan."

"You're an actor?" I said, rhetorically.

"I was an actor. There are not so many roles anymore."

The guy with the trumpet on the sofa said, "You could play that most interesting man in the world."

"I auditioned. They cast a younger guy."

"So what the hell are you doing bothering me?" I asked.

"Now I am a driver. Sometimes I play other roles for my boss, you know, to stay sharp."

"So who's your boss?"

"I am not at liberty to say," he said, dropping right back into character.

Sal stepped forward. "Let's let these boys warm up for their show." He looked at me. "Is there somewhere private we can negotiate?"

I led the way out the back and held the door open for the Mexican actor and Sal. As he stepped out, Sally picked up a phone book that was soaking up the excess water from a potted plant. There was a small courtyard behind the club where the band members could grab a smoke. The actor stepped into the middle of the space and I let Sal follow him down.

Sal whacked the guy in the face with the phone book.

He screamed like a schoolgirl, a high-pitched dog whistle of a noise, and then he cowered. He looked at me like there was something I could do. I had no idea what was going on. I had arrived with a plan, but that had gone up in smoke after the word *telenovela.*

"Take it easy," said Sally. He stepped to the actor and the guy nodded. Sally whacked him again.

"Qué cabrón!" yelled the guy. Sally had slapped him on either cheek and red welts were spreading across his olive skin.

"Um, Sal," I said. "I don't mean to interrupt."

"What?" he asked, like he was watching *Jeopardy* and I wanted to know what he'd like for dinner.

"The guy was trying to buy my house, not murder my family."

"Did the city kick you out of your house?"

"The county, actually."

"And did you find guys measuring up your lawn for a pool?"

"Yes."

"And has this guy been upfront about who he works for?"

"I don't even know his name."

"So. Be cool. He's an actor. They're paranoid about their faces."

Sally turned back to the actor and made a show of rolling the phonebook into a tube, like a bugle or a truncheon.

"Next one's the nose, you get me?"

The actor nodded hastily. This part was going horribly wrong for him.

"What is your name?"

"Domingo."

"Who do you work for?"

"Juan Gotlieb."

"Juan Gotlieb?" asked Sal. "You mean his name is John?"

"No. Is Juan. Juan Gotlieb."

Sal turned to me with an expression that said he just didn't understand the world anymore, and then he focused back on Domingo.

"Who is Juan Gotlieb? And why does he want to buy my friend's house?"

"He is a real estate agent."

"Okay. Why does he want Miami's house?"

"He's a real estate agent."

"Are you saying he is acting for a client?"

"*Sí.*"

"Who?"

Domingo shrugged and shuffled his feet.

"Domingo," said Sally, to regain the actor's attention. He slapped the phone book into his palm like a schoolmaster.

"I don't know who is the client. All I know is he lives in Argentina."

"Argentina?" I said. "Why does he want my house?"

"I don't know, *señor*. He has the house next door. Maybe he wants more space."

"Domingo?" said Sal.

"I think his wife bought the house. For investment, *si*? They get it for retirement, and for when they come to America for shopping."

I said, "I've never seen anyone there."

"He found out it does not have a pool. He thinks every house in Florida must have a pool. So he won't come to it."

"So they want my place to put in a pool?" I asked.

Domingo nodded.

"Did you call the county to come and put the no habitation notice on my door?"

He shuffled his feet and glanced at Sally and the phone book. "I did it."

"You did what?"

"Put the notice. We know the building guy, so I pay him and he gives me the paper and I stick it on your door. Sorry."

"The inspector didn't even visit my house?"

"No, *señor*."

Sal looked at me to confirm if I had anything more to ask. I shook my head.

"You can go," Sal said.

Domingo edged around us like we were dragons. He got to the door near where I stood.

"What was your client offering for my house?" I asked him.

He told me.

"Get out of here, Domingo. And make sure I don't see you again."

"Except on TV." He smiled, and he jumped in through the door before Sally could smack him one last time.

We went back in and Sally returned the phone book under the plant and we left the band to prepare. Danielle was at a table with another couple, at least two drinks in. We refreshed ours and I introduced Sally. The guy at our table was fascinated when Sally told him he had seen Sammy Davis Jr. at The Sands in Vegas.

We kicked back and watched the band file out, and the small crowd applauded and the band burst into *Mack the Knife* and the crowd went ballistic, like they had all been born during the war and had grown up with this music. The only one who had was Sally, and while he didn't go ballistic, he seemed to enjoy it all the same. The band was superb as always, and the guy on the mike should have had a recording contract.

Danielle and I danced below the stage and worked up a sweat in the small room. The band finished their set and we refreshed our drinks; I switched to soda. Plastering my car all over a telephone pole was not my idea of a good time. As we waited for the second set, Sally leaned over to me.

"I forgot to mention," he said. "I heard a little rumble about your car."

"My car?"

"The F-88, was it?"

"Oh, that car."

"The intermediary. I might know who it was."

"You don't say."

He nodded. "He's based in Detroit. But he has a winter home on the Palm Beaches."

"Doesn't everyone? Who is he?"

The band wandered back out from the green room in a haze of sweet smoke and the crowd cheered. Sal leaned in close.

"Call me tomorrow. I'll give you the lowdown."

CHAPTER TWENTY-NINE

I DIDN'T HAVE TO GO FAR TO FIND THE SUSPECTED intermediary in Dale Beadman's car deal. Sally's grapevine worked better than my cell phone service, and his people told him the deal was probably brokered by a guy called Dwight Eckhardt. Eckhardt was, according to Sal, an auctioneer based in Detroit, Michigan, and not surprisingly, he specialized in luxury and collectible vehicles. Eckhardt had a pretty nice setup. He sold cars at his auction rooms in Detroit during the summer, and when the snow came in and the buyers fled south, he followed them to his auction rooms in Fort Lauderdale.

But I didn't have to go to Lauderdale. It turned out Eckhardt's winter home was in one of the high-rise condo developments on Singer Island. Which meant I could have ordinarily walked from my home to his. But as my home was allegedly uninhabitable, I had to drive over from PGA National.

Finding him was one thing. Getting in was another. Unlike the houses around Lake Norman, high-rise condos had doormen and concierges and security guys and lots of apartments with no tenant list. It was like looking for a needle in a haystack with wild bulls running around in the field. Walking in all bold and gung-ho was pointless.

So I did the next best thing. I left a note. I simply scribbled *handling stolen F-88 Oldsmobiles is a crime* and my phone number on a piece of paper and slipped it in an envelope. I told the concierge at the building it was time sensitive because I expected a delay in the reaction, but I really didn't care to wait all day. I wandered over to the Seaside Bar to wait. Seaside is my kind of place. It's dark and there's no view, so the tourists tend to stay across the parking lot, but the beers and the burgers and the people are first class. I was sitting on a bottle of craft brew an hour later when my phone rang. Mr. Eckhardt suggested we chat, and I said I'd be right over. I finished my beer and ordered another and an early lunch of fish dip and crackers before I left. I can keep people waiting with the best of them.

The car auction business must do all right, because Dwight Eckhardt had a penthouse apartment on the ocean side. It had to be worth millions. He met me at the door and ushered me in without a word. The view was expansive. I could practically see Freeport. Eckhardt was also expansive. I tried to come up with a more politically correct way to frame it in my mind, but I couldn't get past *very fat*. He was only about five foot four and almost round. His shoulders joined his head at the ears. He might have sold cars, but I couldn't see him getting in one. He sat next to the kitchen bar on a low stool that he could fall back into. Then the stool rose up like a hydraulic vehicle jack.

"So, Mr. Jones." He took a deep breath before and after every word that sounded like someone in scuba gear. "What is it you think you know?"

"What do I know? I know you're an auctioneer. You sell classic cars, whatever that means. I also know you facilitate the transfer of less legitimate cars. I know you facilitated such a transfer with Dale Beadman and parties unknown."

"And how is it that you think you know all this?"

"Heard it on the grapevine." I was tempted to sing it but I didn't.

"Really." Eckhardt took a drink of water through a mouth that looked altogether too small for his massive head. "The grapevine seems to have led you astray."

"I don't think so. I know you were involved. One hundred percent."

"And how do you think you know this?"

"I'm standing in your living room. If I'm off-base, you don't let me in the door."

"Maybe I like to know things."

"I'm sure you do. I expect it's a pretty crucial part of your business. But you could have asked me questions on the phone. You didn't, because you wanted some time to check me out. See if I really might know anything. And then you asked me in."

"Not exactly a burden of proof."

"I don't need a burden of proof, Mr. Eckhardt. I just need to tell the *Palm Beach Post*. I just need to get my assistant, who is a lot better at these things that I am, to put posts on every relevant social media site that you handle stolen cars. I just need to get that message to every reputation-conscious dealer and collector and car owner in the state. I could probably do a reasonable job of it in Michigan, too."

"And what could I do?"

"I don't know. What could you do?"

"I could pass on information to the State Attorney's office regarding the affairs of a certain Sally Mondavi. I could get photographs, I could get statements. I could provide an open-and-shut case regarding extortion, racketeering and the movement of stolen property that would see Sal Mondavi spend all his last days in prison."

He watched me through slits in his face. I gave him nothing, but I knew I was walking a dangerous line. He knew where I had gotten my information, which meant the grapevine went two ways, which of course it always did. I had to ask myself, what would Sally do?

I pursed my lips and said, "The State Attorney, hey?"

Eckhardt nodded.

"Old Eric Edwards. Yeah, he'd be interested in that all right."

Eckhardt nodded again.

"Of course, knowing Eric as I do, and I know him very well, he's a very pragmatic guy. He's like a big game hunter. He'll take what he can get, but he'll always trade in small game for a shot at something bigger. So I'm wondering what he would go for? Two column inches in the *Palm Beach Post* about the takedown of a two-bit pawnshop on the wrong side of the turnpike, or a lead item in the national section of the *New York Times* about a massive conspiracy in Motown?" I tapped my fingers on my chin like I was considering this great conundrum.

"You're playing a very dangerous game, Mr. Jones."

"Ditto."

"What is it you want, exactly?"

"To get the answers to a few questions."

"Confidentiality is the bedrock of my business."

"I've no doubt. And let's be clear, Mr. Eckhardt. I don't give a damn about your business. I don't care about rich people buying and selling and stealing each other's cars. Except as far as I have been retained to find one such stolen car that I know came via you. The question is, and this is the big question, did it leave via you?"

"Mr. Jones, I don't know what you think it is I do, but I can assure you that I do not steal cars." He said *steal cars* like he'd eaten a bad pickle. "Provenance can be complex, but I would not knowingly handle a vehicle that I knew belonged to one of my clients that was not being sold by said client. I have my standards."

I watched him. Hard. He was tough to read because his eyes were hidden below layers of skin and his facial tics were smothered by flab. But I believed him.

"So I assure you, the vehicle you mentioned in your note did not belong to a current client, and it was transferred to Mr. Beadman in good faith."

"And then stolen."

"What do you mean, then stolen?"

"I mean, I'm not saying it was stolen and then you sold it to Mr. Beadman. I'm saying you sold it to him and then it was stolen."

I thought I saw him flinch, but I couldn't be sure. "The F-88 was stolen?"

"Yes. The day it was delivered, or thereabouts."

"And you think I sold it and then stole it back?"

"There's no honor among thieves."

"As I told you, I do not steal vehicles. And I am a man of honor, Mr. Jones, regardless of what you may think. I had no idea. Mr. Beadman never mentioned . . ."

"I think he's embarrassed about it. He wouldn't even tell me who you were."

"Mr. Beadman is a man of the highest integrity. That is why I chose to do business with him."

"So I have to cross people off my list. You're on it, obviously. But let's assume I believe you and cross you off, I still have two other possibles."

"Who?"

"Whoever sold it, and whoever else wanted to buy it."

"I can't divulge that information. But I can tell you that the seller is most unlikely to be involved."

"Why?"

"Let's just say the seller was a legal structure."

"Like a company?"

"No. A personal legal structure."

"I was away the day we did law school at college, Mr. Eckhardt. Throw me a bone."

"I am not speaking out of turn to say it was an estate."

"An estate? As in someone died and the heirs sold it?"

"That would be a reasonable assumption."

"So why can't they be involved?"

"Let's just say that the estate was only interested in one thing, as a group."

"Money."

"Another reasonable assumption."

"Still doesn't answer my question."

"The individuals were, shall we say, at arm's length. They were not involved in the liquidating of the estate. The attorneys for the estate were under instruction to get what they could and divide up the pie. I'm not even sure they knew that F-88 wasn't a file name for something."

"Okay. So, other buyers."

"I cannot."

"Tell me how many."

"Just the one."

"Why didn't they get it? Price?"

"There is more to these things than price."

"You approached Mr. Beadman because he's a good guy."

"We have dealt with one another at auction. I found him trustworthy and reliable."

"And the other buyer?"

"The attorneys for the estate may have asked some questions about the vehicle before engaging me."

"And this other buyer contacted you?"

"That would be a reasonable assumption."

"And did this other buyer know who the final buyer was?"

"Not from me."

"But maybe the attorneys."

"Unlikely, but I cannot vouch for them completely."

"And this other buyer would be some kind of well-known authority on cars?"

"That would—"

"Be a reasonable assumption, I got it. So would this other buyer have the initials: Ansel Brasher?"

Eckhardt had amazing muscle control. He raised an eyebrow. I'm not sure he meant it. It was hard to say, but it was as close to a tell as I had seen from him.

"Those are not initials, Mr. Jones."

"Right on."

I pushed myself off the back of his sofa and glanced across the water. "Nice view."

"Yes."

"I run down on that beach."

"That sounds awful."

"Depends on the view."

He frowned. He had clearly never run with Danielle.

"Thanks for your time," I said.

He didn't move from the bar. "You were never here."

"What?"

"This conversation never took place."

"What are you, the CIA now?"

"Do you understand what I'm saying?"

"You don't want any of this to get back to anyone and you don't want me to ever speak about it."

"That would be a reasonable assumption."

CHAPTER THIRTY

I had the vague sensation that I needed a shower or to walk through a car wash after meeting with Dwight Eckhardt. I settled for a happy medium. I headed for Longboard Kelly's. For me, it's like going to the spa. It's therapeutic. I was aware that these were the words of a trainee alcoholic, but I was confident that people like Danielle and Muriel and Lizzy would pull me back long before that might ever become a reality.

When I got there, two guys were putting up a new fence between the parking lot and the courtyard. It was cedar and it smelled fantastic. Like my mother's closet. It also served to ensure I got maximum effect from the surprise.

My heart soared when I walked in and saw the freshly restored palapa over my barstool. It wafted gently in the breeze. There were bodies on either side of my stool. Ron was on one side and Danielle on the other. Muriel stood at the taps and when she saw me she stretched her arms out and up like she was a Price is Right model offering me a new car. This was better. I smiled like I'd hit a hole in one and slipped up onto my stool, looking up like I was an astronomer. The fronds were thatched to perfection, as far as my layman's eye could tell.

Muriel put a beer on a mat in front of me, and I looked at it and then looked at her.

"How? When?"

"Two guys showed up. Said they had been working in Palm Beach and said the guy they were working for told them they were needed here. You know anything about that?"

I thought about Dale Beadman and vaguely recalled mentioning it. I didn't even think I had mentioned the name of the bar.

"Nothing to do with me. But this is awesome. I'm so glad Mick didn't go with shiplap."

"And risk losing your business? He's not stupid."

"He's not that."

"I told him you wouldn't have gone anywhere because you'd miss me."

"I wouldn't have missed you."

Muriel's face dropped.

"Because you would have followed to wherever I was drinking. That's where the tips are."

Muriel looked at Danielle. "Do you believe the mouth on this boy?"

Danielle smiled. "I do."

I wasn't sure where to go with that, so I kept quiet.

"Anyway, Mick couldn't say no to a free palapa," said Muriel.

"Free?"

"Yeah. The guys did the work and then refused to take payment. They said it was taken care of."

I took a deep breath and surveyed the courtyard. The table and chairs and umbrellas were back, the longboard with the bite out of it was back on the wall, and there were no jellyfish anywhere to be seen. I turned back to my beer.

"Where's Mick?"

"Out," said Muriel. "He said you'd go and get all mushy over the fact the palapa was back, so he took off."

"He's so sentimental. Here's to Mick."

"To Longboard's," said Ron.

"To Longboard's," said Danielle and Muriel.

We took sips of our drinks. Ron smiled and placed his beer down delicately.

"So I found something out about your real estate guy, Juan Gotlieb."

"Do tell."

"Turns out he is a real estate agent in Boca Raton. But he lives in West Palm, in one of those starter mansions down on Washington Road."

"Must be doing all right for himself."

"Seems to have plenty of good listings, but then so does every other agent. Word is he's leveraged to the hilt to afford the lifestyle."

"How does that get from him to me?"

"I'm getting there."

"I knew you were."

"It looks like a fake-it-'til-you-make-it type thing," Ron said. "He's living like the rich and famous to fast-track into getting the business of the rich and famous."

"Okay."

"That's why he has a driver."

"Domingo."

"Right. As you know, the former telenovela actor and part-time driver for old Juan. Plus he does a bit of hard talking for his boss."

"He's actually a pussycat."

"In the end." Ron nodded. "So it turns out Juan represented the buyer on the house next to yours on Singer Island."

"The wedding cake. Okay, the plot thickens."

"The owner of the house is a C corporation owned by another corporation out of the Bahamas."

"Doesn't anyone just buy a house anymore?"

"But as you learned, the guy behind that corporation is an Argentine."

"Or Argentinian," I said.

"You say potato. So there's not much on him yet."

"Why do I feel like you're building up to the third act?"

"Guess who our estate agent Juan Gotlieb lives next door to?"

I looked at Danielle. "This is going to be good, I can feel it."

Ron drum rolled his fingers on the bar. "Kent Fulsome."

A better man would have seen that coming. "The Great Southeast CEO?"

"The same."

"So piece it together for me, Ronnie, my brain is frazzled."

"Argentine buyer has a property his wife wants to visit, but husband won't come because it doesn't have a pool. Buyer asks real estate agent Juan about the likelihood of expanding. Juan sees the hurricane come in, gets an idea. What if he could get the next-door lot for his buyer? So he sends his actor/driver/henchman over to put an offer."

"Which I don't take."

"Even though it would buy a pool home in Wellington."

"Why would I want to live in Wellington?"

"There are some good schools out there."

"I already finished school."

Ron looked at Danielle, who shrugged. Ron shook his head. "Anyway. Juan's guy, Domingo, sees the Great Southeast claims guy come to your house while he's there to make you the offer. He mentions this to his boss and his boss thinks, aha, that's my neighbor. Juan sticks his head over the side fence, or whatever those mansion types do, and says, 'Hey neighbor, how about a favor? Can you deny the claim on this guy in Singer Island?'"

"Which he was going to do anyway."

"Right. So Kent says, 'Sure neighbor, happy to help.' Maybe Juan offers to pimp for Southeast to his luxury homebuyers. So Kent denies your claim and Juan swoops in to make the sale."

"That didn't quite work out."

"Still might be an offer there."

"I'm not moving, Ron. Now more than ever. I'll pitch a damned tent if I have to."

"But you still don't have the insurance money."

"I've been thinking about that."

"And?"

"Still thinking."

Ron shook his head again and downed his beer. "I must get home to the Lady Cassandra. We have tickets."

"For what?" asked Danielle.

"No idea," said Ron. He slipped off his stool and blew a kiss at Danielle and then tipped a cap he wasn't wearing to me. Then he walked out.

"I love watching you two talk," said Danielle.

"Me, too," said Muriel. "It's like two sides of one dysfunctional brain."

Danielle smiled. "I was going to say a ventriloquist and his dummy."

"But which one's the dummy?" I asked.

"I know," said Muriel.

"So do I," said Danielle. "So do I."

CHAPTER THIRTY-ONE

The regulars were starting to make their way back to Longboard Kelly's. There were two groups of clientele at Longboard's. Those who sat inside and those who sat outside. They were all fine people in my experience, but the two groups didn't really understand each other. But on balance, the inside people were back and the outside people were not. The courtyard sat empty but for Danielle and me, and Muriel got nice and busy in the inside bar. We turned around on our stools and looked at the evening light dropping long shadows across the courtyard.

"How are you getting on with your case?" Danielle asked.

"You know how these things go. I feel like it's moving forward, but you never know if the thing you're pulling on is the thing that will close the case or if it's just a loose thread."

"Where were you today?"

I thought about telling her about Dwight Eckhardt. Danielle knows I walked the line a little closer to the other side than she does. She knows that Sally is no boy scout. But she also knows that he doesn't deal in drugs and he does a lot of good for kids in his community. On balance I think she's comfortable with the fact that none of us is perfect, even in the eyes of the law. But I didn't think she would be so comfortable with Dwight Eckhardt. Vehicles of disputable provenance were one thing. Grand theft auto was not such a big leap from there, despite Eckhardt standing up for his own honor. Me thinks the gentleman doth protest too much. And any investigation of Eckhardt would affect Dale Beadman and I knew from what I'd seen that the scale definitely tipped in his favor. By my measure, anyway.

"Beadman has a rival," I said. "Turns out it's pretty bitter and it's been going for decades. There's a possibility the rival might have been involved in the theft."

"If I can't have it, you can't either?"

"Something like that. These guys have a funny way of keeping score."

"Race wins not enough?"

"Not by a long shot. You won this race, I won that one. Are we one-all or is one race worth more than another? And then you ended up winning the championship but I ended up on television and being famous? You've got a small plane but I've got a lakeside mansion. You've got a car collection and I want it. Or as you say, maybe I don't want it, but I just don't want you to have it."

"The world pines for a man who is a grown-up," she said.

I nodded. No argument from me.

"Why do men end up like that?" she asked. "I mean, how does it get started?"

"A woman," I said.

Danielle slammed her beer down. "Why is it that men always feel the need to blame a woman for something they didn't do?"

"I'm not blaming a woman. Any more than I blame Mount Everest for people who die trying to climb it. The mountain didn't make that decision. Had nothing to do with it. In the grand scheme of things, the mountain would probably prefer people stay the hell away. But people climb and some of them die. It happens because of the mountain, but it isn't the mountain's fault."

"That's a very philosophical argument, MJ. But it smells like hokey baloney."

I shrugged.

"Who is this woman?"

"Missy Beadman."

"Really. Haven't they been married forever?"

"More than forty years. But this thing goes way back. Turns out she was dating someone when she met Dale. This guy took her to the race track, and she met the love of her life there."

"Who was the guy?"

"Ansel Brasher."

"The rival."

"Right."

"So Dale gets the girl and this Brasher stews on it for the rest of his life?"

"More or less."

"Sounds primitive."

"We are that. No doubt. There was plenty of fuel added to the fire over the years, but that was the spark, as far as I could tell."

"Isn't Brasher married, too?"

"He is. Almost as long, I think."

"So his wife isn't the love of his life? That bites." Danielle frowned.

"I don't know. Maybe she is. Maybe he got over Missy but he never got over the slight. We can look at these things however we choose."

"He needs to choose another way to look at it."

"Maybe choose is the wrong word. We see things as we allow ourselves to see them. Some folks win the lottery and complain about the taxes."

Danielle took a sip of her drink. "So Dale lives in Charlotte?"

"No, he lives in Palm Beach."

"He has a house in Palm Beach. It doesn't sound like he lives there. He's at the workshop most weeks, at a race track somewhere most weekends. When is he in Palm Beach? Thanksgiving and Christmas? Doesn't sound like such a great marriage. Sounds lonely."

"They seem happy."

"Do they?"

I put my beer to my mouth but didn't drink. On recollection, they didn't seem happy. Missy seemed distant, and her first conversation with me covered a lot of ancient territory. She had told me how she'd met Dale. I didn't know how most couples met that I had known for years. I knew how my parents met, or at least the version they had developed over the years, and I knew how I had met Danielle and I knew how Ron had met the Lady Cassandra because I was there. Otherwise, I had no idea. But I knew Missy's story, and I had only met her once. It was like she was living in the past, or wanted to be.

Danielle asked the question I didn't want to ask. "Could Missy be cheating on Dale?"

I shook my head.

"Maybe with this Brasher character?"

"No."

"No, you don't think so or no you don't want it to be so?"

"Motive and opportunity. They're not there. Missy spoke to me about Dale. She wasn't angry or even indifferent to it. The opposite. Talking about her early days with Dale was the most human I saw her. The motive just isn't there. And the means.

Brasher is in the Charlotte area just like Dale, but Missy is pretty much a permanent fixture in Palm Beach. She's in the *Post* society pages doing charity stuff all the time."

"It was just an idea."

"Yeah."

We both stared into middle distance with our thoughts. Then Danielle said what I knew she would say.

"What if that's us?"

"That's not us."

"We're apart now."

"We're at Longboard's now."

"You know what I mean, smarty. And I'll be posted somewhere not here."

"Didn't we talk about this already?"

"And you said you'd hunt me down. Which is cute and all, and it's why I love you, but is it realistic? I mean, think about now? When I'm not here? Do you miss me?"

"Of course I do. All the time."

"So how do you cope?"

"I keep busy. I work, I come here to Longboard's. What about you?"

"The same. I'm at the academy. I don't get a lot of downtime. I stay busy, too. So is that how Dale and Missy do it?"

"Maybe."

"Is that what you want? To have a busy life apart and then come together sometime toward the end?"

"Dale and Missy haven't come together at the end. He's still in Charlotte." The words came out of my mouth before I had time to process them in my brain. But once they had, they caused a lightbulb to go off in there. And then the lightbulb exploded.

"I don't want that, MJ."

I slipped off my stool. "Me, either."

"So what do we do?"

"We wait. It's not a lifetime, it's a few more weeks. And then we find out where you get posted. And I've been thinking about Lucas's place."

"What about it?"

"We could get an investment condo. Wherever you get stationed. And I can take cases anywhere. The Palm Beaches aren't the only place with stuff that needs to be solved."

"You've got it all worked out, then."

"Nope. Not by a long shot. But I know as sure as this state is built on a swamp that I don't want to be apart from you any more than I have to be. That's all I need. I know we'll find a solution. Because we want to."

I slammed the last of my beer and pulled my keys out.

"Are you going somewhere now?" asked Danielle.

I nodded.

"You have an interesting sense of timing."

I shook my head.

"Big speech about not being apart and now you're leaving."

"You're coming."

"Where?"

"We need to go see Missy Beadman."

CHAPTER THIRTY-TWO

THE SUN WAS NOTHING BUT A FAINT GLOW AT THE TOP OF the atmosphere when we arrived at the Beadman estate. I wound down the window of my SUV and leaned out toward the inter-com. Through the gates, I could see the darkened silhouettes of men. It took me a moment to comprehend what I was seeing. Then I realized that the guys were finishing up the driveway. They were throwing the last of their equipment into the back of their pickup, and as they did, the headlights burst to life and lit us up like one of the artifacts in Dale Beadman's museum. The pickup started up and then rolled toward us, and the gate opened. The guys in the cabin waved to us as they drove out, and we waved back.

I drove in through the open gate and pulled around to the front of the house. The driveway had been tamped down and didn't even crackle under the tires. I parked behind the Camaro as I had before. Danielle and I wandered up to the front door. The house was quiet. I could see lights burning in the end room. Angie's office. Hard at work, as ever. The rest of the house was dark. I knocked softly. I didn't want to disturb Angie. Mainly because I didn't want to talk to Angie.

There was no response, so I put my hand on the latch and opened the door. I pushed it open and made to step inside.

"There's a doorbell," whispered Danielle.

"I know."

"You can't just walk in."

"Sure I can."

And I did. Danielle followed me and closed the door behind her. Then she flicked the nib to lock the door.

"What are you doing?" she whispered.

"Why are you whispering?" I asked. "We're not cat burglars."

I wandered into the great room. It was darker than the three-quarter moon outside. A lamp was on in the kitchen. I checked it out. It was under-cabinet lighting. Maybe a night-light in case someone got a hankering for a midnight snack. At eight in the evening.

I turned back through the great room to the entrance and looked down the corridor.

"What's down there?" Danielle asked.

"The computer room and Angie's office."

I looked upstairs. The staircase wasn't grand by Palm Beach standards, but it wound up to a landing that overlooked the mandatory chandelier. I started up the stairs.

"MJ," said Danielle. "What are we doing?"

I didn't respond. I didn't have a response. I had wanted to speak with Missy. I preferred to do it without Angie in the room. The rest I was making up on the fly. I reached the landing and broke right. I found three bedrooms, one of which must have been the master. It was huge. I didn't get it. What did people do in their bedrooms that required so much space? A big living room I understood. Even a big kitchen. Everybody ended up in the kitchen at a party. But a big bedroom? It was for sleeping. Did they take tea in there? Bake bread? Practice their cartwheels?

I left the bedrooms and walked past Danielle and headed across to the other wing. The corridor was dark and the only light was coming from a door that stood ajar. I pushed that door open just enough to poke my head in.

It was a media room. At least I thought that was what people called them now. A home cinema. There was a screen that took up the entire wall at the far end from the door. Three rows of seating, four seats per row. The chairs were large recliners that looked like sleeping bears. They had cupholders and little tables between the armrests to put your popcorn on.

Missy Beadman wasn't eating popcorn and she wasn't reclining. She was sitting in the second seat from the end in the front row. Her elbow was on the armrest and her hand was held high, balancing a wineglass between her delicate fingers. She was watching home movies. I watched for a moment and reconsidered. They weren't movies. They were photographs. It was like a slideshow that my father used to do when I was a kid. Once or twice a year, he would get a hankering to revisit my parents' pre-me lives and our family vacations, so he'd pull out his carousel projector and load it up with slides, and we would have to sit through the click and clack of a slide show that was only remotely more interesting than a science slide show at school, at least to a small boy. I had no idea what had happened to the slides or the projector after my father died.

But Missy wasn't watching slides. Her projector was attached to the ceiling at the back of the room and looked like something that might be found in a proper movie theater. There was no click or clack, and the photographs transitioned softly from one to another. It was a hell of a setup. If I ever bothered to watch movies, I could have given up half a bedroom to make space for a room like this.

The photos didn't seem to be in any kind of chronological order. They jumped from color to black-and-white and back again. There were people in seventies costumes that ought to have been illegal and then Angie in her graduation gown and then back to a guy standing on the top of an old-model stock car.

Danielle knocked on the door. I glanced at her and she gave me a look like there was something wrong with us watching Missy watching her memories. Missy didn't jump at the noise. Perhaps she thought it was Angie. She glanced over her shoulder and saw me in the glow of the screen.

"Mr. Jones," she said. "What an unexpected surprise." In certain circles they would have called her well bred. Her good manners were so ingrained that even when she was surprised by strange people appearing unannounced in her darkened home, she was welcoming.

"Missy," I said. "Sorry to disturb."

"Not at all. Come on in. I'm just looking at some old pictures."

I stepped into the room and Danielle came in behind me.

"Hello, ma'am," said Danielle. Her manners were also pretty ingrained. Law enforcement agencies and the military tended to drum those in if a recruit's parents hadn't done it already.

"Why, hello," Missy said, looking back to me.

I got the hint and introduced Danielle as my fiancée, not as a member of the Florida Department of Law Enforcement.

Missy stood and put her drink into the cup holder on her chair. She looked Danielle over.

"Oh my, aren't you a beauty?" She stepped forward and put her hands on Danielle's cheeks the way older women sometimes do. Then she gave Danielle a kiss that might have landed somewhere near her ear or might have been an air-kiss. She stood back to take us both in.

"You are a handsome couple," she said.

"Thanks," I said, as if I was in any way responsible for us being a handsome couple.

"Can I offer you a drink? Some wine?"

She moved toward the side wall, and I noted her movement wasn't as fluid as it had been. It wasn't her first glass of wine for the evening. She stepped to a cabinet I had not seen in the darkness and opened a small bar fridge. She pulled out two glasses and a bottle of something white. She poured and handed us glasses and then she filled her own and picked it up.

"Cheers," she said.

We saluted but I didn't drink. I just held the glass.

"This is quite the setup," I said.

"Why, thank you," she said. "We have a high-definition projector. She's a beauty."

"The photos are in it?" I asked.

"No. I digitized our old photographs and stored them on our server. The projector is linked via Wi-Fi to the server, so I can watch whenever I want."

"All sounds like black magic to me," I said.

"He's a bit of a technophobe," Danielle said.

"My Dale is the same way. He can fix a car to go two hundred miles an hour, but I have to work the remote control. I'm sure you're the same."

Danielle tipped her head. I had nothing to say.

Missy caught me looking at the screen and turned. It was a shot of her, Dale and Angie. Angie must have been two or three years old and was sitting on her daddy's shoulders. They were leaning up against a car. Beadman green.

"Talladega," Missy said. "Dale's first win there."

"Darlington this week," I said.

"Hmm? Oh, yes. Darlington."

"So Dale should be home early. Since it's not too far away."

"Yes. I hope so." Missy leaned against the arm of the end chair and faced us, her back to the screen. It lit her from behind and gave her an aura.

"It must be hard," Danielle said. "With Dale being away so much."

"It's our life. You learn to live with it."

"Do you go to many races?" Danielle asked.

"Not these days. I did, back in the day. Went to most of them." She smiled. Then she dropped it. "But then Angela Jean had to go to school, and we wanted her to have a sense of place, you know?"

Danielle nodded. "Of course."

They both sipped their wine. I watched the screen over Missy's shoulder. Every picture was either Missy and Dale, or the three of them. I didn't recognize Palm Beach in any.

"But now she's grown," said Danielle. "Angela Jean."

"She is that," said Missy. "Her own woman."

"You must be proud."

"Isn't every parent? But she's a good girl. Smart, caring. Pretty, too. I just wish she'd work a little less so she could find a fella."

"These things happen when they're supposed to," said Danielle.

Missy nodded like she agreed, but she didn't say as much. "You just want them to be happy, don't you?"

Missy sipped her wine. As she did, the picture behind her changed from color to black-and-white. I focused on it because I knew it. I had seen it before. It was a digital version of the photograph Missy had shown me the first time we had met. She had said it was from the night she had met Dale. When Ansel Brasher had taken her to the race track in Alabama and she had met the love of her life. The photo on the screen was more vivid than the one in the frame. The effect of the projector, I assumed. The faces in it glowed. They were young and vibrant and the floodlights above made them sparkle with energy. An old race car and a group of young kids. Some looking away. Dale Beadman looking at the camera, already aware of the responsibilities of a team driver. And Missy, eyes for nothing but Dale Beadman.

Then the picture dissolved and another reappeared in its place. Another black-and-white. The same glow, the flare from the same camera lens. The same race car in the background. Clearly the same night. But a different shot. Dale Beadman spraying a beer bottle into the air, a substitute for the champagne bottles on the podium that were years in the future. The people around him were laughing and recoiling from the spray. Except one. The same one. Missy. Her eyes were firmly fixed on Dale. The same look in her eyes. A look that said she had never met a man like Dale and never would again. He was young and indestructible and a winner, and he wore confidence like a greatcoat. She was a planet all of her own, but she was ready to be swept up into his galaxy. Her eyes told the story.

As I looked at her face, I realized that she had an arm around her. An embrace. The man next to her was holding her tight like maybe he was aware she was a planet and he was too, but his gravity was never going to be enough to keep her in near orbit. She was leaning into him. Her body said she was comfortable with the hug, but her face and its laser focus on Dale said she was indifferent to it. I looked at the boy holding her. The boy who had taken her to the race track the night she had met Dale Beadman. I looked at his face. He was younger, much younger. He was flawless and full of hopes and dreams that made him look alive. I had to look again to realize what I was seeing, because I had met the man. After life had revealed the flaws and dashed the hopes and tempered the dreams. I knew who it was. And I knew who it wasn't.

It wasn't Ansel Brasher.

The picture dissolved and was replaced by another. I don't know what the next photograph was. I wasn't looking anymore. I was standing in the dark, reassessing everything. Danielle and Missy were chatting about something, but I couldn't make sense of it. All the blood had rushed to one specific part of my brain. I had no idea which part, but I knew all other senses had become dulled because I was focused on thinking back. On what people had said and what they had done. On the lines they had emphasized and those they had thrown away. I pulled apart the puzzle I had been putting together, and then I started putting it back together. The same pieces in a different order. The picture was going to be a very different picture. If I was seeing it right this time. Which I didn't know for sure.

Missy offered us another glass of wine, but I begged off. I hadn't touched the one I had in my hand. I put it on the cabinet that held the bar fridge and thanked Missy for her hospitality. She said we were welcome anytime. I felt dizzy as we descended the stairs.

We got to the front door when the door to Angie's office opened at the other end of the corridor.

"Miami?" she asked.

"Angie," I said, distracted.

She walked over us and didn't wait for me to introduce her.

"Angie Beadman," she said to Danielle.

"Danielle Castle."

"A pleasure." Angie looked at me. "I didn't know you were here."

"We were in the neighborhood."

"How did you get in?"

"Your mother," I lied.

"Oh." She glanced up in the direction of the cinema room. "Can I help you with something?"

"No," I said. "I think we're good right now."

I opened the door. I wanted to be gone. I needed to think so badly I couldn't stand properly.

"Are you getting somewhere?" Angie asked.

"Possibly."

"I mean really getting somewhere. Do you know who did it?"

"Crystalizing some thoughts."

"Good."

I made to step out, and Angie grabbed my arm. "Miami, can I ask a favor?"

"Sure."

"Once you know—once you're sure—can you come to me first?"

"You?"

"Not my dad. I don't think this would be good for him to deal with."

"He'll need to know."

"Of course. But it would be better if it came from me. Will you do that for me?"

"Sure, Angie. Sure."

We bade her goodnight and I stumbled to my vehicle.

"What was that about?" asked Danielle as I started the SUV and headed for the gate.

"Not sure."

"Are you okay?"

"No. Not okay. I'm an idiot."

"No argument from me." She smiled. "But why this time?"

"Did you see the photo?"

"I saw lots of photos."

"The one from the night Missy met Dale."

"I have no idea which one that would be. A black-and-white one, I suppose."

"Yeah, black-and-white. The night they met. She showed it to me before, the original in a frame. I saw it again, on the screen."

"So?"

I pulled out onto North Ocean Drive and headed for home. I wished I had autopilot. Then I wished I had asked Danielle to drive.

"So there was a second shot. Same night. A guy with his arm around Missy. The guy who took her to the race track the night she met Dale."

"Ansel Brasher."

"No. It wasn't Brasher."

"It wasn't? Who was it?"

I watched the tunnel of light against the hedges either side of the road. I felt like my vision had been that way for too long.

"It was Rex Jennings. The truck driver."

CHAPTER THIRTY-THREE

WE HEADED OFF THE ISLAND ACROSS BINGHAM ISLAND. I rolled my window down to get some breeze on my face. The night air was cool and gave a hint of the season turning.

"So the guy who brought the cars from Michigan was Missy's old flame?" asked Danielle.

I nodded. I had told her about the delivery but left out the bit about there being only one car coming in because of the uncertain provenance.

"So you think he took them away again?"

"I don't see how. But it's a motive. He told me his own wife and kids had left him. He blamed his job. But maybe he never got over Missy."

"Another one."

"Maybe not. I might be wrong about Brasher. Or they both could be in on it."

"Both?"

"The enemy of my enemy is my friend."

"You'll need something better than Sun Tzu."

"I know."

"And what was that with Angie? Don't tell her dad?"

"I don't know what that was. A daughter protecting her father from something?"

"Or a guilty person watching their story fall apart," said Danielle.

"You think it's an inside job?"

"Why would she say that otherwise?"

I had no idea. "The daughter who can't get the top job because her father won't relinquish the position, and the jilted lover of her mother."

"It's not a great movie, but it is a plausible conclusion. You should call Ronzoni."

"Why?"

"They've committed a crime."

"Someone has. I don't know who yet."

"Ronzoni can investigate."

"Ronzoni is investigating, sort of. He can come to his own conclusions. Right now I don't know anything for sure. But there's still a big hole in the story."

"The how."

"Exactly."

We got onto I-95 and headed for home. Or the condo that was playing the part of home right now. I wondered if a condo somewhere was going to become a permanent fixture in my life. I wondered if Missy Beadman would be sitting alone watching old photographs play if she had made that kind of a decision. I wondered if she'd even had that option.

We drove past the offramp for Blue Heron, and I resisted the urge to follow it back to Singer Island. Danielle and I both turned and looked east toward the home that wasn't. I kept going until we got to PGA Boulevard, and I pulled off the freeway and cut back under the overpass toward the golf courses and Lucas's condo.

And then I saw the sign.

A big red sign in the night with the word *Fuelex* on it. High up on a pole so it could be seen from the freeway above. I had been focused on the other side of the freeway, on the exit. Now all I could see was the sign. My Cadillac pulled itself into the gas station.

"We need gas?" Danielle asked.

"No," I said, getting out. Danielle followed me out.

"Why are we stopping? You have a hankering for a bad hot dog?"

"Rex Jennings filled his truck up here."

"When?"

"After leaving the Beadman estate. Before the hurricane."

"How do you know?"

"The woman who does the accounts looked it up. He uses a company gas card."

"So?"

"So gas stations have video. I want to see it."

"What do you think you'll see?"

"I don't know."

"Well, let's go see, then."

Danielle led the way in. It wasn't late, so there were a few customers around. We waited our turn and then approached the girl behind the counter. She smelled like bubble gum.

"Is there a manager on duty?" Danielle asked.

"Yeah. Why?" She chomped on her gum.

Danielle took her FDLE ID out. She was technically only at the academy, but the girl behind the counter didn't know or didn't care. Or both. She picked up a phone and said, "Todd, can you come to the front? Police are here." It wasn't a phone call. The announcement went across the loudspeakers in the store and everyone stared at Danielle and me. Mostly at Danielle.

A kid with pimples came out through a plain door in the back. "Is there a problem?" he asked Danielle.

"No, sir. No problem. Can we talk in the back?"

Todd looked around at the customers, who were all now looking at him. "Yeah, sure."

He led us through the door in the back into a corridor stacked with brown boxes of chips and paper towels and pallets of soda. He led us into a small room that had a desk with a single chair on either side. There was a Fuelex calendar on the wall. The picture was of a green race car. Number 29.

"What's up?" asked Todd.

Danielle explained our need to see the video from the forecourt cameras on the day of the hurricane.

"After eleven a.m.," I said.

The guy hesitated. "Am I going to be in trouble for this?"

"No, sir," said Danielle. "The investigation has nothing to do with you or Fuelex. But what we see might help us with our investigation."

Todd nodded like this was what he wanted to hear, and he pulled his chair around to a console where a small screen sat on a table. It was the kind of screen that comes with a security system, small and with poor resolution. But we weren't trying to spot a man on the moon, so it would do. Todd took a device with a large squash ball-like thing in it and used it to navigate the text menu on the screen. He pulled up a video that was coming from the top of the canopy over the forecourt. We saw the gas pumps and the freeway overpass in the background.

He got the video going, and we watched for a few minutes. Then the big rig pulled into the forecourt at the pumps furthest from the door. The entire truck and trailer didn't fit in the shot. But we saw Rex Jennings step from the cab.

"Diesel pumps," said Todd.

That made sense for a big rig. But something didn't make sense.

"Do you have that from the other side? Looking back the other way?" I asked.

Todd nodded and got to work. It took a bit of doing because the system was old and the interface was clunky, but eventually he got it. The same forecourt looking away from the freeway, west toward PGA National and Lucas's condo. Each camera covered part of the forecourt so the pumps closest to the camera weren't in shot. It didn't matter. I wasn't looking at the pumps. I was looking at the semitrailer coming down PGA Boulevard. As before, it slowed and pulled into the gas station. This time we couldn't see the cabin. We didn't see Rex get out. We waited for a while until the trailer shuddered and then pulled away and rolled out of view.

I asked Todd to go back to the first angle. I should have just watched the video through when he'd had it up the first time, but I was confused. It took him forever to get it back again, but he did so without complaint. We saw the truck appear in the forecourt and stop. We watched as Rex Jennings stepped from the cab and filled the big tank on the truck. We kept watching. He wandered into the store and came out with a soda and then replaced the pump and got in the cab and drove away.

"Keep it going."

The picture wasn't great. At a distance it was pretty grainy. But not that grainy. It showed the truck pull onto PGA Boulevard and then its turn signal came on as it moved under the overpass, and it turned left onto I-95. Headed for Charlotte, North Carolina.

Danielle thanked Todd for valuable assistance and we walked back to the Caddy. We didn't speak until we were in the car.

"So why did the truck come from the west along PGA Boulevard when Palm Beach is east of here?" Danielle asked.

"Good question."

"You said the other day you saw video showing him getting on the freeway at Okeechobee Boulevard. Didn't you?"

"I did," I said. "Leo showed it to me. Rex got on I-95 at Okeechobee. From the east, coming straight from Palm Beach over the bridge at Southern Boulevard."

"So why is he getting back on I-95, this time from the west, only a few miles north of where he got on?"

"That's the thirty-million-dollar question."

CHAPTER THIRTY-FOUR

WE DROVE THE SHORT JOURNEY ALONG PGA BOULEVARD to Lucas's condo. I was looking out past the headlights, out toward the horizon. Wondering. I would have put money on the fact that Danielle was doing the same. We didn't talk until we got back into the townhouse. I dropped my keys on the counter and wandered out onto the small patio. The evening was fresh, and it helped clear my head. Danielle slipped a well-worn Oakland A's sweater on and joined me.

"Let's think this through logically," she said. "Why would he get off?"

"For fuel."

"Right, which he did. But why was he coming from the wrong direction?"

"Maybe he got off early."

"Why?"

"Mistake?"

"You've met him, MJ. Would he make a mistake like that?"

"No."

"Could he have gotten off for fuel and then found himself on the wrong side of the road. Maybe cut up Military Trail?"

"Anything's possible. He knows the family, so he's been here before, but he doesn't live here, so he might have made that mistake."

"Those gas station signs on the poles, they don't really tell you which side they're on. And I imagine pulling a U-turn in a semitrailer is no picnic. So what are the exits he could have gotten off at?"

I said, "He got on at Okeechobee. North from there, it's Palm Beach Gardens, Forty-Fifth, Blue Heron, Northlake and PGA Boulevard."

"Which ones have gas stations?"

"All of them. But he couldn't go to any old gas station. It's in the sponsor agreement that he has to fuel up at a Fuelex station."

"Okay. Where are they?"

"Before PGA? There's one on Blue Heron."

"Is that where you go?"

"Not regularly. Fuelex is expensive."

"So he might have gone there by mistake."

"It feels like we're clutching at straws."

"Why don't we go check?" she asked.

"Check what?"

"The video, dummy. Maybe if he got off at Blue Heron, the Fuelex station will show him doing it."

"And then what?"

"Then you take one more step."

I sighed. "Okay. It's worth a look. Let's do it first thing."

"Let's do it now." Suddenly Danielle seemed to have her second wind.

I didn't. I was exhausted. Physically I was tired from all the driving. Mentally I was tired from the case and being kicked out of my house.

"The video's not going anywhere, hon."

"Do you have official law enforcement ID?" she asked. "Because I don't. I gave back my PBSO badge, and my FDLE ID has me as a trainee."

"Your point being?"

"Tomorrow morning is when the guy who owns the gas station is going to be at work. Not now. You don't do the grave-yard shift if you're the owner. Graveyard shifts are for college kids who don't know a badge from a bullet."

There was not going to be any convincing her otherwise, so I threw her the keys as I should have in Palm Beach and we headed back down to Blue Heron Boulevard. We both worked really hard not to look out toward the dark ocean and our house thereabouts.

The college kid on the graveyard shift turned out to be a middle-aged man with a healthy disrespect of authority. I figure if you worked the graveyard shift in any kind of store, you got robbed sooner or later. Maybe more than once. And that either made you the greatest fan of the local police, or it made you wonder why you were paying their salaries.

The store part was locked up tight and the guy wasn't letting us in. Then he asked for ID. Then he noted that Danielle's ID said she was a trainee, and then he said he wanted to see a warrant. And then I slipped him a fifty. He was alone on the shift, so Danielle offered to stay out front and call if a customer arrived.

I went back to a room the same as the one we had been in with Todd. Fuelex probably had a blueprint on file for putting up their outlets. Like a kit. The security system was the same, right down to the crummy screen. This guy wasn't nearly as adept at using the scrolling squash ball as Todd had been. He took so long I considered calling Todd and asking him to drive over. But the guy eventually got it going. We saw a similar picture as we had at the last Fuelex station. I-95 passed over the top of most of the area, so the video showed a similar overpass. We followed the timestamp on the video and got a few minutes from when we had seen the truck at the next gas station. We saw nothing.

The guy put his hands up like that was all he could do and I told him to back it up and try it fifteen minutes before.

"This is not worth a fifty," he moaned.

"What else would you be doing?"

"Watching Netflix."

"Netflix will wait."

"How about another fifty?"

"How about I tell your boss you already let me in here? Make it play."

He grumbled and made the video start. I had no intention of spending the entire night with this engaging fellow, so I asked him if it could go double time. It could. The cars sped by and we watched for several minutes in fast motion but saw no truck.

It seemed that Rex had not come this way. For the sake of completely covering the bases, I told the guy to go back an hour and roll it fast. I figured we should be able to see a semitrailer. We watched. It was hard on the eyes. Cars zoomed by, and the eye followed across the screen and then zipped back to the other side to watch another car, and so on. It was like watching speed tennis.

And then I saw a truck. Or more specifically the cabin. I had been inside it. I had seen it up nice and close. The guy stopped the speed and slowed the video, and we watched the DBR-badged cabin pull a trailer off the freeway and cut underneath and head west on Blue Heron. It didn't stop at the gas station. I noted the timestamp.

"Is that time accurate?"

"Yeah."

"Okay. Note it. Can you show me the exact same time looking the other way?"

"I'm really gonna need another fifty."

"What's your boss's number again?"

"This is slave labor."

"Dude, you're sitting on your butt getting fifty bucks for twenty minutes' work. You mention slave labor again and I will slap you into tomorrow."

He gave me a look that suggested we weren't going to form a darts team anytime soon and then fumbled with the squash ball. Again it took longer than was necessary. Danielle called out to see if we were okay. I called back that we would be five minutes.

We were less. The guy found the right video and then fast-forwarded to the right time. Then he slowed it down. I watched the DBR cabin zoom by again. It stopped at the next traffic light to the west, Military Trail, which would have been the exact spot Rex would turn right if he wanted to cut back up to the Fuelex on PGA Boulevard.

But he didn't. He stopped at the lights, and then on green he went dead ahead. I watched his taillights until they became nothing more than pixels on the grainy screen.

I told the guy that I was done. I was going to thank him for his time, but I'd given him a fifty and he had given me grief, so I left it. We walked back out into the store, and the guy asked Danielle if any customers had come.

"Three or four," she said. "They all paid at the pump."

"Tough job," I said.

The guy snarled. "You ever had a gun pointed in your face at your work?"

The fact was I had. I didn't like it, not one little bit. And although I hadn't taken a shine to this guy, I didn't like the idea that someone had stuck a gun in his face at his graveyard shift job, either. So I didn't answer his question.

"Thanks for your time," I said.

Danielle took the wheel as we headed home.

"So?" she asked.

"He got off."

"See?"

"And he went straight through the lights. He didn't go up Military Trail."

"He went straight?"

"Yep."

"What's straight?" she asked rhetorically. She knew what was straight ahead from there.

"Beeline Highway."

"That's weird."

"That's not the weird part."

"What's the weird part?"

"The timestamp on the video showed him passing by a half an hour before the timestamp on the video at the Fuelex where he got gas."

"What was he doing for half an hour?"

"Or to put it another way, where did that half hour go?"

"Same question."

I shook my head, to myself as much as anyone. It wasn't the same question. Not the way I was thinking about it.

"Either way, I know what he was doing."

"How?"

"The trailer that came through here? The one that delivered the F-88."

"Yes?"

"Not the same trailer that we see on the video at the PGA Boulevard gas station."

"If it's a different truck, how do you know it's him?"

"Not a different truck, a different trailer. The tractor—the cabin part—that's the same. But the trailer is different. I couldn't see it in the video at Dale Beadman's garage, and I didn't know to look when Leo showed me the video of him getting on the freeway. I should have gotten it when I was in Charlotte. But now, seeing these two videos one after the other? He gets off here with a plain blue soft sided transporter trailer. No DBR signage."

"The trailer at PGA Boulevard had Dale Beadman Racing all over it."

"Exactly. A NASCAR hauler. Fuelex and other sponsors, too. Moving billboards."

"So he swapped trailers?"

"It would seem."

We drove back to the condo. I got tech support to login and set the security video running.

"You're going to watch it again?" Danielle asked.

"I don't need to watch it again. Does the oven have a stop-watch on it?"

"No. It has a countdown timer."

"Need a stopwatch."

"On your phone," Danielle said. She took my phone from me and set the stopwatch running. Then she left the video on the television and brought up a map of West Palm Beach on the laptop screen. She zoomed in so Blue Heron Boulevard was at the bottom and PGA Boulevard was at the top. The Beeline Highway headed off on a northwest route, through miles of nothing toward Indiantown and Okeechobee, on the north end of its namesake lake. Between the two boulevards it formed a triangle.

"What's out there?" asked Danielle, thinking. She knew the county well. She knew what was out there.

So did I. I'd been out there a few times. On cases. There was a lot of nothing out there. Geographically it was the start of the start of the Everglades. "There's some warehouses out there. Distribution-type places."

Danielle used her finger to move the map along the Beeline like she was driving it.

"Aircraft manufacturers," she said. "An airfield. And—"

"What?" I said, leaning into her to see the screen. She pointed at the edge of the screen.

Palm Beach International Raceway.

CHAPTER THIRTY-FIVE

I didn't sleep well. I was like a kid the night before an SAT exam who knew he hadn't studied enough. I knew there were things I knew for sure, and I knew for sure there were things I didn't know. We had agreed that there was no point in heading out in the middle of the night. I got up early and checked the stopwatch on my phone. I looked at the video. It told me exactly what I'd thought it would tell me. We went for a run around the quiet streets of PGA National. The grass on the golf course was glistening. We ran until Danielle decided it was time to turn, and then we ran back. Then we showered and ate breakfast, and Danielle declared she was coming with me.

We drove west from PGA and cut up the Beeline. The further we got from the coast, the less dense the houses became. And then it ended. Just like that. Like there was a line, them and us. Which was true in a manner of speaking. Under the veneer that commercialism had laid over the top, Florida was really just a primordial swamp. And out along the Beeline, you really got to see the difference. One moment it was all houses and golf courses and the next thing the nature was pulsing at the edge of the road, ready to take over if someone forgot just once to cut it back.

In between the wild foliage are pockets of human resistance. We drove up past nondescript buildings that gave no inkling as to what they did, and that made me think of clandestine agencies and biochemical labs creating killer viruses and humanity-destroying robots. I really needed more sleep.

The Palm Beach International Raceway is not all it might seem, if you're just going by the name. The name brings forth images of Daytona and Talladega and Indianapolis all rolled into one. It ain't that. There aren't any stands. There aren't any motels. What there is is a space carved out of the wilds with a blacktop track laid on it. The wide-open parking lot was completely empty when we arrived. There was a sign advertising go-karts that looked like it might have once been legible from the road. The gate to the track stood open, as did the door to a shed just beyond. The place had an end-of-the-world feel to it.

We drove into a shed that might have been a garage. There was a popup canopy out front, just like the one Simon Lees had used when testing at Charlotte. This was not Charlotte. This was where Travis Zanchuk was racing. It was park softball compared to the major leagues. This was a place for low-budget and no-budget race fanatics to come and race their cars. It didn't look like much, but neither did plenty of baseball fields I had played on. It was there to do a job. When the fans all brought their cars in for a few laps or a drag race, they weren't looking at the cracks in the pavement or the peeling paint on the shed. They were racing and that's all they cared about. All I cared about was that this gave them a place to do it that wasn't a public road.

We stopped outside the shed that was the biggest building in sight. There was a banner advertising drag races. A lone guy wandered out and stood by the door. He was lean and wore a hoodie. He looked like he was expecting someone, and he looked like we weren't them.

"Morning," I said.

"Another one," he replied.

"You work here?"

"As much as anyone."

"I'm wondering if you hold cars here?"

"Hold them?"

"You know, store them."

He shook his head. "You see anywhere to store a car?"

"No, I don't."

"You want a storage facility."

"I thought there might be one at a race track."

"Afraid not. How many cars you want to store?"

I shrugged. "Ten?"

"Ten?" He looked surprised. "You want a car lot. Or a hangar."

I glanced at Danielle and she at me. We thanked the guy and headed straight back out to the Beeline. Back toward the coast. Toward civilization.

"Why are you driving so fast?" Danielle asked.

"Sorry, didn't realize."

"Where are we going?"

"Missy Beadman mentioned that they flew their plane out of North Palm Beach County Airport."

"And that guy thought a hangar would be a good idea. Worth a shot. It's down here somewhere."

"Somewhere. These trees are taking over."

"That's what trees do. There!" she yelled.

I hit the skids the same moment as I checked my rearview. We were all alone on the road. The airport was hidden behind throngs of trees and foliage. Even the sign pointing into the airport from the road was half-hidden. I backed up and pulled into the driveway. There was an intercom and a slot for a keycard. I used the intercom.

We got in and pulled up to a building that might loosely have been referred to as the terminal. Private airfields are a different beast. There were rows of hangars surrounding a runaway that didn't look long enough to host the Olympics sprint finals. There were small planes parked on the tarmac. We found a spot and went inside. A guy came out of an office wearing one of those white shirts with the epaulets that pilots like to wear. He was sweating.

"How are you?" he asked.

"Well enough," I said. "Listen, I'm doing an inventory of assets for Dale Beadman Racing."

"Mr. Beadman," he said. I wasn't sure if it was a question or a statement.

"Well, for his daughter. She runs the organization."

"Right, Angie."

"You know Angie?"

"Sure. They fly out of here. Mr. Beadman mostly, but Missus and Angie, too."

"Right. We need to just make sure of the location of their assets."

"Assets?"

"The aircraft."

"The Lear?"

"That's right."

"It's not here. I can tell you that now. Mr. B flew out the other day, and I know for a fact he was staying in Charlotte until Sunday."

"Right. We know that. He's driving down to Darlington and then back up to Charlotte to return here."

"So that's that."

"Well, not quite. See, it's a thing. We have to account for the plane. We know where it is, but we need to tick the box to confirm where it isn't."

"Where it isn't? It's in Charlotte. It isn't everywhere else."

He was a wise one, this guy. I guessed he had earned those epaulets. I looked at Danielle. She took the baton.

"What's your name?" she asked. She was using her floozy voice.

"Adam."

"Adam, that's a nice name."

Adam blushed. I didn't know why. His mother had given him the damned name.

"So this is an IRS thing," said Danielle. "We're trying to make sure Mr. Beadman doesn't run afoul, or worse still, get audited."

Adam visibly shook at the idea of being audited by the IRS.

"So we have to confirm that the aircraft we know is in Charlotte isn't right now, in fact, for tax purposes, in Palm Beach."

"How do you confirm a negative?" he asked.

"We just need to see the empty hangar, Adam," she said. It might have been the fan that was blowing warm air at us from behind the desk, but I thought I saw her bat her eyelids.

"We don't even have to go in," she said. "You just open it, we take a photo for proof, that's it."

He frowned. He didn't look convinced.

"I'd really appreciate it, Adam," Danielle said. "My boss will tear me a new one if I don't get this done and Mr. Beadman gets audited."

Adam glanced down in the direction of Danielle's backside, clearly considering the concept of her getting a new one.

"You don't have to go in?" he confirmed.

"Absolutely not."

He nodded like he wasn't sure, and then he nodded again with more authority. "Okay."

Adam led us out to a small white pickup with a yellow light on top that could flash if there were an emergency. The truck had a bench seat and Danielle sat in the middle, against my better judgment. Not that I was kidding myself that I got any say in where Danielle sat.

He drove us toward the runway. A small plane, maybe a four-seater, was dropping out of the sky for a landing. It sounded like a lawnmower. I thought for a moment it was going to land on top of us, but at the last second, Adam turned hard so Danielle leaned into him, and he directed the pickup to a hangar just off the landing strip.

We got out and Adam stepped forward to open the hangar door. It was a large bifold thing. Too heavy to do by hand. He got some kind of hydraulic system going and it folded in on itself. It was slow going. We waited. And waited. When it was a quarter way open, Adam called us. Danielle and I stepped forward to take a look.

At nothing. It was an empty hangar. It was a large space with room for an aircraft smaller than a jumbo but bigger than the four-seater we had just seen land.

"There you go," Adam said to Danielle.

"Thanks," she replied, deflated.

"Did you want to take a photo?"

Danielle nodded and continued the ruse. "Thanks for reminding me." She took out her phone and took a picture. Then we waited for Adam to close the door. I watched another plane land. This one was bigger. It was a jet of some kind, about five windows long. It didn't sound like a lawn mower. It was the kind of aircraft you could bank on getting you away from a bad storm. It made me think of Dale Beadman's Learjet. And why it hadn't come back for Missy and Angie. And then I turned and looked at the small planes on the tarmac.

Adam came back. "So you got what you need?"

Danielle smiled.

"Not quite," I said. "We need to see the other one."

"The other what?"

"The other hangar."

"This is the Beadman hangar."

"But they had another plane, right? A single prop?"

"Yeah, similar to the one that landed earlier. But they sold it. Upgraded to the Lear that lives here."

"And where did the other plane live?"

"In a smaller hangar. Out back. But I'm telling you they don't have that plane anymore."

"I don't care about the plane. Show me the hangar."

Adam looked a little put out, but a smile from Danielle put it right. I didn't hold that against him. The same thing worked on me. We got back in the pickup, and Adam drove us around the airport to the row of hangars closest to the Beeline Highway. Not that we could see the highway. The foliage was on a rampage. He checked a list and pulled up beside a hangar. We got out again. This hangar looked a little older, like it had been the first row built. Adam worked the door, and it folded in on itself in the same way. He called us over again. We stood next him and looked inside. The space wasn't as large as the hangar for the Learjet.

But it was big enough to hold a blue-sided vehicle transport trailer.

CHAPTER THIRTY-SIX

THE SPACE WAS BARELY BIG ENOUGH TO CONTAIN THE trailer. It had been backed in so it was diagonal across the space. Someone who really knew how to back a trailer had done it. Someone with decades of experience. I took a picture. Danielle told Adam that he needed to close the hangar and not tell anyone about the truck and not let anyone else in. The penalty for doing so might include an IRS audit, which seemed to be a real pain point for him.

"How did you know about the second hangar?" she asked when we got back to my car.

"Missy told me they had upgraded their plane, but I remembered she said they had hangars out here. Hangars, plural."

"We need to call the PBSO," she said.

"No."

"MJ, this guy stole the cars. I don't know how, but he did."

"I know."

"So we need to call the sheriff."

"No. Hon, give me today. There's more going on here than it seems. And for the first time, I think I get it."

"Did he steal those cars or not?"

"It's complicated. But I don't want anyone innocent to get hurt. Just give me today. Tomorrow, if we haven't sorted it out, we call the sheriff."

She wasn't happy about it, but she relented. Danielle drove while I placed calls. I called Angie to say we needed to meet. She said she was in a meeting in Daytona and would be back that evening. She told me to drop by. I said I would.

Then I called Ron. I told him I really needed the address of Great Southeast Permanent. The CEO needed to chat. Urgently. Ron told me that Kent Fulsome had a tee time that afternoon.

"Does that guy ever work?"

"A lot of deals get done on golf courses."

"And they don't get done faster or better in an office?"

"Don't tell anyone," said Ron. "They'll kill you if you let that news out."

I thanked Ron and hung up. Danielle drove back to Lucas's condo to get her truck.

"You want to come?" I asked.

"Tonight?"

"Or now."

"I need to get to work. There are still a lot of people who need help."

"Then tonight."

I left her to go save the world. I couldn't think of a better person to try. I had something else in mind. I slipped into my SUV. I needed some lunch. I decided I felt like a Cuban sandwich. There are lots of good places to get a Cuban sandwich in South Florida. But I had a particular sandwich in mind. I headed down around the airport to a little place behind a strip mall.

Peter Malloy, my errant building inspector, was doing his job from his usual perch at a table outside at Bar Playa. I stopped at the bar and ordered said Cuban sandwich and a beer. The smiling young Latina behind the bar handed me a Tecate and told me she would be happy to bring my sandwich to me. I thanked her and turned to Peter Malloy. He was reading a magazine, eating a Cuban sandwich and drinking a beer, and I wondered how he kept his figure with a diet like that. Maybe his fiancée made him go running as well. I plopped down opposite him and took a sip of beer. He glanced up from his magazine and his mouth dropped open, showing a partially eaten sandwich.

"Didn't your mother ever tell you to eat with your mouth closed?" I said.

To his credit, he did shut it. He badly wanted to say something to me, but now that I had questioned his mother's parenting, he really wanted to swallow first. But the sandwich was thick and bready and needed a lot of mastication. The end result was almost death. He tried to swallow the damned sandwich before it was small enough and it got lodged in his throat. His eyes bulged and he started banging himself in the throat, which really didn't seem to be the right approach. A couple of guys at the bar heard the commotion and pointed. They thought it was pretty funny. Malloy started turning blue.

"You want some help?" I asked him.

He nodded, I think. It was difficult to discern from the chocking. I stood up and moved behind him and then came in hard on his chest with a sudden massive bearhug. The sandwich dislodged and popped up into his mouth and he spat it onto the concrete.

I sat down and sipped my beer. I was having a reasonable day. Life, like cases, is about momentum. You stop moving, you die. Momentum was everything, and I had some now in my case. I also had some with regard to my house. And that was before I had saved Peter Malloy's life. I gave him a good chance to collect himself. It took a while. I had time. The lovely girl from the bar delivered my sandwich and asked if I wanted ketchup. I asked her what kind of heathen put ketchup on a Cuban sandwich. She said Americano. I said nothing to that.

Malloy got his breath back. He sipped some beer and it stung his throat and made him cough.

"Try some honey," I said.

"This doesn't change anything," he said.

A prince among men.

"I don't expect it to. I don't save people's lives in expectation of a return favor. In your case, I did it because I didn't want to spend hours at West Palm Beach police HQ providing a statement to a guy who types with two fingers."

He coughed.

"But let me tell you what does change things. Let's start with Juan Gotlieb. And his actor/driver/hard man, Domingo. I can inform you that they are no longer interested in my property. Further, my new friend, Domingo, has let me know that it was he, and not you, that placed a no habitation order on my house. Paperwork, he tells me, he got from you in return for a cash payment."

"You think you're clever?"

"Not as clever as my better half, but considerably smarter than an oyster."

"You can't touch me. The union won't let you anywhere near me."

"I have no desire to be near you, not the way you eat sandwiches. But let me tell you who might be happy to be near you. How about the *Palm Beach Post?*"

"No one reads that rag anymore."

"Perhaps that's true. Maybe it's all online now, I don't know. But I do know about stories going viral."

"A story about me going viral? You're out of your mind."

"I am. But it doesn't have to go Kardashian viral. It only has to reach your wife. And her church group. And the principal at your kids' schools. And the nasty piece of work who runs the PTA."

"How do you know Lucinda?"

Lucky guess.

"There's no upside here, Pete. You did a dumb thing. We all do dumb things. Me included, as hard as that is to believe. But there's no upside. The guy who paid you has had a change of heart, and he isn't coming back for the money. He's not looking for you to do anything from here. And you know it's a sham order. So all you need to do is rectify it. Call off the dogs. Give me my house back."

He looked at me through smudged glasses. I could tell he was weighing it up. He didn't want to give me a damned thing, lifesaving or not. But he was also the kind of man who avoids hassle like a child avoids broccoli. He was trying to find a way to concede without conceding. Which is pretty hard to do without looking like a complete moron.

I gave him time. I ate half my sandwich while he was thinking. It was food from another planet. A good food planet. The ham was thick and smoky and the pork was roasted to perfection. And there was a cheese in there that was mild but tasty at the same time. I was halfway through the sandwich before Malloy did anything.

He didn't speak. What he did was take a tablet computer out of the satchel at his feet. He fired it up and tap, tap, tapped. Then he spun the screen around to me.

"Violation removed," he said.

There was some horribly formatted page on the screen. But the county logo was at the top, so I took it as read that Malloy had done what he said he had done. If he hadn't, I knew where he lunched.

"But if you don't get that house up to code asap, I will slap an order on it."

"I've already had a contractor in," I said. "Because I don't want to live in a house that isn't to code in a hurricane zone." I sipped my beer. "But, if you slap any kind of order anywhere near my house, I will find you and shove the rest of that sandwich back down your damned throat where it came from."

Malloy went white. Whiter. He again took a moment to compose himself, and I again ate some sandwich.

"Are we done?" he asked.

I nodded.

"Then stay the hell away from me," he said.

"Gladly," I said.

I didn't move. I had a quarter of a sandwich and a half a beer left. The beer was run-of-the-mill but the sandwich was heavenly. I wasn't going anywhere until I was done.

Peter Malloy glared at me through his librarian glasses. Then he stuffed his tablet into his satchel like he was making a point. He stood, gave me a glare that made me think of a book about Ted Williams that I never returned to the New Haven Free Public Library when I was a boy, and he walked out.

CHAPTER THIRTY-SEVEN

I met Ron at South Lakes Country Club. It was a mild afternoon and the breeze was light, so a good number of people had decided that work was for chumps and had left their offices and dental suites and such to hit the fairways. The lot was pretty full, but there was space at the back where I parked. I strode past two men and one woman in three BMWs who were sitting in lanes closer to the clubhouse, waiting to pounce on any spot that was vacated.

I found Ron in the upstairs bar. It was a nice wide-open room with a wonderful view of both sides of the twenty-seven-hole layout. Ron was sitting on a beer at a table by a screened window. I grabbed an iced tea from the bar. I had plenty left to do on this particular day and I needed my wits about me.

We watched a group of golfers in the distance standing on the tee waiting to hit to the fairway, and a group on the fairway waiting to hit to the green, and a group on the green taking their sweet old time over three-foot putts that counted for nothing in the grand scheme of things.

Eventually, I noted that the group waiting on the tee included my old friend, Kent Fulsome. He appeared to have ditched his Miami Dolphins cap in favor of allowing the breeze to ebb through his luxurious hair. He was wearing Ray-Bans and leaned on his driver.

A guy on the green hit a two-foot putt to ten feet past the cup, and the groan from the group on the fairway was audible through the mesh bug screens in the bar. The guy walked a wide circle around the green to analyze why things had gone so badly. He got down on his haunches and assessed the angle of the green like it was one of those unreadable monsters at Augusta National. It was no such thing. The green ran down-hill, back to front. Gary Player could have read that green from his home in South Africa, or Arizona or wherever it was he lived now. Everyone on the course knew it was an easy read.

Including Kent Fulsome. The pain of watching someone pull off a Band-Aid one hair at a time was too much for him. I watched him from my perch in the bar. He bullied his way to the tee box and he mounted his ball on a high tee and then he took one, two, three waggles of his backside and he whacked the ball right up the middle of the fairway. He was good under pressure. He was fired up and the blood was pumping and the shot was straight up the middle. Proof positive that golf was played in the mind, not on the course. Score one for not thinking and just doing.

The guys on the fairway were not impressed. In their defense, they were not the reason for the holdup. They were waiting for the schmo on the green like everyone else. So when Fulsome's ball went flying through their group at head height and landed on the fairway just ahead of them, they weren't all that happy. Three of them turned and started yelling abuse back at the tee. Fulsome gave them a mouthful back. The fourth guy in the group took a fairway wood from his bag and stormed up to Fulsome's ball. He faced the wrong way—back toward the tee

—dug his heels into the lush fairway and smacked the ball right back at Fulsome.

It didn't make it. The guy on the fairway had used a shorter club and had hit off the fairway, not off a tee, but he hit a decent shot. And his point was made. The next thing that happened was Custer and Sitting Bull. The group on the tee jumped into their two carts and tore along the cart path as fast as their electric motors would go. The guys on the fairway saw this and got in their two carts and took off the wrong way, straight up the fairway.

Ron's mouth dropped. He was old-school and very big on golf course decorum. He didn't abide drinking, cursing or betting on a golf course. I wasn't sure where jousting fell on his list. Not high. His face went white as he watched the two sets of carts closing in on each other.

Then they met. They zoomed past each other, clubs flailing outside the carts like swords. Each of the carts did a wide turn and came back for a second shot, two-on-two. The left pair flew by each other again, the click of graphite shafts connecting echoing up the fairway. The right pair did not. I wasn't sure if it was a miscalculation or if one of the drivers was a demon at playing chicken, but the two carts smashed into each other head-on.

Golf carts go fast but not that fast. Especially on thick fairway grass. But it was enough for the passenger of the cart coming toward us to end up in the lap of the guy driving the cart headed away. The other driver got out, wielding a putter like it was a lightsaber. It was Kent Fulsome. He was doing that time-honored move of boorish morons the world over and begging his companions to hold him back from beating the daylight out of someone while simultaneously making no attempt to move in and do any such thing.

"I think we need to call the police," said Ron.

"Nah," I said. "Leave it with me."

I walked out of the bar and down the stairs that came out in front of the green, where the guy who had missed the putt was still trying to assess his next attempt and was most aggrieved with the fuss that was disturbing his concentration. I wandered past him and headed for the melee. I ambled down the fairway with my hands in my pockets, a glorious sunny day to take a walk.

By the time I got there, the fight had descended into name-calling. That's one thing about golf players and fans. They're generally not big fighters. You don't see a lot of that action at the PGA. So once the bluster and the testosterone had been worked through, they really didn't know what to do.

So I decided to the throw some gasoline on the fire.

"Kent Fulsome, imagine finding you here!"

I marched toward him with a big grin. He frowned, dropped his shades and squinted over them like he needed a new prescription, and then the penny dropped.

"What the hell are you doing here?"

"I was thinking the same thing about you. Do you ever work?"

"This is work, genius."

"Only if you're Phil Mickelson, and you're not."

"This is harassment, pal. I'll call the cops."

"That's okay, the cops have already been called. You dunderheads are all on video. You're gonna go viral." I smiled even wider. I was having a better time than I thought I would. Every one of the knuckleheads on the fairway spun toward the clubhouse, where a decent-sized gathering had formed to watch the idiocy. Contrition was rapid. Clubs were slipped back into their bags and guys from both groups starting shaking hands in truce. Foreign diplomacy should happen so easily. Of course, it does. When you have a common enemy. Apologies were offered and accepted and then, as one, they all turned their thoughts on the guy up on the green, who had just putted again. And missed.

I focused on Kent. He had offered no such apology. He was the big man on campus. The financial wunderkind who had started an insurance business from scratch and turned it into an enterprise worth hundreds of millions. A lot of those hundreds of millions had evaporated in the winds of the hurricane. Even with his business on the line, he stood firm. He saw it as his greatest strength. Weaker men could not have done what he had done. He was the alpha male. He was about to learn about being beta.

"How's business, Kent?"

"Great."

"Cashed up, are you? No? I hear you're wearing a mountain of debt."

"You don't know what you're talking about."

"Don't I? Then I guess I don't know that you don't have the cash to cover the claims on you. And without cash, you can't even pay the lawyers you'll need to hire to defend all the lawsuits from people like me. And then the regulators will come in. And they'll freeze everything. And they'll take your nice little mansion on Washington Street."

"You don't know anything. The house isn't a company asset. Dream on."

"I will. You know what I'm dreaming of? I'm dreaming of a guy who needs a bit of extra finance to paper over his losses. And I'm dreaming that the only way a guy could get that sort of financing is to offer a director's guarantee. Using his home as collateral."

He didn't fold, but his veneer cracked a little. "You're crazy," he said, but it wasn't very convincing.

"Am I?"

"You think my problems get fixed by paying your claim? Do the math. The smart play is to pay nothing."

"So you're not going to pay out Dale Beadman's thirty million?"

Now he did go pale. I knew why. Ron had explained it to me. Palm Beach was a small community, especially at the top end. Friends helped friends. But they also ate their young. If Fulsome failed to pay Palm Beach royalty like the famous and well-liked Dale Beadman, then not only was his business done, but so was he. He could declare the company bankrupt and then form another company to buy the assets of the old business and then carry on as if nothing happened. But he couldn't do that without money, and he couldn't get any money if he became a Palm Beach pariah. He needed friends. Sure, he could move to Seattle and start again there, but his wife was a Palm Beach native and his kids were in school. She wasn't keen to move. Ron knew that for a fact, too. The Lady Cassandra had told him as much. So old Kent could deny me, but denying Dale Beadman was the last act he would do as a business mover and shaker. Unless they started selling insurance in North Korea. It was time to real the fish in.

"I can save you thirty million dollars," I said.

"What?"

"Thirty million. It might not save you, but it might tip the scales. Thirty million in cash that you don't have to pay out this week."

"You can't."

"I can, Kent."

He went quiet. I heard birds chirping in the trees around the fairway.

"How?"

"What's the standard bounty for recovering insured property?"

"Five percent."

"I have it on good authority it's ten percent."

"Maybe."

"Even twenty percent on a high-value item."

"What's your point?"

"What if I can find Beadman's cars?"

"What?"

"What would that be worth?"

"You know where they are?"

"No. I haven't seen them at all."

"Then you're full of it."

"I was retained by Mr. Beadman to find them. He doesn't want your insurance payout. He wants his cars. And I have good reason to believe that I can make that happen. Excellent reason."

"Then tell us. If you don't, you're obstructing an investigation and you'll go to jail."

"I don't know what you're talking about, Kent."

"Yes, you do."

"I have no recollection of that, Senator."

Fulsome stepped toward me. He thought he had a winning hand.

"All right," he said. "You bring me the cars, I'll give you ten percent."

He held out his hand for me to shake. I didn't.

"I don't think so, Kent. I only do gentlemen's agreements with gentlemen."

He dropped the hand. "Well, I'm not giving you ten percent on your say-so."

"No, you're not. Ten percent of thirty million is what, three million dollars?"

He said nothing. I think he was okay with the math.

I said, "The claim that you owe me is fifty thousand."

He waited.

"So I'll agree to find your insured cars for the fifty thousand you owe me."

He frowned. Now he didn't get the math. It didn't compute.

"You're saying you'll find the cars, and instead of the three million bounty, you want a fifty thousand bounty?"

"No. I'm saying I don't want any bounty at all. All I want is the fifty thousand that my policy covered me for."

He looked perplexed.

"And I should add that I know why you denied the claim. Apart from the fact that you're a scumbag lowlife. I know Juan Gotlieb asked you to. He wanted my house for a client. He has been dissuaded of the value of pursuing my property."

Kent Fulsome smiled. Like a shark. He had a winning smile normally. I bet he had worked on it in front of the mirror for all of his college years. But this smile wasn't a facial expression. It came from within.

"All right, pal. You got a deal. Hell, that guy's just a neighbor, not a damned fraternity brother. Get me the cars and I'll give you your fifty."

"I'll expect a cashier's check at my office today."

"You think I'm paying before you produce the cars?" He laughed.

"I do," I said. "One of us is good to his word. One of us is a scumbag insurance huckster. We'll be siding with me."

He said nothing. He was weighing it up. He was an insurance guy. He understood risk. It was everywhere. It was a risk to leave your house every day because you might get hit by a car. It was a risk to stay home because the gas line might get a leak and explode. Risk was unavoidable. So it was always a balance between risk and reward. Fulsome was balancing my fifty thousand against his thirty million. It wasn't much of a risk.

"You'll have a check this afternoon," he said, eventually.

"Cashier's check," I said. "None of your company paper."

"Cashier's check," he said. "When will I get the cars?"

I turned toward the green, where Ron was watching me from the upstairs bar.

"As soon as I get the money," I said, striding away.

CHAPTER THIRTY-EIGHT

THE GATE WAS CLOSED THIS TIME. I BUZZED, AND ANGIE Beadman answered and she let us in. The Camaro was in the driveway. Danielle, Ron and I got to the top of the steps before the door opened. Angie stood before us in a blue work shirt with the DBR logo on it.

"What's happened?" she asked. "You sounded kind of urgent on the phone."

I looked at the time on my phone. "Not that urgent," I said. "Your dad's in Darlington, right?"

"Until Sunday night."

Angie let us in and I led the way into the great room. Missy Beadman stepped out of the kitchen.

"Mr. Jones," she said.

"Missy," I said. I introduced Ron to her.

"Can I offer you all a bite to eat? I was making sandwiches."

"Perhaps later," I said. "Let's go over to the pub."

Being in the pub would suit my purpose. There was also a chance of a beer. I led Missy into the kitchen. The room looked ready for a magazine shoot. When I prepare food, my kitchen looks a teenager's bedroom. I saw no evidence of sandwiches being made. Perhaps she had just gotten the hankering as we arrived.

I walked out the kitchen door and across the lawn with Missy, Angie and Danielle in tow. I didn't wait for Ron. I strode across the deck with the outdoor kitchen and under the palapa and into the pub. The sun was dropping to the west, so the easterly aspect of the French doors gave a gloom to the interior of the pub. Angie Beadman offered us a stool at the bar. Danielle and Angie sat. I chose to stand. Missy was in behind the bar. I felt a beer offer coming on.

"Would anyone like some sweet tea?"

It was sweet tea all around.

"So why have you dragged us out here, Miami?" asked Angie. "Have you learned something?"

"I've learned plenty," I said. "More about cars than I ever felt I needed."

"I meant about our burglary?"

"I know what you meant, Angie. And you know what I learned about that? It's hard to find a good suspect when everyone seems to love the victim."

"What does that mean?"

"When I see a crime that clearly involves a degree of planning, I always look for the people who had something to gain from it. Best and first are people who have an issue with the victim. So I look at the victim's enemies. But there was a problem."

"A problem with Dad's enemies? What enemies?"

"That's kind of the problem. A guy like him, a go-getter, successful. You get a few enemies along the way. You don't have to be a bad person to get enemies because you are not responsible for your enemies. They're responsible for becoming such. Some folks can feel wronged for the dumbest reasons. And Dale had given people reasons. But Dale's enemies were poor excuses for enemies."

"Poor enemies?" asked Angie. The look on her face suggested she was starting to consider whether I was a lunatic. Missy Beadman laid four napkins on the bar.

"What happened to Ron?" Missy asked, realizing that Ron had not joined us in the bar.

"He had to take a call," I said. "And, yes, there were two enemies that stuck out. And they were poor enemies because they just weren't very good at it. One was a guy called Travis Zanchuk. He had been a top engineer for your dad's vehicle engineering business."

"I remember Travis," Angie said.

"I'm surprised. He's not that memorable, even as an enemy. He sued the business because he felt wronged about the development of a new technology. He had aspirations of being a NASCAR crew chief, but now he builds cars for local race meets. Good candidate, except that even he knew that his dream wasn't going to come true. There's a lot more to being a crew chief than just being a good engineer. The lawsuit was a cry for recognition. But legally he knew there was no basis for it."

"Doesn't mean he couldn't hold a grudge," Danielle said.

"You're right about that. And he does. He blames Dale. But he doesn't believe. Not down in his guts. He doesn't have the drive to pull off a crime like this. So I looked at some guys who did have the drive. And the capability. Rory Lobe and Winton Gifford."

"Those old guys?" Angie asked.

"Yeah, my thoughts exactly. Like Travis, they had been involved in legal action against your dad's company. But they just saw it as a business move. They're not buddies anymore, that's for sure, but they moved on a long time ago. Besides, your dad actually settled with them, and I'm willing to bet they did well enough out of it to be placated."

"They did just fine," Angie said.

"Do you like lemon with your tea?" Missy asked Danielle.

"Yes, ma'am."

"Mr. Jones?"

"Yes, ma'am."

Missy nodded like that was the correct answer. She began slicing a lemon that had appeared from the bar refrigerator.

"So not WinLobe?" said Angie.

"Nope," I said. "But while I was in Charlotte I had a couple of opinions repeated to me by people. One of those regarded not an enemy, but a rival. Ansel Brasher."

I watched both Angie and Missy for reaction. Angie gave none. Missy spoke.

"You think old Ansel Brasher did this?" She said like it wasn't possible.

"He's a good rival. They'll make a movie about Dale and Brasher's rivalry someday. It's got everything. Fast cars, bright lights, rival racing organizations, glamorous locations. And a woman's affection, mixed in there for good measure."

"A woman's affection?" asked Angie. "What are you talking about?"

I took a breath, in through the nose and out through the mouth. I spoke to Angie. "When I first visited, your mother mentioned that she had been taken to the race track the night she first met your father."

"So?"

"Taken by a boy."

"Again, so?"

"I learned in Charlotte that Ansel Brasher had a thing for your mother."

Angie frowned. "A thing?" She looked at her mother. Missy's face said nothing.

"You think Ansel Brasher took Dad's cars because he had a thing for Mom?" asked Angie.

"Men have done worse for less," I said. "And then, of course, I learned about the taunt in Monaco about who was the better driver, and the subsequent race at Indy. And the accident that killed Brasher's chances of the Triple Crown."

"You learned about it?" Angie looked at Danielle and then back at me. "You didn't know about that before?"

"I'd heard the story but I didn't recall the drivers. Or the particulars. And then I learned the reason why Dale wasn't here the day the F-88 was delivered."

"He got delayed in Charlotte," said Missy, placing tall glasses of tea onto the napkins.

"He did," I said. "Because of filming. It turned out he was filming a piece for a movie that was being produced, or executive produced, or something, by Ansel Brasher."

"You think Brasher kept Dad in Charlotte so he could take the cars?" asked Angie, but again she didn't look like she was buying it.

"I do. I did. I really liked Brasher for it. I met him. He's an easy guy to hate. But there was a big question I couldn't answer. How did he know the F-88 was even here?"

"He couldn't," said Angie. "Could he?"

"I did some digging and found out that he was interested in the F-88 as well."

"He was?"

"He was. I found the intermediary that no one wanted to tell me about." I looked at Danielle, and she was frowning because this was news to her. "He wasn't very keen to talk. He was very big into client confidentiality. Like he was a lawyer. Which he definitely was not. But I could see how his business kind of relied on it. He said he never told the loser who won a bid for a car. He never told Brasher. I believed him. So I couldn't answer how Brasher even knew the car was here."

"So how did he?" Danielle asked.

"He didn't. Because it was then that I learned that everything I knew about Ansel Brasher was wrong."

"Everything?"

"Almost everything. He's a major pain in the backside and a total narcissist. That much is true. But if it wasn't him—the rival —and it wasn't an enemy, then the next logical suspect was a friend."

"How is a friend logical?" asked Angie.

"It takes some twisted logic. But it didn't matter. I spoke to a lot of people at the workshop. Dale has a lot of friends there. They love him. But none of them were good for the burglary. So I moved to the next logical choice."

"Who's left?" asked Angie.

"Family."

"Family?" she repeated.

"That's right. It occurred to me right back at the beginning that this whole thing might be a case of insurance fraud."

"Insurance fraud?" Angie spat.

"Yeah. It happens. More often in Palm Beach than people might think. A company falls on hard times, someone loses a job. Appearances must be kept up. Lifestyles maintained. So suddenly valuable possessions get stolen or a warehouse gets burned to the ground. Insurance is claimed. And then the cops find out that the fire was arson, or the businessman is found in a pawn shop hocking the allegedly stolen items. It happens."

"You're kidding me." Angie looked at her mother and then at Danielle. "This is what you've come up with? Dad committed insurance fraud?"

"Like I say, it happens. The option had to be canvassed. But

Ron found out that the company was healthy. Nothing irregular there. The technologies that Beadman Automotive Engineering created are still patented and are still being used by a large percentage of manufacturers. There's a good income stream there."

"Damned right there is," said Angie. "So you're saying it wasn't fraud after all."

"I decided it probably wasn't your father committing fraud. But he didn't handle the paperwork."

Angie leaned back in her stool. They had little backs on them to prevent her falling back onto the floor.

"You think I committed insurance fraud?"

"It was a possibility, you've got to admit. But then I found out that you hadn't even put in a claim. Hard to commit insurance fraud when you don't put in a claim."

"You didn't claim?" asked Missy. She was looking at Angie.

"No. Eventually, I did."

"You did," I said. "After I pushed you into doing it. If anyone was committing insurance fraud it was me, unwittingly."

"Are you saying you took my dad's cars?"

"I was in a hotel in Palm Beach when that happened," I said. I stayed standing and made no attempt to pick up my sweet tea. Danielle and Angie took a sip. Missy watched from behind the bar like it was her night job.

I kept going while they were drinking. "I said I heard a couple of things repeatedly when I was in Charlotte. You know what the other was? It was that Angie should be the CEO at DBR. It was pretty much a consensus. Dale was loved up there, no doubt about it. But pretty much everyone thought it was your time, Angie. Time for Dale to step down. Everyone except for Dale."

"Miami, are you saying that I stole my dad's cars to

somehow get his job? I hope not, because I don't want to believe that you're that messed up."

"Angie, I'm afraid that was more or less where the logic trail ended. Everyone thought you should be at the reins. I believe the cars were stolen in an attempt to divert his attention, to shake him loose. Kidnap his cars and get his focus off the racing team."

I waited. I had nothing more to say. Not for a moment, anyway. When you beat the bushes, you have to give the birds a chance to flee. Angie looked me in the eye. She held her drink halfway to her mouth, and her mouth hung open ready to receive it but she had frozen in motion. She was like a statue. She wanted to say something, and her lips tried to form the words but none came. She was stuck between a rock and a hard place. But I wasn't hearing what I wanted to hear, so I drove home my point.

"Did I mention that Danielle is an agent for the Florida Department of Law Enforcement?" I left out the bit about being a trainee at the academy. Never let the facts get in the way.

Angie didn't move. She didn't speak.

Missy Beadman spoke for her. "Mr. Jones, you can't seriously think Angela Jean took her father's cars."

"I believe what the evidence tells me, Missy."

"She can't have done this."

"Can't have?"

"She didn't."

"Mom," said Angie. "Let me deal with this."

"No, Angela Jean, this is not right. I can't let you get into trouble for something you didn't do."

Angie turned on her stool to her mother. They each tried to speak, but again the words didn't come.

"How do you know she didn't do it?" Danielle asked Missy.

"I'm her mother," Missy said quietly. Then with more effort, she said, "Eleven cars off the island. She couldn't. It doesn't make sense."

"It didn't," I said. "Until I realized it wasn't Ansel Brasher. The exact second I knew it wasn't him was the same second I knew who it was. I figured it out last night. When we visited with you, Missy. You were watching old photographs. And everything fell into place. See, I thought Brasher was the guy who took you to the race track when you met Dale, but last night I saw a photograph from that night. Up on your big screen. The guy who took you that night was Rex Jennings. The guy who drives the development cars for Dale. The guy who he trusted to deliver his F-88 from Michigan."

"Rex is a family friend," said Angie, spinning back on her stool to me. "He's known my dad forever, and despite what you think he would never hurt Dad."

"I agree. And that's why nothing made sense at first. But I met Rex. He drove me to the track in Charlotte. He looks the part, but he's not your stereotypical truck driver. Or maybe he is. Maybe they're all hard-looking guys with soft marshmallow centers. Either way, he told me how he'd been around at the beginning, when Missy and Dale met. It didn't click then how he knew that. Because he was the guy who took her there. But unlike Ansel Brasher, he didn't harbor a grudge." I stepped to the bar, and reached between Danielle and Missy and picked up the sweet tea that Missy had left there for me. It was too sweet for my liking, but it wet the whistle. Not as well as a beer, but enough to do the job. I stepped back and leaned on the end of one of the booths.

"Quite the opposite. Missy, you told me that the guy who brought you the night you met Dale probably didn't want the job of being your boyfriend. I thought it was false modesty. But it wasn't. He didn't want the job. You and Rex dated, but like lots of young couples, the spark just wasn't there. But you remained friends."

"Lifelong friends," she said.

"He spoke of you and Dale like lifelong friends do. And he told me how he met someone else. The love of his life. The woman he married and had kids with. But he told me how the life on the road destroyed his family. He lost them before he realized what he was losing. I guess they got tired of never having a husband and a father at home. He told Dale what was happening, and Dale took him off the long-haul routes and had him drive locally for the development team. But it was too late. His family had already checked out, emotionally if not physically. And he knew that it was his fault."

"He's a good man," said Missy.

"You know, I think he is. He's sad about the mistake he made, but he's a good man. And that's why he didn't want Dale to make the same mistake. To ruin his life—and yours—by making the same mistake he made. That's why when you asked him to, he agreed to steal Dale's F-88 Oldsmobile."

CHAPTER THIRTY-NINE

"MIAMI, THIS IS GETTING TIRESOME," ANGIE SAID.

"There's a method to the madness," I said. "But I assure you that Rex did take the cars. I have video evidence of him leaving the island carrying a transporter trailer with no race team signage, and then reappearing with a DBR-branded NASCAR hauler. The vehicle transporter was big enough to hold all of Dale's cars, but the NASCAR hauler couldn't fit more than two or three. They're designed to carry a lot of other stuff. And there's a half-hour time gap between the two."

"Time enough to switch trailers," said Danielle.

"That doesn't prove anything," said Angie.

"It does, I'm afraid," I said. "There's proof enough to put him away."

"You can't do that," said Missy.

"Why?"

"Because you're right. He did it for me."

Angie dropped her sweet tea onto the bar. "Mom?"

"I'm sorry, Angela Jean. You must think me a fool."

"No, Mom, I don't." Angie looked her mother over. Missy

had aged years in seconds. The pep that permeated her had gone. "Why?" whispered Angie.

"For you and for me. Mr. Jones was right. Everyone at the race team knows you should be running the team. You do the important things anyway, but you have to do it from Palm Beach instead of being in Charlotte and getting the credit you deserve."

"Mom, I'm happy enough."

"No, you're not, Angela Jean, and neither am I. I spoke with Rex many times after his family left for Colorado. It nearly killed him. It's hard when a man loses everything through his own negligence and he knows it's no one's fault but his."

"But. . ."

"And he didn't want Dale to make the same mistake, did he?" I said, watching Missy. "He didn't want his lifelong friends to feel his pain. He knew you were unhappy, Missy."

"But you weren't unhappy," said Angie. "Were you?"

Missy looked at me, the messenger, and then at her daughter. "I haven't had a husband for a long time. I'm not complaining about my life, sweetheart. I've had a wonderful life. I've got you. We've had a lot of good times. But I have more days behind than in front of me. And I don't want to spend them watching old photographs of the glory days. I want to go and do things that don't involve race tracks. I want to take walks on the beach, I want to sip drinks while overlooking, I don't know. . ."

"The Champs-Élysées," I said, recalling her trip to Monaco.

"Yes," she said. "I haven't seen Paris, or London or Tokyo. I'd like to. And I'd prefer not to do it alone."

"Why didn't you talk to him?" Angie asked.

Missy smiled but said nothing.

I said, "Same reason you haven't told him to move aside. Because you both love your dad, and you both know that he's petrified."

"Petrified?" asked Danielle, and then she put her hand over her mouth to push the words back.

"Yeah, he's scared out of his mind. Because like Missy, he knows the days ahead are fewer. And he knows that he isn't required at DBR anymore. He knows Angie runs the show already, in truth. I saw the place. It's a well-oiled machine. He's the reason it exists at all, but now he's not needed. And he can keep denying the truth as long as he holds on to the mantle." I let Angie think about that for a while and punched some words into my phone and sent a text message. Then I said, "What I don't get is whose call it was to take all the cars?"

"It was a joint thing," said Missy. "Originally I planned to remove only the F-88. When Dale said he was having Rex truck it in, it was the last straw. He spends more time with his silly cars than he does with me." Missy took a sip of tea. "Dale was supposed to be here for the delivery, but then he would fly back to Charlotte as he always did. There would be time for Rex to wait and then come back to the house. But the hurricane came and Dale wasn't here and Rex delivered the car and he saw the opportunity. He called me."

"I saw that on the video," I said. "He makes a call just before he closes the garage door."

"Yes. He said if taking the F-88 didn't do it, surely taking all the cars would make a point. I agreed."

"What point?" asked Angie.

Missy shook her head. "I don't know, honestly. Rex and I talked it through and it seemed to make sense. If we took his latest car, maybe he would focus more time at home. And I guess if we took them all, he might focus more time on me." She sighed. "It all seems so foolish, now."

"Wait," said Angie. "We have video. Rex didn't take the cars. They're there on the video."

Missy looked at me. "Mr. Jones?"

"I think you've been underestimated all your life, Missy," I said. "You have the college degree, not Dale. You did the books back in the beginning, and I'll bet you could be running the show now if you hadn't let your daughter take on that role. Everyone sees the pretty race driver's wife. No one would suspect that you could learn to operate the video security system. But you did."

Missy nodded. "It's amazing what you can teach yourself on the internet."

"It is," I said. "You learned how to operate the servers and the video. Then when Rex closed the door, having delivered the F-88, you stopped the video."

"But I went back to my office," said Angie. "You weren't in the computer room."

"She did it remotely," I said. "Just how you set me up to view it." I said to Missy, "Where were you? In the bedroom?"

"Kitchen," she said. "Watching the truck."

"So Rex goes in and gets all the cars into the truck. Must have taken a while."

"Less than half an hour. He's been doing it for forty years."

"And all the while the video isn't going. But then there's a problem. If you start it again, we'll all see the missing cars."

"Exactly," said Angie.

"So I'm guessing you took some video from the previous day and pasted it in place."

"I don't think it's a cut-and-paste thing," said Angie.

"It's not," said Missy. "It's more complicated than that, but that is essentially the idea. It was raining already the day before, so the driveway was wet."

"And the driveway was the only evidence of the hurricane," said Danielle. "And it was sheltered. The other video is inside, behind hurricane shutters."

"So how did you know, Mr. Jones?" asked Missy. "That the video wasn't real?"

"Two things. The first was the palapa." I gestured outside the French doors. "I could see the reflection of the palapa in that television. There's a security light on the deck and I noticed it. But we have one, just the same at our local bar. The owner, Mick, said it got blown away before it even got dark. Yours got blown away, too. But not on the video. It was still there when the power went out. Which didn't make sense. It's on the windward side of the garage. Longboard's Kelly's is a ways back from the water. So if Mick's got blown away, why didn't yours? Because the video wasn't live."

"Not exactly conclusive," said Angie.

"No, but it got me thinking. So I timed the video. There was no timestamp on it, which I understand isn't unusual with home security. But the timer didn't match the end of the video. See, I was on top of The Mornington hotel just after the power went out there. The whole island was black. So your power had to have gone out as well, at the same time. But the hotel's video had a timestamp on it. According to it, there was a half hour difference between when their power went out and when yours did. A missing half hour. The half hour it took Rex to load the cars and get away."

I looked at Missy to confirm I had it right. I had it right. She was looking at the top of the bar, or through it. She was looking somewhere I couldn't see.

"It's over," she said. She took a deep breath. Then she looked at me with a determination in her eyes that I hadn't seen before. A resolve. "Angela Jean had nothing to do with this," she said. "It's all me. Not Rex, either. He was an unwilling accomplice. Whatever happens now, Dale, the police, the insurance. It's on me. Angela Jean knew nothing."

I liked her style. She was a mother protecting her child, yes, but she was also taking responsibility for her actions. The world needed a few more people who did that. So I walked over to the bar and flicked a button on the console. The garage burst into light. White and antiseptic and empty.

"She might not have been involved, Missy, but she knew. That's why she never put in the insurance claim. Because she knew something was up, but she couldn't reconcile what her brain told her that thing was."

I left the pub. I opened the door to the garage, then just walked out. I ambled across the vacant space. My boat shoes squeaked on the polished concrete. I walked three-quarters of the way to the roller door and I waited. I hoped they were following. Nothing feels as foolish as making the big dramatic gesture that nobody understands. But they did. Or maybe Danielle directed them out. She understood me and my dramatic gestures.

Danielle and Angie and Missy Beadman gathered around me. Danielle smiled like she wondered what the hell I thought I was doing. Angie looked exhausted and perplexed. Missy looked worn but relieved that the truth had broken free of the cage.

"What happens now, Mr. Jones?" Missy asked. "I am willing to cooperate with the police. I understand you are duty-bound to let the insurance company know what has happened, but I do ask that you don't implicate Angela Jean."

"There's a problem there, Missy," I said.

"Which is?"

"I can't think why police should come. Technically, I suppose, you wasted their time, and I'm sure they've got some kind of rule against that. In your favor, it's Palm Beach, and the only person's time you wasted was Detective Ronzoni's, and it's hard to tell wasted time from useful time with him. Otherwise, I'm not sure what crime you committed. You didn't legally steal the cars. They might be your husband's toys but any judge is going to call them communal property, and you can't steal something you own."

"But Rex took them," Missy said.

"Because you asked him to. That's not burglary, that's delivery."

Missy looked at Angie and then back at me. "What about you, Mr. Jones?"

"What about me?"

"We wasted your time."

"Unfortunately, not a crime. Besides, you'll get an invoice from me."

"What about the cars?" Angie asked.

"Indeed," I said, wandering over and hitting the button to raise the roller door. It was a long, slow reveal. The door took forever. Eventually, it opened. The transporter trailer sat with the back ramp down onto the driveway. It was full of collectible cars. Ron stood by the ramp like a showcase model, waving his palms out at the cars. Lucas stood on the other side of the ramp, arms crossed. He was the only guy I knew who could drive a big rig. There wasn't much he couldn't do. We had borrowed the rig from the guy who had delivered the wood for Mick's new fence at Longboard's. The cost for a couple hours was a tank of diesel and two cases of beer.

Lucas stepped up into the trailer and unclipped the first car. It was a Model T. He wheeled it down and Ron helped him get it into the position it had been before the hurricane.

"I don't understand," said Missy. "You found them?"

"Of course," I said.

"Will you tell Dad what happened?" asked Angie.

"You asked me to tell you first if I found the cars. I know you did that because you were protecting your mom. So I'm telling you first. I found the cars."

"But Dad?"

"He's my client," I said. "I have to tell him I found the cars."

Both Angie and Missy nodded.

"The where, how, why and when, I leave to you."

"Mr. Jones?" Missy looked at me like I was telling a joke she didn't understand.

"Mrs. Beadman, I'm just a PI. I'm not a counselor and I don't profess to have the secrets of the world all worked out. But if you're asking, I'll tell you that I think you need to have a chat, as a family. You need to lay it all on the line. Because right now there's a thread of sorrow running through your family, and from the outside looking in, I can't help feel like you're just one tough conversation away from all being pretty damned happy."

CHAPTER FORTY

DEMOLITION CREWS ARE A FORCE OF NATURE. THE GUYS
working for Rucci the contractor showed up the next day ready
for action. They looked like a lynch mob without the torches.
Rucci told them where to start and they hit my house hard. They
removed all the furniture that remained, and the appliances and
leftover belongings, and carried them up into a moving van, which
disappeared to an undisclosed location that Rucci assured me
would be safe for the duration. Then the guys entered with crow-
bars and sledgehammers, and before I knew what was happening,
the living room floor was gone and the kitchen cabinets were in a
waste hopper that had taken up residence in my driveway.

I handed Rucci the cashier's check that had been delivered
by courier from Great Southeast Permanent. I hoped for the
sake of all the other people whose homes lay in pieces that
Great Southeast was indeed more permanent for the thirty
million they would not have to cough up to Dale Beadman.

"I can't bank a cashier's check made out to you," he said.

"Okay," I said. "I'll go to the bank right now."

"No hurry. We'll be here for a few weeks."

"About the kitchen," I said.

He cocked an eyebrow.

"I didn't think it was damaged," I said.

"Sal thinks you need a new kitchen."

"Sal thinks?"

"It'll be better. You'll see."

I didn't see. It looked like a bomb had hit my house. My mouth just sat open as I watched it get ripped down to the studs. Rucci slapped my back.

"Don't worry. It always looks worse before it looks better."

He strode into the house to direct traffic. I wandered out the back. Two guys were maneuvering a boat trailer down the side of the yard. It was a tight fit but they got it through. One of the guys hitched a line to the boat that lay on my grass. I helped him keep it straight as the other guy worked the winch to pull the boat up onto the trailer. The speedboat looked in fine condition considering it had run aground. The guy behind the winch stepped off the trailer and shook my hand.

"Thanks for calling," he said. "I didn't think I'd see her again."

"Glad to help," I said. Ron had used the boat's registration to track down the owner, and I was glad to have my unobstructed water view back.

It didn't stay unobstructed for long. Lucas dropped off a tent that he used to go what he called *bushwhacking* in the Everglades. It was a good size. A main room in front with no floor and then two bedrooms with plastic floors. I put it up facing the water, not the house. It took me longer than was necessary to erect it, but once it was done I had a place to live. I had kept back the mattress off my bed from the moving truck, and it took the entire area of one of the bedrooms. I put sheets and pillows in there and then I dragged two loungers across the lawn and positioned them overlooking the water. Right where my neighbor's pool would have been.

Danielle arrived home just as Rucci's guys were cleaning up. Her t-shirt was covered in grime and her khakis were stained. She looked tired and disheveled. I thought she'd be horrified by the idea of giving up Lucas's condo for a tent. But I underestimated her again.

"I get it," she said. "You want to be home."

"Something like that."

"No skin off my nose. I've got four walls and a roof in Tallahassee."

We popped a bottle of wine and drank from plastic tumblers, laying back on our loungers. The sun gave a great show as it fell below the horizon beyond Riviera Beach.

"Did you tell Dale Beadman about his cars?" Danielle asked.

"I did. And I thanked him for the new palapa at Longboard's. That was classy."

"It was. But he must have had a lot of questions."

"I'm sure. I told him he'd get answers from his wife and daughter."

"You think they'll tell him they took the cars?"

"I don't know. I think they should. I think it might pound the message home to Dale, and it seems to me they've been dancing around the truth for too long."

"Dancing around the truth never ends well."

That thought hung on the air as we sipped our drinks.

"So when are you heading back to those four walls in Tallahassee?" I asked.

"Tomorrow," she said. "When will I see you again?"

"Next weekend. I'll come up."

"I'll show you the sights."

"Can't wait."

"And then what?" she asked.

"The weekend after, we could meet at Epcot. See the house of tomorrow, get some ideas."

"I'm not sure that is what you think it is."

"We could walk over to the France pavilion, eat a croissant."

"And after that?"

"After that, you'll graduate."

"And end up somewhere."

"Of course. We've all got to be somewhere."

Danielle sipped her wine and then played with the ring on her finger. Her engagement ring.

"You having doubts?" I asked her.

"No," she said. "None. I'm just thinking about Missy and Dale Beadman. I don't want to live some great life but have to wait fifty years to have you in it."

"If you're not in it, it won't be a great life."

"Sort of my point," she said.

"So they are not us and we are not them."

"Are you sure?"

"Positive. This very conversation is proof of it. We're planning opportunities to be together. They didn't do that."

"Maybe they did, in the early days."

"They didn't do it hard enough. They should have spent more time at Epcot."

Danielle smiled. "You're not going to take this seriously, are you?"

"Nope. Not for a second. Because taking it seriously suggests there's something to be concerned about, and there's not. When you worked for the PBSO, did we work together?"

"Not usually."

"And were there days when we didn't see each other?"

"Yes, some."

"And did you doubt how I felt about you or whether we'd lead separate lives because of it?"

"No. But we're talking bigger distances and more days apart, aren't we?"

"No, we're not. That's what you're worried about, but what I'm saying is that there aren't more days apart in the future. I know because you're not some discretionary part of my life, like beer or nachos. You're crucial to life, like oxygen or water. And sure, I can go days and days without water. But I don't like the feeling it gives me because my body is telling me that I can't do that forever. I'll die. That's how I feel about you. It's not optional. I lost Lenny, and I promise you I would have curled up and died as well, and the only reason I didn't, *the only reason*, is that you came into my life right then. Right when I needed you, you were there. Then and every time since. So don't go thinking that you can get away from me, because I can't afford for that to happen."

Danielle looked me over. The X-ray look. I don't know if she was looking for a false note in my symphony or just wanted to imprint my mug on her mind before she returned to Tallahassee. She looked for the longest time. And I waited for her to do it. Then she smiled. That half smile that turned handsprings in my guts.

We both looked toward the water and Riviera Beach beyond. The sun was playing out its final notes of the day and the sky grew pink and then purple. The lights across the water twinkled and I heard the sounds of yacht rigging slapping against masts. A flock of gulls flew low over the water. The birds were returning. The tourists would follow. Then the neighborhood burst to life. Lights exploded on and the sounds of air conditioners and televisions permeated the silence. The power was restored. Life would go on.

Our place stayed dark. We had no AC, no appliances. No

floor, no kitchen. The power was off at the breaker box. We felt like an island of silence in an ocean of white noise. Or perhaps the opposite. A black hole in a starry galaxy. We didn't care. We sat in the dark and watched the lights, and I hoped that Missy and Dale Beadman were doing the same. We drank our wine. The bottle got emptied.

Danielle stood. She stretched her back out and looked at the view. Then she turned and walked away. I wasn't sure where she planned to go. There was no fridge in the house. There was no more wine. Just an old mattress in an older tent. I heard the zip to the tent. Then something landed on my head. It was a dirty t-shirt. Then I was hit by a pair of stained khakis. I dropped my empty tumbler onto the grass by my lounger and stood. I had said I wouldn't leave her alone.

I am nothing if not true to my word.

ACKNOWLEDGMENTS

Thanks to Eliza Dee for the editorial support. Thanks to Wayne, Bob and Charlene for the above and beyond feedback.

As always, any and all errors and omissions are mine, especially but not limited to not obeying the speed limit on I-95 outside Daytona. That's just asking for trouble.

ABOUT THE AUTHOR

A.J. Stewart is the USA Today bestselling author of the Miami Jones series and the John Flynn thriller series.

He has lived and worked in Australia, Japan, UK, Norway, and South Africa, as well as San Francisco, Connecticut and of course Florida. He currently resides in Los Angeles with his two favorite people, his wife and son.

AJ is working on a screenplay that he never plans to produce, but it gives him something to talk about at parties in LA.

You can find AJ online at
www.ajstewartbooks.com